Orbach.

What was it about O

He was a big man, m
effect, a man of gothic
man of apparent – but
command not only of h
a manipulator; at times I thought the word that fibest was
monster; at other times, despite myself, I still lied him,
sensing that one day the lid had to come off, and when it
did it would cause him a lot of hurt.

Above all, he was an arrogant man. He was a brilliant
man. His arrogance was surpassed by his single-minded
ability, and his ability by his extraordinary ambition. He
had enjoyed supreme professional success, and corresponding wealth. But he was probably the loneliest and
unhappiest man I ever met, and certainly the most cruel.
He made enemies first thing in the morning the way others
made their beds, and left them just as tidily ordered.

Though patently a driven man, with a centrifugal energy
that swept lesser mortals out of his way, I had struggled
long and hard to identify his code and his direction. He
lacked any identifiable morality. In this sense he was, of
course, the perfect lawyer and an even better judge; but
he was a wholly imperfect human being.

# ORBACH'S JUDGEMENT

**Bernard Bannerman**

SPHERE BOOKS LIMITED

A *Sphere* Book

First published in Great Britain by Sphere Books Ltd 1991
© Copyright Bernard Bannerman 1991

Printed and bound in Great Britain by
BPCC Hazell Books
Aylesbury, Bucks, England
Member of BPCC Ltd.

ISBN 0 7474 0521 2

Sphere Books Ltd
A Division of
Macdonald & Co (Publishers) Ltd
Orbit House
1 New Fetter Lane
London EC4A 1AR
A member of Maxwell Macmillan Pergamon Publishing Corporation

For long-suffering, longer-complaining Ruthie:
a long overdue dedication!

# Acknowledgements

A number of people helped me with information which I have in equal parts used and misused: my thanks, and apologies, to – Chris Peach (medical), Tom Dykes (dental), Lorna Dade (Southend) and Tracey Platt (Southend Rochford).

# CHAPTER ONE

I was exhausted by the time I finished the manuscript. It was nearly three o'clock: a cold night early in the new year. No one was left in the club, save Natalie, a waiter and a couple who didn't want to go home to their separate apartments and separate partners.

I was sitting behind the desk in the office, as I had been since I had started to read, some five or more hours before. I had drunk the best part of a bottle of Southern Comfort and either I had hardly smoked at all or I was on my second pack of Camels. I felt like I'd run a marathon, got up before ten in the morning, made love twice in a month or done something else equally exhausting but exhilarating.

I couldn't at first work out why, but the mood I was in reminded me of Bob Dylan's 'Desolation Row'. I remember the first time I heard it: the first time, the second, the third and on and on until I was equally exhausted. Exhausted, yet relieved, as if I had just discovered that a secret wasn't as dark and as dirty as I'd always believed. There was something about the song that made it for me the greatest Dylan of all. It was a glorification of depression; an exuberant celebration of despair; an anthem to the awful; a theme tune for the intense loneliness I then suffered from, and continued to suffer from for many years after; a song about people driven mad by loneliness, the mad I was often on the verge of, the mad that sometimes made me think I could murder for the sake of feeling someone's warm body next to mine.

Sometimes I would listen stoned or drunk, on occasions with a companion, too often alone. It didn't always bring me relief. Sometimes, it made things worse. Nonetheless,

1

it reflected and gave a tangible form to the balance of my own mania. In those days I saw only the downside of life. Moments of joy nestled uncomfortably and unnaturally between visions of hell. If it wasn't going to beat me – and there were many times it came close to doing so – I had to be able to relate to it other than out of a bottle of pills. That's what the song did for me: it spaced out my despair.

Times changed. Me too. I grew up – some say less than others, everyone says less than I ought to have. I could find what I wanted in music instead; jazz, classical, recently, thanks to the private tapes Lewis left in the club, I've even begun to listen to opera, which gives you some idea of how old I am and comparatively settled. Thanks for the latter go mostly to Sandy, and of course always and above all to Alton.

Sandy is the woman I used to live with, and the mother of our son, Alton, the child I'd never believed I was going to have, in part for reasons medical, in part because it had been an article of my faith that the kindest thing I could do for the world was to leave nothing of myself behind.

Alton's odd name derives from my friend Lewis, who owned the club before me and who had died in the middle of my last case. Fat old faggot, ubiquitous usurer, conniving club-owner and erstwhile gangster, he had been a shoulder for me to lean on, a source of information when others had dried up, a name to get me through doors, and once or twice the principal reason I hadn't achieved my main objective in life: to take up residence as a handful of ashes in an imitation Grecian urn.

Lewis was only ever known as Lewis. I found out why when I read his will. His full name was Lewis Alexander Altonspritzer. The way the club came to me is long and complicated and – as a matter of fact – I'm not the person he intended to get it. A lot of people played a part in its devolution onto my shoulders: Malcolm, Lewis' ex- and the then manager of the club, who was supposed to benefit but didn't stay around long enough; Tim Dowell; and Tom, Malcolm's tantalising toy-boy. Tom was the only one who

2

might've objected to the chicanery that left me in charge, but it wouldn't have benefited him anyhow: the club would have gone to some obscure relative in Malcolm's native Glasgow, no friend of Lewis, nor Malcolm, nor even of mine. I gave Tom a job in the club and the club was paying for him to go to private classes to get some paper qualifications with which to help Natalie keep the books.

Natalie? Well, that's another part of what'd been happening but if I tell you about it now, I'll never begin. This is supposed to be about how come my son's got a weird name like Alton.

In a separate letter to me which was with his will, Lewis said of our then unborn child – if it's a girl, call her after me; if it's a boy, give him a kiss. He had also left him ten thousand in the will itself. 'It' was a boy, and I gave him a kiss, but it wasn't enough, so Sandy suggested we give him half Lewis's last name as well, as a sort of compromise. We couldn't call him Alexander: that was a name already appropriated by Alex Keenan, one of Sandy's former lovers. I had protested about encumbering our child with such an awesomely awkward name. Sandy said:

'You wanna call him Spritzer?'

Lewis itself was out; it would've been tempting fate. Liberals we might well be but we wanted OUR son to be NORMAL. I suggested lamely:

'Elton?' She'd been known not to turn the radio off.

'Alton,' she repeated, and that was the end of the discussion. Sorry, kid, I thought: you'll understand when you're older.

\* \* \*

It had begun just a few days before. I was at work. This itself would once upon a time have been cause for comment, but in the year and a quarter since Alton had been born I'd gone back into and stayed in practice as a lawyer with Sandy. She was now only working part-time. The practice was the same one I'd set up with her after we'd finished all our qualifying stages, more years ago than she'd forgive me for telling. It was called Nichol and Co. Nichol is Sandy. My name's Dave Woolf. Sandy's authority over the names we use goes back a long way.

I'd been in it at the beginning for maybe four-five years before she kicked me out. Seemed to think I ought to be paid in cash instead of coke. When all our debts and assets were totalled up, I got less back out of the partnership than I'd put in. I set up as a private investigator. After a while getting by on process serving and divorce work, I ran out of steam altogether.

I picked up a big case: Disraeli Chambers, the serial killings of a bunch of loony-tunes lefties. That was when I met Dowell: he's a policeman, then a detective sergeant, now a detective inspector. It was when I re-encountered Russel Orbach, the barrister, who I'd known years before in a much less tortured lifetime when he was himself a member of those Chambers. It was when Lewis saved my life.

It was also when Sandy'n'I'd made up our long-standing dispute, discovering as I'd long suspected that the aggro between us all those years before had Freudian undertones. For a while after that we were on and off. She wanted me to come back to work as a lawyer. I was always finding an excuse not to. The excuses ran out when she told me she was pregnant, and my last case as a private eye finished the day Alton was born. I'd been going straight since.

Mostly what going straight meant was legal aid work. Our practice is in North London where a lot of people are still tenants of private landlords, or employed on terms and in conditions that would make Edwin Chadwick, the nineteenth century public health reformer, shudder; many of them, maybe a majority, are black and in that part of London this is a criminal offence in its own right, which gave me a lot of time in the magistrates' courts.

It wasn't boring work in itself, but it bored me. It was routine, and I hate routine. It was a time-warp. It felt like I'd gone back a decade or more. It was the same sort of work I was doing that had driven me to dope. We made a profit out of young, fairly recently qualified solicitors we didn't make up into partners, and outdoor and articled clerks who couldn't be; we made some too on conveyancing and out of a couple of housing associations who wanted, as public landlords, to show whose side they were really on when they got us to evict one of their tenants in rent arrears.

What we didn't do was commercial work, heavy landlord activity, setting up or advising companies, patent, copyright, shipping, tax or anything else that made real money – or libel.

'Why does he want to see me?'

'I think he'd rather explain that himself. We'll pay for the interview, of course.'

I shrugged, but as this was a telephone conversation, his secretary couldn't see. I said:

'Yeah, sure, why not.' And made an appointment for Nigel Morris, managing director of Aldwych House the publishers, to come see me. My best guess was: when he saw the location and state of our offices, he'd turn right around and go back to the city solicitors his firm usually hired, where the carpets come up to your knees, the coffee is freshly ground, they've even got a couple of law-books and the opening 'how are you?' cost three figures.

Three days later, after the weekend, at the end of the day, the first man ever to make me feel physically insubstantial was ushered into my room.

What I mean is that he squeezed through the door sideways while my receptionist shoved from one side and I pulled from the other. He was six four, weighed at least twenty stone, his belly so big I thought he might be pregnant; he had a nose my grandfather would've been proud of; he was close-bearded, a light brown, almost ginger colour; his face formed a perfect circle; his shirts were made by a marquee manufacturer; he wore boats on his feet and that part of his girth that didn't overlap them was contained in *schmatter* enough for three pairs of normal trousers.

5

'Sit there,' I quickly pointed to a chair I'd long hated and was looking for an excuse to get rid of: 'We take no liability for physical injuries to our clients. Is that clear?'

He chuckled knowingly:

'Are you trying to make the point that I'm f-f-fat?'

I retreated around my desk. He said:

'How much has this cost us so far?' He held up a hand: 'No, I know, lawyers don't like to talk about money. Ah, it's so different in the world of publishing where our der-der-derisory emoluments mean we can't afford to do anything else but engage in baroque conversations about it. That's why all publishing deals take place over lunch: it's the only way we can eat. This,' he placed his hands on his stomach: 'Re-re-represents fifteen years of expense account.

'Have you ever been to F-f-f-frankfurt? Of course you haven't. Why should you have? Everybody hates it. It's become a major st-st-status symbol not to go. There's a huge hall, like a giant who-who-whorehouse for coal-miners who haven't seen, the surface since they were Bevin boys at the beginning of the wa-wa-war . . .'

I held up my hand:

'Stop.'

He jerked back in his chair. The back cracked. At least, I think it was the chair's back, not his own.

'I di-di-digress. You're a busy man. You don't want to hear about Frankfurt. You probably have a hundred hungry clients desperate for you to take their cases: criminals with con-convictions as long as your face; wives dr-drooling at the prospect of divorce; pa-pa-paternity suits; ha-ha-half the city needs you to ha-ha-handle a merger; it's an exciting life as a lawyer. Publishing. People think it's exciting. They thinks it's d-d-deals made in exotic parts; mi-mi-millions of p-p-pounds . . .'

The stammer was brilliant. I hesitated to interrupt again, because I couldn't be sure what was coming next: something interesting, something relevant; or just more of the same.

'Lunch in M-m-maxims, a flight to New York, a ca-ca-cadillac to a writer's Con-con-connecticut estate, a black

6

butler serving di-di-dinner to a li-li-liberal conscience, the publisher's cheque-book tucked neatly into his tuxedo . . .'

'*Genug,*' I could guess from the nose and the verbal diarrhoea what we had in common; it might be more effective than English.

'That's very cl-cl-clever of you. Very few people g-g-g-guess that I'm Je-je-jewish. I'm only half-Jewish actually; half-Irish. My mother was Irish. My father was a sp-sp-sports journalist . . .'

I lowered my head into my hands and began to cry.

'You w-w-want me to tell you what I'm doing here?' He seemed surprised.

For the barest second, he stopped. Before I could help myself, I asked:

'Have you always stammered?'

'Al-al-always. You should have heard me when I was y-y-y-younger. Wh-when I was about ten I . . .'

'I'm sorry. I shouldn't have asked; it was my fault. Please stop. I mean, you can stop, can't you? Is there some special trick to make you stop? It's late, I'm tired, I want to go home. I want to get home before my child goes to secondary school,' I pleaded.

'How old is your child? Is it a boy or a girl? Let me show you.' No one, but no one, carried pictures of their family in their wallets anymore. (In my part of town, they were well advised not even to carry wallets: I, too, digress). Nigel Morris passed over a picture of an admittedly pretty little girl, maybe two or so. 'This is Mimi,' I thought he was stammering again. 'Miriam really. The l-l-l-love of my life. June and I tried for a l-l-l-long time . . .'

'Do you want a divorce?'

'Good Lord, no. Why on earth should you . . .?'

'Do you want to have your child adopted? Do you want to sue little Mimi? Do you want me to put a contract out on her? What's it got to do with anything?' I howled.

The door to my office burst open and Ruth, one of our junior solicitors, put her head nervously inside. Behind her I could see two others: James and Neil. They weren't stupid. Ruth said:

'Is everything alright?'

'Fine, fine,' I said wearily. 'Nigel Morris meet Ruth Binder. The two behind her are James Coatman and Neil O'Rourke. They're solicitors in the firm. They're all very good. Very, very good. Much better than me. Wouldn't you really rather discuss your problem with one of them? They're cheaper too,' I appealed again to common heritage.

'No, it's definitely you I want to see,' he said without the slightest hint of a stammer. 'Well,' he explained, 'it comes and then it g-g-g-goes.'

The staff backed out in unison, like an orchestration from the detective show *Blue Moon* that I'd taken up watching after the tragic demise of *Hill Street Blues*. They couldn't be less alike, which was good, because I couldn't stand to be reminded of what I was missing.

I leaned back in my chair:

'Mr Morris, so far I've cost you or your firm the better part of a hundred pounds, and I have not heard anything about what I can do for you.'

'Ah, yes, lawyers' legal charges never cease to amaze me: the der-der-derisory . . .'

'Derisory emoluments. We've done that bit already. And I know you're half-Jewish, half-Irish, and you had a child late in life and she's beautiful – which I freely admit – and named Miriam or Mimi affectionately and that sometimes you stammer and sometimes you don't and that it's a much harder life in publishing than people like to think and, oh, yeah, you've a wife called June and what else? Nothing else. Nothing at all. It's not that I really mind, I mean you're paying for my time, or your firm is, and if it's your firm why, why, why should they be paying? Please. Pretty please?'

I stopped, exhausted. It wasn't one of my better speeches but they rarely are before I get the chance to polish them for posterity.

He sighed. At that moment, I finally took to him. He reminded me of Lewis. The room shook, the building shook. I hung onto the arms of my chair and held my breath until it stopped. When it did so, he began:

'Do you know the name Jada Jarrynge? Of course you do. Ev-ev-everyone knows her name.' This didn't stop him telling me about her.

Jada (long 'a', short 'a') Jarrynge (pronounced as in fat syringe) had bounced onto the airwaves only a year before. She was a tall, stunningly beautiful, black woman – Dominican in origin – who was still at art college at the time her first album was released.

I don't know what they call that sort of music. I've heard it called soul, but it's got nothing to do with the sort of soul I grew up with. I only listened to it to begin with because you couldn't turn on the radio or television without. Gradually, it grew on me like it grew on many others and when her second album (is a compact disc an album?) came out, I went out and bought it – not merely to leer at the cover – and, also like everyone else, including Nigel Morris, had to admit that it was even better than the first.

Most of this Nigel Morris told me, even though I already knew it, at far greater length than I've now set it out and interspersed with metaphor, allegory, personal reminiscence and miscellaneous observations I couldn't categorise.

He also reminded me that she had quit art college, and – wholly out of order for the normal career development of her peers, if there were any – had immediately taken the principal supporting role in a short-run television mini-serial to display an acting agility probably as substantial as her voice. She had since made a movie and though, of course, it was too early to be sure, it seemed as if she was here to stay.

What he didn't tell me was something else I happened to know about her, which I didn't think he'd know, so I told him.

Jada Jarrynge was the daughter of Eartha Mellor and step-daughter of Mick Mellor. Eartha and Mick had a child together, called Frankie. A few years ago, Eartha and Mick died in a plane crash. Under the terms of their wills, they had appointed as testamentary guardian Mick's best friend, the Honourable Mr Justice Sir Russel Orbach,

High Court Judge, although at the time still plain Russel Orbach, Queen's Counsel. Jada had gone to live with her father; so far as I knew, Frankie was still living with Orbach, which is where and how I'd met her. By now, she probably ate ground glass for breakfast.

'You're wrong. I did know. That's why I've come to see you.' Another whole sentence without a stammer. 'I also know that you and Orbach – er – how shall I put it?' It was the first time he'd been stuck for words, so I didn't help him out. 'Have a relationship,' he concluded uncharacteristically unimaginatively.

'It's one way of putting it,' I said dryly. 'A better way to put it would be that we enjoy a state of love-hate: one per cent love. Can you work the rest out for yourself or do you need to borrow a calculator?'

He didn't ask me why, which suggested he knew more about my business than he ought to have. But then, the affairs in which Orbach and I have both been involved, while never in their full glory making the front pages – where they belonged – made good gossip, maybe as much as ten or fifteen per cent of it accurate, and I'd long since ceased to be amazed by how many people had a slice of the story. Morris was a publisher: a lot of lawyers write. Aldwych House was part of a conglomerate which owned newspapers: journalists know a lot they can't print and don't hesitate to talk about it. He was my generation: I'd learned he lived in Hackney, during one of his conversational cul-de-sacs, and so did a lot of lawyers I knew; he would have friends amongst them.

Orbach had lurked like a moving shadow in the background of the Disraeli Chambers case. Had he killed any of them? Certainly not. Had he hired anyone to kill any of them? Certainly not. Had he conspired with anyone to kill any of them? Certainly not. Had he done anything in connection with any of those grisly deaths for which he could be indicted, or even subject to civil suit? Certainly not. Was he responsible for all of them? Waddaya think.

He'd done me a favour during the Mather's case, mostly – I thought at the time – to show off how powerful and knowledgeable he was: the aura of omniscience. I'd come to rethink his reasons a while later when he called up and asked me to carry out an investigation for him; the Pulleyne case. If he hadn't offered me so much money, really a ludicrous amount, at a time when – in anticipation of Alton – I needed it, I wouldn't have worked for him.

The fact that I'd worked for him and his elevation to the bench were a lot closer than kissing cousins. The last time I'd seen him, the day of his promotion, I'd punched out his lunch and taken a good shot at re-arranging his jawline by way of saying good-bye, I'd hoped for the last time ever.

'Now are you going to tell me why you're here?'

'Jada Jarrynge writes.'

This, I confess, came as a surprise. She'd been at art college, she was a singer and an actress. I would have expected her to sign her contracts with an 'x'.

'Jada Jarrynge writes bri-bri-brilliantly. She has written a book. Her ag-agent sent me the book. He wants half a mill-mill-million pounds for it. That's a lot of money. People think pub-pub-publishing is gl-gl-glamorous, we're always flying off to make mill-mill-mill . . .'

'You've told me. You've told me at least once. Maybe you've told me twice. You've also told me about cadillacs in Connecticut, the Frankfurt Book Fair and Bevan boys. It's not fair. We were just beginning to get somewhere.'

'Bevin,' he corrected. He leaned back again and the chair cracked again and I held my breath again as this time he sunk slowly and surprisingly gracefully to the floor. It had obviously happened to him before. His arms were behind him to break the fall and he lay there, like Gulliver, his belly about the same height as my desk, in sublime and peaceful silence. For a moment, I thought he was going to doze off.

Fortunately, there was no one left in the office. I helped him up and, reluctantly, proffered the other chair in my room, one I was quite fond of. He sat on it gingerly, mentioning that I could add the d-d-d-damage to my b-b-b-bill. I waved a hand in the air as if I wouldn't dream of it, and made a note on my pad to do just that. Aldwych House was a big enough publisher in its own right and the group as a whole qualified for the description multi-national. They could afford the hundred quid I'd charge for a chair I'd've paid someone a fiver to cart away.

'What're we talking here? Autobiography? I mean, ain't she a bit young to write her life-story; she's only just out of diapers?'

'It's not just an autobiography. At least, it says it isn't. I'm not sure how to describe it. It's called "Where I'm C-c-c-coming From". It's a co-co-collage, in a way. There's poetry, songs, drawings, a play, stories, re-col-col-collections.'

'Sounds yuk. You really wanna publish it? A bit pre-pretentious, isn't it?' Now he'd got me stammering.

Actually, I found it quite attractive, and above all disarming. I couldn't escape the idea that he'd deliberately adopted a stammer to compensate for his weight. Big people are quite intimidating to most of us. They loom over us, invading the personal space we expect to be allowed around us, often not realising how far they're intruding and how much we mind.

But I hadn't felt that with Morris and maybe the stammer was why. Who can feel threatened by someone with a stammer? It's a disability, isn't it? Like only having one leg or being deaf or diseased? I mean, basically, they're crips, ain't they?

'No, you're wrong. I do want to pu-pu-publish it. I haven't described it very well. The things that are in it flow into each other; they're extremely well cr-crafted, well connected; the theme, the title, flows through it like, well, like an air that flows through a group of medieval madrigals; that's what makes it a problem.'

I shook my head; he'd lost me. It wasn't the first time but it was the first time I thought it might matter.

'There's a part of it, a part of it she won't con-contemplate cutting, that pur-purports – but only thinly – to be fiction, in which she writes about the death of her m-m-m-mother, her mother and her step-father. She b-b-basically is s-s-s-saying it was m-m-m-murder.'

I raised my eyebrows but didn't say anything. My heart was beating, as if I knew where the conversation was going, and I knew where I'd go with it.

'She-she-she's accusing the man who her ha-ha- . . .'

'Who her half-sister – Frankie – went to live with, right?' There was no way I could wait for him to finish for himself. 'It's crazy, it's bizarre, she's mad, she must be, there's no way, I mean, I know he's a disturbed man, maybe a bad man, yes, I'd say he was a bad man, but this is too much.'

And I was protesting too much.

\* \* \*

Orbach.

What was it about Orbach?

He was a big man, not physically but in emphasis and effect, a man of gothic proportions, a man of mystery, a man of apparent – but I emphasise only apparent – total command not only of himself but of everyone about him, a manipulator; at times I thought the word that fit best was monster; at other times, despite myself, I still liked him, sensing that one day the lid had to come off, and when it did it would cause him a lot of hurt.

Above all, he was an arrogant man. He was a brilliant man. His arrogance was surpassed by his single-minded ability, and his ability by his extraordinary ambition. He had enjoyed supreme professional success, and corresponding wealth. But he was probably the loneliest and unhappiest man I ever met, and certainly the most cruel. He made enemies first thing in the morning the way others made their beds, and left them just as tidily ordered.

Though patently a driven man, with a centrifugal energy that swept lesser mortals out of his way, I had struggled long and hard to identify his code and his direction. He lacked any identifiable morality. In this sense he was, of course, the perfect lawyer and an even better judge; but he was a wholly imperfect human being.

When I had re-encountered Orbach during Disraeli Chambers, he had been an isolated, bitter man, obsessed by age-old grudges, a man who had broken up with his lady friend in order to be left alone to pursue his revenge, living in his silent Highgate apartment and spending his holidays inspecting the Munch Museum in Oslo in company with a woman old enough to be his mother and who indeed he called 'Mor', which I'd learned was Norwegian for mother.

It was difficult not to contrast this with the fond father-figure I had met at his new house in Barnsbury, enjoying life with his adoptive daughter, who had finally found someone to love who couldn't hurt him back. A man who had discovered, at last, a way to live with himself and with someone else.

I remembered him telling me how Mick and Eartha had died in a small Cessna they'd all owned together, on which they'd learned to fly when Frankie's parents were planning to emigrate to Bolivia, and which Orbach had planned to buy them out of when they went. I remembered him telling me there'd never been any explanation for the crash: something shorn through, but perhaps it had been broken when or as they came down.

And I remembered something he had said during Disraeli Chambers, something so chilling that it had accidentally helped me fill in the missing pieces. I'd been at his home, still the flat in Highgate then. We'd been discussing the deaths: I can't remember now how many had happened by then; three or four or five. He had baldly stated that he had no objection to his former colleagues dying.

I had challenged him. He stood his ground: they were hypocrites, they were scum, it was better they were dead. I'd got up to leave and as I did so I copped out of the discussion by saying it was a good thing we didn't have to make those decisions:

'Because gods and governments do it for us.'

He hadn't answered. He hadn't wanted to lie. I was quite clear at the time what he meant: he considered himself bound by the decisions of neither.

It was a dangerous starting-point for an investigator. A lawyer is supposed to believe his client, and not care how much of his account is true: he is only concerned with the probably untrue. But an investigator needs to start with an open mind or else he'll see evidence where there is none, and fail to spot the fallacy lying at his feet.

14

\* \* \*

Morris left the manuscript with me. There were more reasons involved in his wish to publish than the book's alleged intrinsic quality. For one thing, even if it was garbage, it would have a guaranteed sale that would recover the advance being asked for several times over. Serial rights, as well as hardback and paperback rights, both in this country and in much of the remainder of the English-speaking world.

For another, it had become a matter of interest to the man who owned the publishing conglomerate. Morris had of course discussed the book with him; initially, he had been horrified. He saw his knighthood, ennoblement and eternal hotel reservation in heaven disappearing out the window. Morris had persuaded him to read the book and indeed to meet Jada Jarrynge privately before making up his mind.

'Do I get to do the same?' I grinned.

He held up a hand.

'No, he's not like that. Not at all.'

I got the impression it wasn't blind loyalty so I didn't push the point. 'He spent an hour with her. I don't know what went on. But he was moved by it; I mean personally moved. He's still frightened of publishing it, but tempted. Both as a book, and in one of the group newspapers, *The Sunday*. But he's scared of what the lawyers will say. You know your lot, by the time they've finished li-li-libel-reading a book, there's nothing left but the title.'

He'd reached an agreement with his boss. Before they reached a final decision on publication, it had been decided that they would carry out their own investigation, to see how much of it they would be able to support when the proverbial hit the air-conditioning. Morris'd asked around who might be suitable and my name had come up. It had come up in two different ways. For one thing, I was reputed to be the best, if not the only, investigator who specialised in the misconduct of members of the legal profession itself. For another, I was linked to Orbach.

'Are you saying you – or your boss – believes her?'

15

'I'm not sure. She clearly believes it herself. Something happened. You'll have to make up your own mi-mi-mind.'

For the sake of form, I told him I wasn't investigating anymore. I had to say that, or Alton would be enjoying life without father: Sandy'd kill me. But it was only form: I never had any real doubt I'd take the job: the notion had been planted in my mind; I had to find out, one way or the other.

\* \* \*

The compromise we reached meant I would be retained as a lawyer, and that I would accordingly be paid on a hourly rate which, once I worked it out, meant I'd be paid more even than Orbach had paid me. Given time, the right mood and something to offer in exchange, I stood at least a chance of securing Sandy's consent. Sandy liked best butter on better bread.

I didn't take the manuscript home with me that night, or at all. I wasn't ready to broach it with her yet. Instead, I took it down to the club on one of the routine twice-weekly visits I was allowed: allowed by Sandy, both for the sake of my liver and so I couldn't linger too long over Natalie; and allowed by Natalie, who'd finally got fed up with my interfering with her management of the club and threatened to quit if I didn't stop coming around so often. The only times I went more frequently were when I had to cover during her holidays.

Natalie was a friend of Carson, my former investigative assistant who was now in Australia. There were times when I had wondered whether they'd maybe been a bit more to each other but I never found out for sure and decided, wishfully, probably not. A beautiful Jewess of Russian extraction, a sometime dancer, sometime actress, commonly waitress, she'd been sharing a squat in Islington with Carson and a couple of others, in which I'd stayed for a short time while hiding out from some people who didn't like me anymore.

At that time, she had plans to open her own restaurant or at least a cafe of some sort. When I'd first asked her

16

about the club, she'd refused. But shortly afterwards, they'd all been evicted from the squat and her meagre savings were going to have to go into house purchase if she didn't take up my offer, which came with a small flat at the top of the building on the Old Brompton Road where the club is situated and where once upon a time Lewis had seduced not only Malcolm but many of his other employees and not a few of his customers.

In the last years of his life, though, the flat had been used as a storeroom, or sometimes for a homeless member of staff to live in, and Lewis himself had an apartment elsewhere, considerably more opulent than this. We argued long and hard about it, and eventually I agreed she could spend a few thousand doing the flat up. She moved in, occasionally but never for long joined by a friend, and took control of the club.

She was surprisingly successful. Though Lewis was gay, and so were many of the staff and customers, the club was not exclusively homosexual. It's principal purpose was to provide people with somewhere suitably sleazy but not exorbitantly expensive to go after the pubs shut at the excruciatingly early hour of eleven o'clock. Lewis had kept it open during the afternoons as well, in the days when pubs also shut from three o'clock to five-thirty, but now they could open all day there was insufficient business and we'd quickly dropped the daylight hours.

In Lewis' time, the club was darkly-lit, gloomily-decorated and, until the last customer had gone, the music he played was what he thought contemptuously they wanted to hear. After they left, I'd learned the night of his death, he would often stay behind for what was left of the night, listening to opera, counting his money and brooding about his weight, his lost sexual capacity, gang-wars he'd won and a few he had lost.

I formed a company to run the club, made Natalie a director and appointed an accountant to serve as secretary. I told her I didn't care if it made a profit, but I didn't want to make a loss and I didn't want anything to happen that made us liable for any real damage, like poisoning a guest or physical harm from the condition of the premises or the customers. I didn't want to get sued for anything, not even non-payment of bills. I don't think she was robbing me, because there would have been a substantial excess income over expenditure but for what she was spending to make the place over into her own image.

I hate to admit it, but I liked it better these days. There were still pockets that were discreetly lighted, so people could enjoy their clandestine affairs or encounters which for other reasons they didn't want witnessed. She'd rewired throughout, and brought in a sound-engineer to restructure the music system so it could be heard evenly almost everywhere, without deafening some and leaving others straining to listen.

She'd also done amazing things with the menu. We had to serve food, by the terms of our licence, but during Lewis's tenure it had been so bad no one ever ate there twice. Now, I looked forward to my meal on my evenings at the club, and a couple of times when we'd found a baby-sitter and managed to tear ourselves away from the child who was going one day to rule the world, Sandy'd eaten there with me too.

Normally, I went home first and came down around nine o'clock, still before the place really woke up. I'd eat a meal with Natalie and we'd discuss problems that hadn't been serious enough to ring me about, the latest dilemma in her love-life, and what I thought of whatever she was wearing. Natalie'd look good in a nun's outfit so she never took much notice of my answer: it was just her way of reminding me she knew that if I wasn't straining to remain faithful to Sandy I'd be lapping at her heels. After we'd eaten, we'd retreat to the office for an hour or so to go over the books, before emerging, proud of our proprietorship, to see how many of our customers we could out-drink.

This night, though, I went to the club from the office and asked Natalie to go through the books with me as soon as I arrived. Then I asked her to send my meal in to eat alone and to make sure that I remained undisturbed.

Then I settled down to read what Jada Jarrynge had to say for herself.

# CHAPTER TWO

If she was right, it was a tale of extravagant evil. A man who had selected his own happiness over and above the lives of his best friends. A man who had viewed as an object to be fought over and fought for, a child he claimed to love. A man who considered not at all what might be best for the child, only what was best for himself. Put like that, maybe it wasn't so different from a million other murders.

After I looked out into the club the first time, and saw Natalie still had company, I returned to the office for a final smoke and brood. When I came back out, only Natalie was left. Pointedly, there was a bottle of Southern Comfort on her table. In that subtle, reticent, coy style she had learned from her friend the sophisticated conversationalist Carson, she said:

'So what's up?'

I said, 'Tell me about Carson.'

Carson had been my assistant. She had taken off within a week of the end of the last case. She didn't tell me why. Just left a note at the office during the Christmas-New Year break saying she'd probably be back some day, with probably underlined.

I didn't know if it had something to do with all the deaths; or because during the case she'd begun to reflect on how she'd conducted her life and needed to sort some things out about it that were still in Australia; or because at one point of high tension we'd made love and she didn't want to face Sandy back at the office. I expect it was just because she felt like it.

Once during the past fourteen months, Sandy and I had received a postcard from Tasmania: it said 'down under but not down'.

'I see.' Natalie knew enough about what I used to do, and what I did with Carson, to understand that my question was also a sort of answer to hers. She'd been peripherally involved in our last case, and shown herself a solid trooper when it counted.

'Do you know the Dylan song "Desolation Row"?'

She shook her head. Of course not. She didn't draw a pension either.

'It's about loneliness, at least that's what I think it's about; about people driven mad by loneliness; mad enough maybe to kill.'

On another subject, she might've mocked my pretension. But she knew enough of loneliness herself not to do so now.

'What does it mean?'

'What do you mean?'

'What does it mean for you, now? This is a case, right?'

'Right. Have you been in touch with her?' Twice I had asked her if Carson had written or if she knew where she was and she'd denied it. Now I wasn't sure: 'Do you know where she is?'

She flushed.

The first period I knew Natalie, I fancied her so badly I'm still not sure why I didn't try: probably because I couldn't believe I'd ever get that lucky. When she moved into the club, the emphasis went out of it, partly because of Sandy and Alton, partly also because the club, like the office, had become a routine. Now, for no reason I could explain, I was sitting there as turned on by her as ever I had been.

She knew. She reached around the table and squeezed lightly. My turn to flush. She said:

'Thanks, but, uh, it's not a good idea is it?'

'You've grown old this last year or so, Nat.' For old read wise.

'It makes you, a place like this. They're not happy people who come here, or they wouldn't be here: they'd be at home, holding hands and watching television, listening to music, making love in front of the fire, the way it's supposed to be.'

20

'You haven't answered my question.'

'No more I have,' she admitted tacitly that she knew where Carson was.

'Do you have an address?'

'No, but I have a number where I can leave a message.'

'And, uh, are you willing to disclose this number to me? Why've you never told me before; why've you actually lied about it?'

She shrugged. The effect was as extravagant as when Morris did so, but much more erotic.

'She didn't want you to ring her for a while. But she wanted me to be able to make contact for you when you really needed her. I guess she thought you'd stay in touch with me,' she added with a broad grin.

It was late; maybe that was why I was confused. She explained:

'She thought you'd have a hard time of it, settling down at the office, settling down with Sandy and Alton; she thought you'd want her around because of that – not need her, want her – but that if she was, it would actually be harder for you. I don't know, I'm not explaining very well. Maybe she meant you bring something out in each other.'

Oh, yeah, we do.

'But, of course, she knew there might come a time when you really needed her, and that would be different.'

'And that's now, right?'

'Well, that's what I'm asking you. It could be. I don't know, do I? You haven't told me what it's about.'

No more I had.

'Well? Are you going to?'

I had no doubts about trusting her. Nor did I want to hurt her by giving her the impression that I didn't trust her. But it was still all too fresh in my mind, I still hadn't worked out where I was going with it – or why. So I told her no, I wasn't going to tell her what it was about, and yes, could I please have Carson's number in Australia and yes, I'd probably tell her about it soon.

She sat for a while, evenly divided between agreeing and refusing, between demanding to know and trusting me that it wasn't time yet.

21

Then she got up and went into the office, to her desk I suppose, and returned with the number written on a memo-sheet.

'Tell her she can stay with me,' was all she said.

* * *

I got to meet Jada Jarrynge. I didn't get to meet her alone. I got to meet her in the company and at the office of her agent. I didn't know they made agents like that anymore. He was a prematurely balding, bespectacled, fundamentally slight man but with a middle-aged spread he wasn't prepared to acknowledge by wearing shirts and trousers quite big enough. He had a disproportionately large moustache and looked as if he ought to be behind the counter of a pornographic bookshop, picking his nose and pressing a buzzer under the counter to admit favoured customers to the back room where the really hard stuff was on display. He introduced himself by so many names I promptly forgot them all.

Jada Jarrynge was something else. She was at one and the same time the entire stock of the bookshop in question and an open-faced, innocent child, devoid of any make-up so far as I could tell, wearing faded jeans and a faded denim jacket with floral-patches sewn on, underneath which was an off-white, Greek-style peasant blouse cut just low enough so I could see where her breasts began to slope downhill into heaven. She was very tall indeed: maybe six foot, six foot one in flat running-shoes; her skin was rough yet lustrous; from her ears hung silver spirals and sprays; her hair was a natural phenomenon of wiry black spikes; she was alternately animated and sulky.

'I can see the family resemblance,' I said.

'With whom?'

Note: whom. I shouldn't've been surprised. I'd read her book. Nothing Morris had said about it was an exaggeration.

'Your sister. Frankie.'

'How do you know her?'

'I've been to Orbach's house. I met her there. Oh, this

22

was a couple of years ago, a bit less.'

I started to light a cigarette.

'Please don't. It's bad for my voice,' she said.

I didn't argue but put the cigarette back in its pack. I once started to walk out on a case because the client didn't want me to smoke and only came back when he sent for an ashtray. Morris, the other night, during one of his detours, had expressed regret that I was trying to kill him before he could watch Mimi grow up to win the Nobel Prize for Peace, Literature and Science. His ambitions were, beside mine for Alton, so very modest.

'How old are you, Jada?'

'She's twenty-two,' her agent answered. He had to do something to earn his percentage.

'How old were you when your parents died?'

'It was my mother and step-father. I was nearly eighteen; just over four years ago. My father's still alive. I lived with him until last year.'

'I presume you bought your own place?'

'Of course,' the agent interrupted: 'It's very important for her to put as much as she can into property.'

'Advising her on other property deals, are you?' I snapped.

He looked startled, then laughed easily.

'No. It's what I tell my own daughters.' He made more points in one sentence than I had time to count so I let it go. Besides, I was more interested in the address. I asked. She said, with due suspicion:

'What do you need it for?'

'If I'm going to work on this, I may need to contact you urgently, to check something out or, hell, just to talk it through. I know you're not my legal client, but in effect you're the one whose hunches I'm working out.'

She pondered this for a while and conceded her phone number. If I failed on the case, I could probably make money selling it.

'I want to ask you about . . .' I withdrew from my briefcase the copy Morris had allowed me to take of the manuscript: 'Your mother's letter. On page eighty-three. The one to . . .'

'Yes. I know what you mean. It's the only letter that matters.'

I looked at her, wide-eyed and sad: it was maybe the first time I ever appreciated the naivety with which I had gone through my student years or the meaning of the phrase 'sublime ignorance'.

'Is it real?'

It was the key question.

She seemed surprised I should ask.

'Of course.'

The letter had been sent to Mick Mellor, then in Bolivia looking at land they might buy. It read, in part:

'He came around again last night. If he was anyone else, I think he was trying to get with me. He's been sitting as a judge. He was very tired.

'He was still going on about it, trying to change my mind, talking about Frankie, why it wasn't good for her, how he'd miss her, how he'd miss us. He's so lonely, Mick, I feel sorry for him, but he won't face it's his problem not us. He wants something from us he shouldn't ask. He wants answers from us no one else has. He frightens me. He can be so persuading, I can't answer him. He has hundred reasons why it's bad for Frankie bad for us all of which bad for him. One time, I went for drinks, when I came back he was talking to himself – say, it won't happen, it won't happen. I say, don't take on so; you'll visit; we'll visit; you don't lose us, don't lose her. I feel frightened. Something's going to happen. I feel it. Come home. Please.'

'I'm curious about something,' I said to Jada.

She nodded graceful permission to ask.

'You write beautifully yourself. This is your mother's letter, your dead mother's letter. I don't know if it's word-for-word the way it was written. There's a lot of, well, bad English in it. Why didn't you clean it up?'

Her eyes flashed. I flinched.

'My mother was the best woman I knew. This was her English. Who says what's right and wrong English? She wrote like she spoke and she spoke like she was and a West Indian she was, I am. She had very little formal education, not until later when she went to college through

24

her work.' Like Mellor, she had worked in housing. 'Did you have any difficulty understanding? Could you put it better?'

'No. I'm sorry. I just wanted to understand.'

'Try harder,' she hissed. 'You've got a hard job, you're going to have to work hard at it, all of it. Do you understand me?'

I grinned.

'Oh, yeah, I understand you alright. Maybe I understood already. Maybe my way of understanding wouldn't've been the same as yours. OK?'

She settled back on the sofa satisfied for the time being, both with her own answer and, I liked to think, with mine.

'Does Orbach know you're writing a book?'

'Sure. I told him. I told him he was in it.'

'Why?'

She beamed:

'I want him to read it; I want him to look forward to reading it.'

I nodded:

'Yeah, that I understand.' The greater the shock. 'But it's sort of dangerous: he's a dangerous man, you know.'

'I do know,' she whispered, 'I know, don't I?' Then: 'Do you? How do you know? What do you know?'

I made a decision. Perhaps I'd made it before I came, but I hadn't known it until then. I was going to break all the rules with her, for her. I glanced at the agent, then back at Jada. I said to him:

'Would you let me talk to Jada in private for a bit? I want to tell her some things. They're, well, privileged really. Things I shouldn't be saying. Things I want to tell her.'

They exchanged a glance and she nodded. He rose and said he'd go and make some tea. I asked for coffee.

I told her then the story of Disraeli Chambers. I told her too how Orbach had succeeded to the High Court judgeship of which he was so proud. Then I told her what mood her book had put me in and she knew the song and she knew what I meant. I told her I knew it was possible that she had written the truth. I didn't say I believed her, because I still didn't know if I did: just that it might be true that somewhere along the line his arrogance and his ambition and his loneliness and his pain had snapped into harmony, he had crossed the line between knowing right from wrong.

'You sound as if you're sorry for him – are you?'

'Maybe,' though it wasn't something I'd thought about.

'Will that stop you?'

'Sometimes I feel sorry for Adolf Hitler. There's no evidence he ever had a happy day in his life: to the contrary. But it wouldn't have stopped me killing him if I'd had the chance.' My courage is inexhaustible when my enemies are already dead.

The agent returned with two cups. She looked at me and it was my turn to nod assent. She said it was alright for him to come back in now. While he fetched his own cup, she said, 'You can smoke a cigarette if you want.'

I laughed out loud; she knew as much about handling people as I'd failed to learn. I lit up.

'How did you get the letter? If it was in Mick's things, surely . . .' If it went to anyone, it would have gone to Frankie – Mick wasn't Jada's father.

'I stole it,' she said without hesitation. 'I knew, you see, I knew when he'd been, the time she was writing about. My mother talked to me. I wasn't a child anymore. The letter was, well, I should say about six months before it happened. When it happened, I was already suspicious. Why did he buy the plane with them? Why had he agreed to learn to fly with them? Why was he helping them get ready to emigrate when he didn't want them to? I've written all of this in the book.'

'Yes, I remember.' There was nothing in the relevant parts of her book that wasn't already engraved on my memory.

'So when it happened, I took the letter. Before anyone else could do so. I wanted proof.'

It was a frightening picture; the seventeen-year-old child already plotting revenge for her mother's death.

'Did you never try and talk to anyone else about it? I mean, about your, well, suspicions.'

'I talked to my father. He . . .' She hesitated. She was looking for a way to say it that would not sound disloyal. 'My father told me not to say anything. He said no one would believe me. He said I would make a lot of trouble, and would be hurt by it.'

'Did he believe you?'

'Does it matter?'

'Do you know anything about what the letter says at the beginning – sitting as a judge? I think she must have meant as an Assistant Recorder, that's a part-time judge. A lot of barristers do it, especially if they're trying to impress the Lord Chancellor in the hopes of further promotion. Why would she have remarked on it?'

She shrugged:

'That's what I want to know too. When I've visited with Frankie, sometimes I've stayed in the house; once, no twice, we went on holidays together, he's talked to me a lot.' She meant that she'd used the opportunities to get him to talk. Who'd've believed it? The great manipulator outwitted by a girl less than half his age; that would be the greatest humiliation of all. 'He likes me; he trusts me. But I don't know anything else about it. Is it important?' She was intellectually concerned she might have missed something significant.

'I don't know. I can find out.'

'What do you think, Mr Woolf?' the agent asked.

'What I think is, Jada's father was right. There's a real risk involved'. I told Jada: 'I once did a job for Orbach. I learned something during it. They – the establishment – whatever you want to call them – the legal establishment, the government, the civil service, whatever – they'll go to any lengths to prevent any dirt attaching to a judge, especially a senior, a High Court judge; to prevent anyone finding anything out; and if it's getting close, to cover it up; even then, they'd let a judge get away with it – resign, disappear from public life – rather than see him in court, or a word in the papers. It's fundamental to the system: you can't have a crooked judge.'

When I had seen Orbach at his chambers, right after his appointment to the bench was announced, he told me that he had wanted to become a judge so as to not have to work the long hours of a successful Q.C., to have more time for Frankie: 'What I think now is – if Jada's right,' I entered the continuing caveat, 'if she's right, then the real reason would've been because he knew that a judge would be untouchable: not just from when he became a judge, but for always.'

'You're a practising lawyer, they could do you more harm than they could do Jada, couldn't they?' the agent persisted.

'I suppose so.'

'But you still want to take it on?'

'Yes, yes of course.' I was surprised by the question.

'Why?' Jada asked.

'I'm not entirely sure I can explain. I just need to know.'

It was complicated. It wasn't entirely to do with the fact that Orbach had – for a while – conned me during Disraeli Chambers. Nor that he had used me during the investigation I'd carried out for him: after all, he'd paid the piper, and handsomely. Nor was it about something Tim Dowell used to say, that Orbach and I were alike, two versions of the same difference. Nor, for sure, after the outcome of my last case, was it because of any residual commitment to the Law and its integrity. These were the things it wasn't. Now I had to find out what it was.

\* \* \*

Alton was fast asleep in the buggy that looked like it had been built on Mars – I was glad, he was far too young to meet him; Sandy was still enthusing about the house we'd been to see; I waited nervously to see if he answered the door, half-hoping he wouldn't.

Therefore, he did.

He was growing old and casual: he didn't bother to conceal his surprise. In days gone by, he would've felt obliged to act like he'd been expecting us.

'What are you doing here?'

He didn't invite us in immediately. Our last parting had not been a promising indication of future warm relations.

We had more reason for surprise than he: he had lost a lot of weight and had shaven his beard, though not his moustache; he reminded me slightly of one of the recent vice-chancellors, also moustachioed, who in turn used to remind me of Rumpole of the Bailey on the television. I had seen other members of the bar who had similarly lost weight when they went onto the bench. The Law is an essentially sedentary occupation, but while in practice it calls for a lot of energy – usually generated by excessive food and/or drink. Once on the bench, there aren't the same strains; it is easier to follow a physically more disciplined life-style.

'Well, uh, we came to look at a house, down the road in fact, and I, uh, thought we'd come and say hallo.'

He studied me like I was also something from outer space totally ignoring Sandy until she said:

'Hallo, Russel. Or am I supposed to call you Sir Russel? Judge? God? You look better without the beard – or the belly. Less awesome.'

Despite himself he contrived a smile; he smiled rarely – he viewed it as a sign of weakness:

'Same old Sandy. You'd better come in, I suppose.'

'This is Alton,' she introduced. 'But knowing how you used to feel about children, I don't suppose you'll be calling him anything anyway.'

'It's different now,' he answered. He didn't query the name so things couldn't've changed that much – he hadn't been listening.

'Where's Frankie?' I asked as he led us down to the kitchen.

'Out. Tea? Coffee? Drink, I suppose, for you, Dave?' He said dryly. Ouch. I was tempted to remark that I, too, had changed, but it was asking too much of myself.

He knew what I drank. He hadn't finished the bottle he'd bought in during the time I was working for him. Nor had anyone else since. Frankie must be eleven or twelve by now: I was surprised she hadn't drunk it. Orbach was not himself what I call a great drinker but then there are very few people who I do.

'Perhaps, Sandy, a glass of wine?'

29

There was a time – maybe fifteen or so years before – when there would have been nothing noteworthy about us sitting around together, drinking. We'd all been part of the same, early seventies, so-called radical legal movement: fighting the landlords, the bosses and the police in the name of sixties' idealism. That was when Russel was at Disraeli Chambers, I was at Nichol and Co., and we as solicitors briefed them as barristers. So much had changed, barristers didn't even need to be instructed by solicitors anymore, but could take instructions from other professionals like accountants or surveyors and, soon, would probably be able to do so from lay clients direct.

Then Russel had left Disraeli Chambers; I'd left Nichol & Co.; Sandy had stopped instructing him; he'd become a Q.C.; the last time the three of us were together in one place our other companions were Alexander Keenan, Orbach's oldest and best enemy but Sandy's sometime lover, and a jittery German with a penchant for automatic pistols. Today, he was a judge. Orbach, that is: not the German.

'Sure.'

'I'll open a bottle.'

Sandy made a half-hearted protest, which he properly ignored. He said: 'Perhaps the living-room would be more comfortable.'

As we followed, both of us compared his house with the one we had just been to see. There were surprisingly many differences. His kitchen led through french-windows onto the back garden and his living-room was entirely separate. The one we'd seen was much larger and the whole of the ground floor was open-plan, with the kitchen in the front of the basement, an intervening dining-area and steps up to the living-room on the garden level.

On the ground floor in 'our' house, where Orbach's living-room was, there was a room at the front that would serve well as a study, and a second bathroom. On the middle floor, two more rooms, one for Alton and one for prospective Nanny. On the top floor, in a recessed attic addition, the bedroom that would be ours, with its own *en suite* bathroom. I don't know why; everyone's got their personal idea of luxury; mine's always been an *en suite* bathroom.

Once he had settled us into the living-room, he went to fetch a bottle of wine. He took a long time. Suddenly, we heard an anguished curse, a howl of protest at an inconsiderate, scatological deity, followed by the shattering of glass. Sandy and I exchanged a look. Neither of us wanted to go and see what had happened; for all we knew, he might've found Frankie helping herself to a glass of milk without asking. Reluctantly, I went down to the kitchen to see what was going on. Russel was kneeling down, brushing into a dustpan what was left of the bottle.

'Problem?'

He looked up surprised, like a naughty child caught in the act, then recovered himself to say:

'No, not at all. I dropped the bottle. That's all.'

But in the pan I could see the remnants of a cork still firmly ensconced in the remnants of a neck, and by the sink I saw the corkscrew, with half a cork part-way up it. Also, the shattered glass and the spilled wine spread across not only the floor but the work-surface and into the sink. The cork had split, and so had Orbach's control.

I backed to the kitchen door, afraid despite myself.

'You don't need any help, then?'

'No,' he hissed between gritted teeth. 'I'll be right up. I don't need your help.' Yours or anyone's.

There wasn't enough time to tell Sandy what had happened before he finally emerged, glasses and new bottle in hand. He raised his own after he poured for her:

'Cheers.'

Nothing had happened. I had dreamed it. I said, ignoring the incident in the kitchen, 'No hard feelings, Russel?'

He smiled, 'You know me, Dave, I don't bear grudges.'

I choked on my Southern Comfort.

'How come you're looking at houses around here?'

\* \* \*

As ever, Orbach had put his finger on the contradiction.

The one thing we were not supposed to be doing was looking at houses around there.

For a start, they were far too expensive. Sandy might have money, but it was going to take me a while to catch up on the missing decade of my own earning career.

For another, who'd want to live near Orbach? It'd be like leaving school and moving in next to the headmaster, or getting out of a gaol and taking up residence as a neighbour of the chief warden: forever on parole. Every time I looked up, he'd be there, watching, knowing, disapproving; when I changed channels on the television, drank milk from the bottle, picked my nose, jerked off. Hell, no, not like parole at all – a life sentence.

But as a matter of fact we were looking at houses around there.

The answer – as to so many mysteries in my life – lies with Sandy. Sandy had not been at all impressed by my account of Nigel Morris' visit; she didn't even find my imitation of his stammer funny. Nor was she impressed with Jada Jarrynge's manuscript which, contrary to my express instructions not to show it to anyone, I offered her to read. Nor did she want her autograph. Nor even – most uncharacteristic, of all – was she overwhelmed by how much money I would earn running up the hours of a private investigator, at the charges of a solicitor. I got the message. She didn't want me investigating – anyone, at any price, and especially not Russel Orbach.

My first attempt accordingly fell on deaf ears. My second did a little better. I resorted to our usual method of cohabiting. We were both lawyers. I offered a deal. Sandy had wanted to move out of her house since before the baby was born. In the way of these things, the actuality of Alton had overtaken the aspiration and she had been too tired and too busy and just too plain absorbed in him to pursue it. If she would let me delve a little way into the new case, I said I would make the time to go house-hunting with her; even better, if we actually found somewhere I could afford a share of – an important qualification – I might actually agree to buy it.

'Whereabouts?' she asked suspiciously.

What I had in mind was Crouch End, Hackney, maybe even North Islington – places you didn't need a computer to count your bank balance. But as we had been talking, I had an idea how to merge my interests.

'How about South Islington?' I said brightly. 'Barnsbury, for example?'

She shook her head in amazement.

'You're about as subtle as a child on Christmas morning. You can't afford it; you don't want to live near him; and, no, I won't let you use us as a coy excuse to happen to bump into him or pop in and say hallo.'

I smiled winningly. She flung a pack of nappies at me.

'And change Alton for the rest of the week?'

I love my son, I hate his excrement.

Like most of my plans, this one had already begun to backfire. Two minutes after we went inside the house I had picked on his street – one of many with a For Sale sign up – Sandy handed me Alton and pulled out her calculator, looking pointedly at me as she began to punch buttons. She could do that: she used to go with an accountant. There was an irony lurking in the near-distance that was so sweet and so terrifying I knew it was about to take over.

\* \* \*

'Which house have you been to see?'

Sandy told him. It was on the same side of the street as his, but closer to Copenhagen Street, and the Sainsbury and Marks and Spencer on the other side: about an equal distance from the Crown pub, but in the other direction.

'The one with the show-garden? I didn't know it was up for sale.'

'No. It's got a funny shaped garden, and I think it backs onto the show-garden at one point, but it's a few houses along. The garden's fabulous: walled, goes off in every direction, it may be the best feature.'

He explained didactically, 'There used to be businesses in the middle of what are now the gardens; some of them were stables; the properties went wholly residential at different times; it has led to some odd shapes; some of the gardens are tiny; I'm quite lucky, but if it's the one I'm thinking of, I can see why you're excited.'

It had been his area of practice: land, planning, development. He knew Mick Mellor because they worked on cases together. Orbach as barrister, Mellor as surveyor.

'You must be doing well,' he added condescendingly.

Sandy and I exchanged a look. I changed the subject quickly.

'Tell us what it's like, being on the bench.'

If you'd asked me the last time I saw him whether I'd ever again be willing to sit and chat politely, I would have sworn on the grave my father didn't yet occupy that it would never happen.

'It's pleasant, really, compared to practice. There isn't the insecurity of wondering where the next case is coming from, nor the lurking guilt when you get time off; we're supposed to be concerned about appeals, and about the prospects of promotion to the Court of Appeal, but I would have thought I've gone as far as I'm ever likely to, wouldn't you?'

He had already gone a lot further than he had any right to do.

'It can be hard work; it calls for a lot of concentration, and there's much more preparation than people realise, both before a case and when it comes to writing judgements. But on the other hand, it's not that difficult to know what decision to reach.'

'No? I would have thought that was the hardest thing of all: people are so unpredictable.'

'Rubbish,' he dismissed my sentimental proposition briskly. 'People are the most predictable animals of all. All you have to do is to work out what they wanted to do; people only do what they want; people can always be made to do what they wanted to do; once they start on a course of conduct, they can't get off it.'

'Still sounds to me like hard work – sussing out what they want to do.'

He stepped off his rostrum.

'I can't complain; it's what I wanted; it gives me time for Frankie.'

34

'How is she?'

'She's wonderful. She's doing brilliantly at school, she had the lead part in the play last year, she's on the running team, she's . . .'

Sandy shook her head in awe; 'Dave told me you'd turned into a doting father but I didn't believe him. Is it really you in there, Russel?'

He laughed mirthlessly.

'I've changed, Sandy, I've changed a lot. Before, well, I never really knew what happiness was, a normal life.'

'Margot?' I asked.

'Margot? That was an affair of the mind. We were intellectual partners, and, of definition, that required considerable independence, separateness. I thought I'd lost all chance of knowing, well . . .' he laughed again, but this time nervously, embarrassed to talk of such intimate matters, 'Well, I mean knowing a way of life like others always seemed to manage to find.'

'When do we get to see this paragon?' Sandy asked.

'Not today, I'm afraid. I've let her stay with her sister. Do you know who that is?' He asked proudly, 'Jada Jarrynge. The singer. And actress. Of course, she's only her half-sister, and I had no part in her upbringing, but she's turned out very well and I like to think perhaps I helped a little. After all, her father,' he waved a hand dismissively. I couldn't remember what her father did, but I got the point.

'Does she write her own material?' I asked out of a bloody-minded refusal not to have some fun at his expense, not to feel in the slightest way that I knew something he didn't.

'Certainly. She writes very well. She's writing a book, you know, about her life; she says she's going to put me in it,' he beamed.

'Really?' I managed to sound surprised. 'That'll be interesting.'

# CHAPTER THREE

There was one question left over from the investigation I had carried out for Orbach: whose side had Tim Dowell been on? I knew the facile answer – his own, as always. I also knew that the way things had ended might be considered proof that he, as much as Orbach, had been playing me for a patsy. He'd done it before. But it wasn't so clear this time around; certainly, it wasn't clear that he'd intended to use me until very late on, when perhaps there were no real choices left.

Between my second and my third major cases, I'd avoided Tim, angry at the way he'd conned me. This time I'd seen him a couple times. I saw him soon after we took Alton home. He came around to discuss the club. It wasn't his business, but that never stopped him interfering. In his will, Lewis had left it to me: I wasn't supposed to keep it; it was to be passed on to Malcolm – once an old violence conviction had been spent and he could qualify to hold the liquor licence. All of this was to be found in the side-letter. Tim had acquired the letter. Now that Malcolm wasn't going to see the time out, he proposed to tear it up. That left the club in my name without qualification.

We'd stood on the doorstep, arguing the ethics of what we were about to do, and in the end it was he who had torn the letter into tiny pieces and thrust them deep into the dustbin to be carted away. He'd come back once more, with a present for Alton: the pram that could convert into buggy and that was carry-cot as well. It was, for a copper, an expensive gift, and I'd read it at the time as some sort of apology.

'Nah,' he said now, 'I just thought, you don't have much family, do you. I mean, your mother's dead, you hardly speak to your sisters and you and your father haven't been in touch as long as I've known you. And, well, with Lewis gone . . .' He was about all I had left for a friend.

He wasn't far off.

I didn't say thanks. Sandy'd said it when he brought it to the house and I didn't want to spoil him.

'How's your zoo?'

He was a vicious, deceitful, hard-drinking, wholly incorruptible in any conventional sense, successful Detective Inspector, with a tiny head that would'nt've looked big on a weasel and a university degree in Law he didn't like too many people to know about. Most of the time he was kept on stand-by for the dirtiest jobs, where neither the Marquess of Queensbury nor the Judge's Rules had anything to do with how the case was handled. Nonetheless, or perhaps because of it, he was happily married, to the best of my knowledge and belief never unfaithful, and from the occasional remark a thoughtful and sensitive father.

'Good. Sandy? And Elton?'

'Alton's fine,' I corrected, ignoring the deliberate slip. 'Sandy's headaches have started again, but otherwise she's alright; she's working part-time now.' As long as I'd known her, Sandy had suffered from occasional headaches. They weren't at the front of the head, nor at the sides like a migraine, but at the back, at the top of her neck. They didn't last long and for the first year after Alton was born, they went away, but recently they'd returned.

'She should see a doctor.'

'You know Sandy.' Bad news happens when you go looking for it.

He eyed me suspiciously, this desultory chatter was not why I'd called him up.

'Well?'

I sighed:

'Don't you want another drink?'

We were at the club. In the past, we'd spent many hours there, alone or with Lewis. He hadn't been in since the

37

night of Lewis' death. When he arrived, he sniffed around, like a dog marking out his space. He had been surprised to see Natalie, but polite and had yet to make any of the more obvious remarks I would have expected of him. Perhaps he was growing up too.

'Alright.' This was what he and I had in common, Southern Comfort. He always drank it with me – his wife wouldn't let him keep it at home. 'I'll do you a favour.'

'Do me another? Could you get me the police report on a plane crash?'

All plane crashes which result in deaths, whether or not of the pilot or passengers, and whether or not involving commercial aircraft, are investigated by the Civil Aviation Authority. Save where the crash involves the Royal Air Force, or when there is litigation as yet unresolved and one or other of the parties injuncts to prevent it, these reports are published. They are obtainable through Her Majesty's Stationery Office, and I had already read – though barely understood – that concerning the Mellors.

The police will also normally conduct an investigation, on behalf of the coroner. That report will not be made public, save insofar as it produces evidence in a case, whether in front of the coroner or otherwise. The verdict returned by the coroner – accidental death – was itself valueless. It wasn't conclusive that there had been no human intervention. It was merely the most probable explanation in the absence of any other. Jada had reproduced the local newspaper reports of the inquest: they were neither of them more than two paragraphs, and contained no useful information at all. The crash didn't make the nationals.

'What do you know about planes?'

'Nothing.' This was true. I know they used to have four wings and now only have two, which is terrifying enough in itself. I know they go up in the sky with lots of foolish people in them, and whenever I can I make sure I'm not one of them.

I once flew to America, by *Loftleidir*, the Icelandic airline which in those days was the only cheap service. It was a night flight and I didn't see the aircraft as we boarded.

38

But we had to touch down in Iceland. Though it was by then after midnight, it was spring or summer and very light. That was when I realised the plane ran on propellors: they had to give me a tranquillizer and carry me back on board to continue the journey.

The Mellors' plane, I had learned from Jada's book, was a Cessna six-seater, a single span light turboprop they'd bought with Orbach, second-hand, and parked – if that's what you do with a plane – at Southend Rochford where there were private club facilities. I knew they got tuition there too, and that by the time of the crash, Mick – a faster learner than either Eartha or Russel – had secured his licence. I knew they had filed a flight plan to Pont-toise, outside Paris, but were barely across the Thames Estuary when they crashed.

'So? What would you do with the report? Get Alton to explain it to you?'

'Uh, let me rephrase the question: could you get me the police report and someone to help me understand it?'

'You want something more than the usual, bland, C.A.A. guff, huh? This is a personal injuries case, right? A death claim? Manufacturer's negligence? That sort of thing? I mean, it must be, 'cos you're a solicitor now, Dave, and that's all. Right?'

'Uh, yeah, right, definitely.'

He sighed and downed his drink, but hung onto the glass.

'I wondered how long it'd last.'

'Is that why you've been keeping away?'

'Could be.' Like Carson, we brought something out in each other. 'Then again, could be I wasn't sure what you were thinking.'

'About Pulleyne?'

'Yup.'

He was asking me the left-over question I was supposed to be asking him.

'I'm not sure. I believed, I believe, right up until the end, you wanted the same thing I did. After that . . . I don't know. Do you?'

He thought about it for a while then shrugged.

39

'I think, at the end, I knew we wouldn't get everything, so I settled for something. That make sense to you?'

'About.'

'Will it do?'

While I was still an investigator, the roles were reversed: he wasn't supposed to care what I thought; I was supposed to curry his favour; that's the way it's always been between the police and a private eye. Now he wasn't sure whether to treat me the same way, or as a solicitor. Me neither.

I didn't answer.

After a long silence, he said, 'Are you going to tell me about it?'

'An old friend of ours. Now a High Court judge. That make any difference to you?'

'Orbach.' He and Orbach went way back. A lot of people went way back with Orbach – few of them went forward.

I nodded.

He blinked about a dozen times:

'You never learn, do you? You working for him or agin' him and is there a difference?'

'Agin'.'

'Why're you doing it, Dave?'

'I thought you might tell me, Tim.' I held the bottle out to him, but he shook his head.

'You've got a very destructive streak, Dave . . .'

'Tell me something new . . .'

'I thought, maybe, you know, with a child . . . It'd have an effect.'

'Some,' I conceded. 'Just not enough. So?'

'I'm not your shrink . . .'

'Never stopped you before . . .'

'It isn't funny, Dave. You could do yourself a lot of harm. And Sandy. And Alton. You just can't accept . . . the idea of someone you can't understand. It frightens you; he frightens you.'

I pondered this for a while, and poured myself another shot while I did so, though he again refused.

'Hell, there's lots of people I don't understand. I don't even understand myself half the time.'

'That's exactly my point.'

I half-understood but was too proud to admit the other half.

'So? You gonna help?'

'Like I said, Dave, you never learn.'

He put his glass down on the table, got up from his seat, turned casually as if looking to see where the door to the lavatory now was, and walked out of the club.

* * *

I couldn't do anything for the next couple of weeks. A Crown Court trial came suddenly into the list and I had to spend most of each day at court, sitting behind a barrister who knew less about the case than I, who'd been handed it at the last moment when the woman I'd originally instructed couldn't get out of another case she was in. Despite his worst efforts, we got an acquittal, but they'd allow me on legal aid only the same low rate for my constant attendance as they'd allow for an articled clerk.

I rang Carson once, the day after Natalie's given me the number. I got through alright: it was nine hours ahead of us. I got through to a man with a middle-european accent who sounded old enough to be her father if I didn't know her father was dead and who told me Carson had gone on a trek into Gibson and couldn't be reached. No, he had no idea when she'd be back; could be a week, could be a month. Did I want to leave a message? Sure: tell her Dave called. She didn't ring back.

I went down to the Temple on a conference in another case, which I'd deliberately allocated to a barrister in Orbach's old Chambers. His clerk seemed surprised to see me: we hadn't briefed any of his barristers for many years. As I went in to the con, I said, 'If you're around when we finish, have a drink?'

'Certainly, Mr Woolf. It'd be a pleasure.' He was yet more surprised. Usually, clerks cruised solicitors to come for a drink. Gone were the grand old days of Marshall Hall when solicitors had to persuade barristers to accept a case: with a few exceptions, most of the bar now touted outrageously for work, themselves or through their clerks, and it was a rare conference which didn't end with an offer to me of a drink from one or other. Most sets of chambers found an excuse for a party half a dozen times a year, to which they invited all those solicitors they hadn't seen since the one before.

We went to a wine bar, itself called Chambers, above the Witness Box pub. Orbach's former clerk was called Edward. Neither Ed nor Ned nor least of all Ted or Teddy. He wore a suit more expensive than that of the barrister with whom I had been in conference, and a watch-chain of solid gold. He was balding, pompous, in his late forties and lived in Essex. It is unnecessary to say more.

He selected carefully a claret at the top end of the price-range. I thought about asking for a Southern Comfort but it would be interesting to see what the rest of the world drank. I even quite liked it. He asked me:

'How did you find Mr Davies, sir?'

'Alright,' I said grudgingly.

Theoretically, all barristers are supposed to be equally brilliant, distinguished, absolute masters and mistresses of any area of law on which they are asked to advise and advocates to the gentry who make their services available to the general public out of the goodness of their hearts rather than for fees the size of which most clients didn't complain about because they had been stunned into shocked silence.

Solicitors and barristers' clerks know better. They know that cases have to be switched around at the last moment. They know they can't always have the barrister of choice. If he was that available, he wouldn't be that good. So a lot of the time, by silent agreement, we settle for someone with an average degree of competence rather than start over in other chambers, again and again, looking for a brief with more positive qualities. 'Alright' was praise enough for a Davies. Edward nodded gravely. He wasn't looking for more.

'Do you see much of Sir Russel?' I asked idly.

'You knew him quite well, didn't you, Mr Woolf?' I presumed he had some idea of the state in which I'd left

Orbach the last time I'd been at his chambers – maybe he'd even helped him up off the floor.

'No, we're fine, a little misunderstanding was all. I was at his home the other day.'

'Camden, isn't it?' I forgot to mention that barristers' clerks are also the most suspicious people on earth – because they are themselves so thoroughly untrustworthy, they don't think anyone can be trusted.

'Islington,' I corrected dryly, so he poured me another glass of claret. 'Thanks. Cheers.'

'Your health, sir. He doesn't come into chambers often. He had a party at his house after his appointment. Naturally, I was invited.'

'Yes, but did you go?' I chuckled maliciously.

He smiled forlornly, but judges don't bring their former clerks any income, while solicitors do, so he shifted gear into a broad grin intended to look boyish but that would've made Boris Karloff look amiable.

'Have you ever seen him in court?'

'No, sir, I haven't. Too busy.'

'Not even when he sat before his full-time appointment? As an Assistant Recorder, I mean?' This was what I was after.

He shook his head. We were almost at the end of the first bottle and he'd drunk more of it than me. I offered to buy another.

'Let me, sir.'

'If you insist.' It wouldn't stop me claiming it on expenses from Aldwych House.

'Where did he sit in those days?' I asked when he had returned and refilled our glasses.

'South-Eastern Circuit, if my memory serves.'

'Yes,' I said: 'I think that's what I remember, too.'

\* \* \*

She didn't return my call, but when I arrived home for dinner after my drinking session with Edward, she was sitting in the kitchen, Alton on her lap, Sandy fussing to feed her.

'You called, master,' was her opening remark.

I sat down opposite her. We'd neither kissed nor shaken hands. We were still sizing each other up.

'I might've called to check you were still far enough away.'

'You wouldn't've spent the money. Unless of course,' her eyes glinted, 'you had a client paying expenses.'

'You've already talked to Natalie,' I accused.

She pointed with her foot to the rucksack behind the door: she'd come straight here.

We examined each other openly and curiously. I never had a partner in an investigation before Carson – assistant, partner, it was all the same and not always clear who was in charge or, at least, in control. The first time I'd seen her, she'd terrified me. From her reaction, I wasn't sure it wasn't entirely mutual. Most of the time she was surly if not downright sour, scowling instead of speaking, or mumbling monosyllabically. Then she would switch mode and talk without end at as great a length as, but more to the point than, Nigel Morris. Initially, she'd been secretive with me. Now we were secretive together.

'Lost the mop, I see.'

'Wearing contacts, are we?'

When I first knew her, she had a blue hedge standing upright in the middle of her otherwise close-cropped, dyed-platinum blonde head, and wore a blue leather bomber jacket to match. Her hair had grown out, and it was now somewhere between blonde and mouse, maybe even its natural colour; her jacket, too, was now a boring and undistinguished tan.

She was about five nine, a couple of inches shorter than I, but even without heels walked so tall I always felt she was hovering over me. She was built big, too, and every inch of it was solid. Her Australian accent came and went with her moods. No one would ever call her beautiful, or pretty, nor maybe even turn a head to watch after her on the street; they were the ones who were missing out, not her.

'If you two want to go outside and punch each other for a while, that's fine – dinner'll be a bit yet,' Sandy said.

Alton started to cry. He didn't like violence.

I've never been sure if Sandy sensed what had happened between us. She was jealous enough to suspect I slept with anything less macho than Rambo. I think she usually assumed I had unless and until the opposite was proven beyond any doubt at all; reason doesn't come into it. But there'd been a hint or two beyond the generality, coupled to the slightest suggestion that she might even understand and, in this one, exceptional case, excuse.

It was a balmy spring evening so we took our drinks and doing half what Sandy suggested, took them outside. We leaned against the fence at the end of the garden, not talking, until she put her drink down on the grass, stood up and came and put her arms right around me, almost as if she was pleased to see me. I got no opportunity to put my glass down, so I drank it over her shoulder, lowered it as far as I could, and let it plop straight down, base first, to the dewy ground where, as I had hoped, it didn't break. We held each other's face in our hands and grinned and giggled and kissed just once, mainly chastely but mouths a fraction open, on the lips.

We didn't speak about that other time. We'd agreed after it happened that it wasn't necessary, and in the brief period before she'd disappeared to dingo-heaven we'd hardly seen each other. It was just after Alton was born and I had other things to occupy my mind – like, where to learn to be a father, and quickly. We both began to speak at once –

'It's great to see . . .'

'It feels like coming . . .'

Then we hugged again, picked up our glasses and went back inside. Sandy examined us critically: as Carson never wore makeup, she couldn't've been looking for lipstick; she must've been looking for blood. She bit her lower lip, nodded once in satisfaction and gestured with her head to the table, where Alton was already belted into his high chair.

We didn't talk about the case over the meal. Conversations at the dinner table, one of life's few true pleasures, were a sacrifice to the child. We couldn't complete a sentence without a howl from Alton, or from Sandy as food dribbled disdainfully down his chin. As often as not he needed changing half-way through, which didn't do much to enhance my appetite.

After, Alton decided suddenly it was bed-time which meant also that we were only going to get a quarter of a night's sleep. We retreated to the living-room while Sandy took him upstairs, graciously waving away an offer to do the honours I hadn't made.

'How was it?' I asked.

'OK Better than I expected.'

'Whose phone was it?'

'He was a sort of third cousin five times removed.' There was not much left of her immediate family. 'I stayed there mostly.'

Our eyes caught. When you know someone that well, the most banal sentence can carry a host of meaning. I just said:

'Weird.'

She shrugged:

'I never did old before.'

'Thanks,' I broke our rule.

She giggled. She can do that, giggle without seeming silly or childish or, worst of all, girlish. That was something else no one would ever call her.

I didn't mind. I suppose what I'd learned most in the time since she'd been gone was that I could handle the one thing that had always terrified me: compromise. I got it off Alton, I guess. I found I couldn't always have my own way, but that it didn't matter anymore. I'd never been faithful to a woman before Sandy, nor indeed for the first years with Sandy, because I couldn't reconcile the need to do so with the inevitable and not-so-occasional sexual desire for someone else which, being of my generation, it never used to occur to me didn't necessarily have to be acted on.

'Stay here tonight; move to the club tomorrow,' I urged. I wanted her under the same roof.

'OK,' she said unquestioningly. 'You gonna tell me what it's all about?'

'Sure. They have electricity in Australia yet?'

'A bit.'

'Steam-radios?'

46

'Trannies.'

'Television: like, uh, radio with pictures?'

'Moving pictures?'

'Yup. Moving pictures.'

'No. But it's coming soon – in the next ten, twenty years, soon as someone kills Kylie Minogue.'

'They got Jada Jarrynge?'

'Right. What're we doing for her . . . Or should I say to her?'

'Which'd you rather?'

'For. I like her music. I like her.'

'You ought to. You've got a lot in common.' I meant they both had a childhood experience that threatened to take over for good. At fifteen, Carson had killed her uncle, who had attacked her crippled father with a meat-cleaver. It was part of what she'd gone back to Australia to sort her head out about. It was what she meant when she said it'd been better than she expected.

'What's the scam?'

'She thinks someone killed her parents.'

'And did they?'

'The man she thinks did it goes by the name of Orbach.'

'Yuk,' she observed intelligently. 'Really?'

'Really what? Really does she think it or really did he do it?'

'Whatever.'

'Really she thinks it. I don't know about the other. Talked to Tim – seems to think I've got a bit of a bee in my bonnet about Orbach, some reason. What do you think?'

'Where do we start? When?'

* * *

It's all and always and only about connections. There's no crime that isn't. That's why the perfect crime is said to be the murder of a complete stranger. Even then, there's a momentary connection, however fleeting, however distant, as, for example, between the random sniper and his victims. They are still together in a connected place, and the connection takes tangible form as a bullet. Similarly,

47

the person who poisons a stranger, a number of people, or a whole city. They're connected too.

One difficulty lies in how deeply the connection is buried; the slighter the connection, the shallower the grave it calls for. But the main problem is knowing where to dig. I knew approximately from when to when: a six month period in Orbach's life, when he was still a barrister, sitting some of the time as an Assistant Recorder, between the letter Jada'd quoted in her book and the day the Mellors' Cessna came down. I knew he'd still been living in Highgate, because he moved to Barnsbury on account of the space needed for Frankie. I knew therefore there would be little purpose plodding around his private life of that point in time: he had none.

Assistant Recorders sit mainly in the criminal courts. That is to say, the Crown Court, not the magistrates' courts which don't have real judges. They also sit in county courts, where minor civil actions are heard, and very occasionally in the High Court itself, where Orbach was now a permanent, full-time judge. Mostly, though, it is the Crown Court. That's where the volume work is, and where the backlog that matters builds up. The Law has always regarded as far more important whether a person should be fined tuppence-halfpenny for stealing a bottle of milk – which is the sort of petty offence part-time judges try – than whether or not he should be evicted from his home.

They especially tend to put people to sit in crime when someone has, or has had, a left wing reputation, as Orbach was tagged because of his one-time membership of Disraeli Chambers. They want to see just how liberally they will perform on the bench. Usually, they're the hardest bastards of all. They are motivated not by such paltry considerations as justice, fairness, or the economic or psychological deprivation of the accused, but by the really important matters, like how quickly they can achieve their own professional advancement which is bound to be of greater value to society than letting off another little villain.

In an unfair division of labour, I sent Carson to play with airplanes, and concentrated myself on pinning down Orbach's professional activities, on and off the bench.

48

Perusing the law reports helped: he had appeared as leading counsel in a long-running building contract dispute for much of the time. My mind winged tangentially to the moon: builders are Freemasons; Freemasons are, as I had discovered during the Mather's case, at least potentially a criminal and invariably a conspiratorial crew; builders also have the opportunity to bury people in concrete, so I'd read in a hundred thrillers and seen in many more movies.

The trouble was, the Mellors had died in the air, not at the bottom of the sea-bed, and what I knew of builders suggested they would be wholly incapable of doing anything technical to an airplane. Especially if they were Freemasons, who rode on their broomsticks instead.

As for Carson, she didn't do a whole bunch better. There was a flying club at Southend Rochford Airport, which I already knew; there were several flying clubs at Southend Rochford, which I didn't know. Tuition could be arranged at any of them. So could parking space.

She finally tracked down the club through which the Mellor-Orbach Flying Circus had functioned, but the man in charge of tuition was new, and could neither remember who his predecessor of that time would have been, nor where his records were. An outside firm did their small plane maintenance; he knew little about them. She rang to ask whether it was worth the cost of staying in an hotel to make further enquiries. I told her to cash in her return ticket and hitch-hike back to town.

I wasn't too worried. For a change, even absent the assistance of the cowardly Dowell, I had alternative resources. I rang Nigel Morris.

'You still thinking in terms of running this in one of the newspapers?'

'Uh, yes. *The Sunday*. Did you see last week's ed-ed-edition? There was a full-page story about a country I'd never heard of. I'm not su-sure if it even exists. It was ab-about . . .'

'Nigel,' I cautioned, 'I'm charging for this call.'

With his usual lack of direction, we discussed the possibility of tapping into the investigative resources of the paper. An hour or two into the conversation, he confirmed that he could ask whether they could be made available to me. An hour after that, still in the same conversation, he confirmed that he would so ask.

The next day, he rang to give me the name of a contact, Brian Battle. I didn't try ringing straight away; it was twelve o'clock and if he was any good as a journalist he'd already be in the pub. I left it until four and we arranged to meet that evening at the club.

For the duration of the case, and of Carson's stay with Natalie, the usual restrictions did not apply: I could go as often as I liked, provided I did not interfere in club management more than usual. Someone told me it is profoundly sexist to surround myself with women who tell me what I can and can't do; I understand the theory – it means I'm worth their time, trouble and attention; the difference is, my lot mean it.

Battle was a tall, lean, gangling man, in his thirties but already greying, with a wrinkled shirt and a stain-spotted tie, but smartly pressed slacks which, he explained, he had bought that afternoon to replace those over which he had spilled his liquid lunch. I told him he could order food if he wanted, but didn't tell him he wouldn't have to pay until after he'd selected what he wanted. I chose the wine for him – chateau cheapo.

'This your place, then?' He asked, licking his lips as he watched Natalie return to the bar with at least one unnecessary, sarcastic tweak of her backside. 'Nice.'

'The place is; not the people in it.'

'Pity. How did you come to own a club like this?'

'It's a long story. You wanna join?'

'What's it cost?' His eyes narrowed.

I told him. He barked. I wasn't going to be able to compensate the accounts for what my extra visits were costing the club.

'What do you know?' I asked.

'Nothing. Memo from the chairman. Find an investigative journalist; lend him to Aldwych House. Then I got a call from a man named Morris: talker, stammerer . . .'

'I know. Don't remind me. He told you what?'

50

'By way of his ignorance of new technology, his honey-moon on a canal boat, a bestseller he'd failed to buy and his daughter's medical history, to take a call from you and do whatever you asked me that was legal. He said you were a lawyer, so I should worry a lot and consult the group's legal eagle if in doubt.'

'You know what an Assistant Recorder is?'

He nodded.

'How would you go about finding whether and where he was sitting at a particular time?'

'Ring the Lord Chancellor's Office?'

I shook my head.

'Chat up his clerk.'

'Tried it.'

'Ask him.'

'They say tomorrow never comes, but I don't see why I should make it a sure thing.'

'This got anything to do with Pulleyne?'

Another one with a name, a slice of a story and a shot at the annual 'What The Papers Say' award.

'Who?'

He grinned:

'Worth a try.'

'You've tried. Now try to answer my question.'

'They sit on circuits, don't they? You know which?'

I told him.

'And you said you know when?'

'Within six months . . .'

He groaned.

'Do you know how many local papers that means I have to plough through?'

'Start in Southend-on-Sea.'

# CHAPTER FOUR

'It's, er, hardly the best way to choose a neighbourhood,' I proffered lamely. 'I could understand better if it was his house you wanted to buy.'

Sandy was still going on about the property in Cloudesley Road.

I understood well enough. I liked the place about as much as she did. I could remember the impression the street had made on me the first time I'd visited Orbach's, waiting for him sitting outside the pub nearly opposite his house. Very few streets in London have what can properly be called a discernible ambience. Cloudesley Road did. It was a light street, with double-width pavements but a narrow road that could only be entered from one end so that there was relatively little traffic. In the middle, next door to the pub, there was a general store. People wandered casually from their houses almost as if they weren't going outside at all.

It was a village and as such it was as close as people like us ever got to the ideal of the sixties like it was sung: back to the country.

Sandy said, suddenly serious:

'Sometimes I get frightened, Dave. I get frightened by the things you do. I get frightened you won't be here all that time ahead. I want us to have some of the good life now, instead of saving it up for a future which isn't there when we arrive. You know what I'm saying?'

'Not a chance; I'll outlive the lot of you.'

We were in the kitchen. B.A., the kitchen was not the focal point of our home life. It was used for its specific purposes, but we'd sit and talk and often eat in the living-room. Since his fall to earth, the increase in kitchen chores – cooking, feeding him, washing clothes – meant there was often so little time left at the end of the day it wasn't worth moving to another room.

This was another reason for buying a new house. The kitchen was not designed for living in. The house was the one Sandy had bought, years and years (and years) before and done up for the lifestyle of a single person. There were plenty of work-tops but not enough places comfortably to put our bottoms. She'd always assumed that if she ever had a family, she and whomever would find somewhere together that would be theirs not just hers. She hadn't reckoned the whomever might be me, with attendant problems like absence of capital, a mortal fear of commitment and a concentration span too short for England's archaic conveyancing process.

'We can't really afford it, can we?'

I hadn't a clue what we were worth. I drew cash from the firm, to spend, and everything else was handled between Sandy and Naomi. Naomi was at the College of Law with us but after practising for a while, she'd quit, married, had kids and now came in two days a week to do the office books and accounts and some of the bills. If I was short, I borrowed from the till at the club. If I was really short, I borrowed from petty cash at the office. No one had caught me yet.

'We'd have to borrow most of it. I mean you will.' She grinned comfortably: 'I can afford my end.'

'I thought I could too,' afford her end, I meant. 'For richer and poorer?'

'We're not married.'

'For Alton's sake?'

'Precisely.'

It was a straightforward, conservative proposition. If I invested heavily in property, a house I'd actually want to hang onto, I'd have a real incentive to stick at steady work.

'What about Orbach? You really want to live spitting close?' Orbach could spit. 'We can hardly ask him to move out for our sakes.'

53

'We don't have to have anything to do with him. This is London. Do you know who lives two doors away? Hell, do you know who lives next door? Besides, if Jada Jarrynge's right, he's not going to be around for long, is he.' It was the first time she had conceded that there might be something in the accusation. I said so. She said, 'That's not what I'm saying. I said "if".'

'What do you think, though, San?'

She scowled.

'. . . Times I have to tell you. . . ?' Not to abbreviate her abbreviation. 'I think . . . I think you have to find out; I think you have to satisfy yourself one way or the other; I think, maybe, you're going to come a cropper, but as long as you don't get hurt too badly, well. . .' she smiled sweetly and didn't finish her sentence.

'You think it'll teach me a lesson?'

'Something like that. Either way, he's not a problem.'

'He won't go to jail,' I said flatly. 'He'll still have to live somewhere.'

She shook her head.

'If he's disgraced, he'll move away, somewhere he's not known, people always do.'

'Orbach ain't people.' Nonetheless, she was probably right: his temper tantrum over the broken cork confirmed what I had always believed – that somewhere deep inside was a man scared of shame. 'What if you're right and I don't prove anything, or I actually prove her wrong?'

'Then he'll never know you even tried,' she said smugly.

'Bullshit.' These things always come out. Orbach was a man who had made an art-form out of knowing things he wasn't supposed to. 'He'd know.'

'He's not God, Dave – just a High Court judge,' she sighed.

'You tell him; I shan't.'

'You'll do it, then?' She ignored my objections.

'Do I have a choice?'

'That's good. They accepted our offer.'

I should have known. She'd already bid on the house and for all I knew had exchanged a binding contract to buy it.

'No. The surveyor's going round tomorrow.' She didn't mean Mick Mellor.

'What about this house?'

She shook her head sadly.

'You're some detective. Really.'

I guessed then, or else I had unconsciously noticed as I came in, that there was already a sign outside.

'What if you don't sell it in time?'

She shrugged, 'I'll bridge. These houses go like hot cakes.'

'And you're a jammy bugger,' I muttered.

On the baby-mike, we heard Alton begin to cry. I smiled. I was a jammy bugger too. I loved him and I loved her and they both knew it better than I did. One way or the other, I had about a month to finish off the case if I was going to be able to see Orbach on the street without crossing to the other side.

\* \* \*

During my discussion with Brian Battle, Carson had been watching from another table, at an angle, from where she could see him but where he wouldn't see her unless by chance. Battle stayed until after one, until my third offer of another cup of coffee told him I wasn't good for anything stronger. As soon as he left, she joined me. Never the dissembler, she said:

'Don't trust him.'

'Why?' I didn't, instinctively, but I wanted her to tell me the reason.

'I don't know. The way he was looking at Natalie, maybe.'

'On that basis . . .'

'Yeah, I wouldn't trust anyone. Including you. Hey: it's me. Remember? I don't.'

Thanks, I thought.

I wanted to go home. With a bit of luck for me, less so for Sandy, Alton would wake up just before I got back. I wanted to hold him for a while, then I wanted to hold Sandy for a while longer.

I pondered Carson's remark – her opening remark, not the sarcastic ones that followed – and told her to go back to Southend herself, hang around the local newspaper back-issue libraries, pick up on whatever he did, shadow him. I suppose I could've told her to do the job herself, now Battle'd given me the idea, but she wouldn't've been grateful and I could see no reason to look a gift horse in the mouth.

While she was in Southend, I went to see Alex Keenan. Keenan and Orbach had been friends long ago, then enemies. Keenan had been a Q.C. many years before Orbach; he was some years more senior. But now Orbach was a High Court judge and Keenan still only a barrister. I didn't imagine Keenan minded – to the contrary, he'd lose whatever little credibility he had with the left if he accepted an appointment.

He wasn't happy to see me. On the other hand, he could hardly refuse an interview. I knew far too much about him. He wouldn't come to the club to talk. I had to go to his new chambers late one evening, not just after court but after he'd already finished a lengthy conference on another matter. It was so late there weren't even any clerks around. It was so late there weren't even any other barristers around. I got the point: he didn't want to be seen talking to me.

'Have you ever seen him since?'

Since meant since the night at Sandy's house when we'd last been together.

'No.'

'Not even in court?'

Keenan did mostly crime, but he got a little High Court work too.

'I think . . . It's generally known that I couldn't appear in front of him. Not why, of course.' He added: 'Just that there's sufficient proper cause to keep my cases out of his list.' On such understandings did the Law tick over.

I toyed with asking him about the Lady Helen, his wife; I'd heard a rumour they'd split up. I decided uncommonly in favour of discretion.

'Did you know Orbach moved house?'

'I heard,' his eyes narrowed. 'What's this about, Dave?'

He wouldn't descend to use of my surname alone: it's part of his man-of-the-people pose. But it didn't sound any different than if he had called me Woolf.

'We're buying a house in the same street as him. You knew about . . .'

He nodded curtly:

'I heard. Congratulations,' he said dryly.

I tried to keep the smug, superior, winner's grin off my face. I didn't succeed. But then, I didn't try very hard.

'Is that what this is about?'

'No, of course not. I want to ask what you know about Mellor, Mick Mellor. His child went to live with Orbach after he died.'

'I heard,' he repeated. 'I knew him. Why?'

Mellor had originally been a housing surveyor, doing legal aid work for tenants who wanted their landlords to indulge them in such luxuries as windows that shut, tiles on roofs, floorboards you could walk on, working lavatories, an absence of rodents and of algae.

'Did you know they were that close?'

'Yes. They were friends for a long time. As long as I can remember.'

'You said you heard; did it surprise you?'

'Yes and no. Yes, because Russel always professed not to like children – but no, because I always thought it was an act, because he couldn't have them himself. He could be very good with them. Talk to them seriously without being condescending, take time to listen to them, get them to express themselves better, clearer, so they understood themselves more. I think it was a great shame he couldn't have children. I think . . . More than anything, I think that's what made him such a bitter man.'

Despite my intended discretion, I said:

'That and the way his friends treated him.'

His lips puckered.

'That made it worse. Perhaps what I meant was, that's what made him such an unhappy man; the way he handled his unhappiness antagonised people; they felt put down by

57

him, when really he was putting himself down; so then they turned on him. The bitterness followed.'

It was an acute analysis.

'You still haven't told me what this is about, Dave.' The Dave didn't sound quite so four-letter this time.

'I'm . . . Well, let's just say I'm curious – why should anyone have named him testamentary guardian? Given what you've said: he was a single man, whoever's fault it was by then he was also a bitter man, he was very unhappy, he was very lonely too. I remember visiting him at home.'

'He was always lonely. As long as I knew him.'

'What does he do for sex? I've never really figured him out that way.'

'That may be true of him too. I don't think he's gay; anyway, no more than most of us are capable of. When he was younger he went out with a lot of women. But I don't know. Russel keeps a lot to himself, or at any rate he doesn't let it show to those around him.'

He didn't use to, but the mini-incident in his house, when the cork wouldn't come out of the wine, suggested to me that he was on the turn. I said nothing, so he continued:

'I think, because of his sterility, he was incapable of seeing sex as anything other than fun, a game, a hobby – ultimately, therefore, an indulgence and, as such, a weakness to be despised. It was hard, especially in the late sixties and early seventies, to imagine sex as a love-medium that could last as such in its own right. Once you also have to rule it out as a means of procreation . . .' He tailed off.

'Tell me more about Mellor: did you know his wife?'

'No, I never met her. Not that I remember. I don't know what to tell you. He was a good-looking man, amusing, very dedicated, serious about his work. Perhaps that's what he and Orbach had in common: a sense of professionalism, setting themselves the highest standards. There's an implicit arrogance in it: only I recognise the true standards that are capable of being achieved; only I strive hard enough to attain them. Perhaps that could account for appointing him his child's guardian, so it'd . . .'

'She.'

58

'So she'd be brought up by someone with the same sort of approach to life, at least to work.' Then he thought about my correction, 'She? You're not suggesting . . .'

'No. She's only eleven or twelve years old.' That didn't make it impossible, but Keenan knew it was highly unlikely. 'Do you think . . . I know he wouldn't, probably couldn't, forge a will or anything like that. But do you think he'd be capable of . . . well, finding a way to make them appoint him the guardian, as it were against their better judgment, against their true wishes even?'

'I see. You're working for a relative? Someone else with a claim to the child?'

'Something like that.' I could afford to go this far with Keenan – he was the last person who would run to Orbach with the tale.

'Well, you know as well as I do, from Disraeli Chambers, he's a skilful manipulator. So I'd have to say yes, but not I think in any way that could be proved in Law, especially not against a High Court judge. To upset a will like that, you'd need to show such a degree of undue influence, or blackmail, or drugs, that the court recognises that the will does not express the intentions of the testator; it's not enough just to show that someone influenced someone else, or persuaded them; after all, most of our decisions are not wholly independent, we don't exist in a vacuum; other things and other people bring us or help bring us to our answers.'

'Would he be capable of that, then? Not drugs: there're two wills involved, Mick's and his wife's. But – what about your example? Blackmail, say?'

He thought about it for a long time. Though he and Orbach were enemies, and both had ample cause to despise the other, neither of them had ever, to my knowledge, descended to cheap insult or unfounded criticism. They were respectful foes.

'I'm trying to think about it objectively. I think I would have to say that in the right circumstances, given the right incentive, Russel is capable of blackmail. Wouldn't you?'

I nodded. A nod cannot be taken down and used in evidence.

'But I can't imagine what that could be. I mean, to blackmail or even bully someone into naming you as your child's guardian – well, what would be the purpose anyway? It's only going to be effective if they die. I've been presuming that they didn't both have some deadly illness at the time. They died in a car crash, right?'

'Plane crash. And, no, they didn't have a deadly disease either.'

'So what's the end gain, if it will not and cannot be rendered effective except by chance? That's what I'm trying to say. It's a game without a winner. Isn't it?'

I didn't say anything. I wanted to see if he filled in the missing link for himself. He, more than most, had reason to do so. Gradually – much more slowly than he would have done in years gone by – he saw the point. The blood drained out of his face. His eyes looked haunted.

'Good Lord,' was all he said though.

I said:

'And could you believe that?' Even though what 'that' was remained unspoken. 'Suppose – take your thesis – unhappy man, because he can't have children, lonely man, somehow becomes testamentary guardian – throw in: this is the closest thing he has to family – they're planning to emigrate, far away, South America – could a combination of circumstances like that trigger something off in him, something as extreme as . . . that? I ought to say: he was a part-owner of the plane; he had access to it he was learning to fly with them.'

He shook his head.

'No. I don't think so. As you know, I have more reason than most not to be impressed by his respect for human life. But I don't think he's capable of violence himself, not personally. He's a complex man; what he does is to play on others' weaknesses, perhaps encourage things to happen, perhaps even make them happen – but only at second-hand. You could call it hypocrisy: I would; but don't forget what a good lawyer he is – and a good civil lawyer – he understands everything there is to know about cause and consequence, and I don't mean only legally. Without someone in the middle, a buffer if you like, to absorb the responsibility, I don't think he'd go that far.'

As if it had suddenly dawned on him that we had been discussing the possibility that a High Court judge was a murderer, he rose firmly:

'I don't think I can help you any further, Dave. I'd have to say, no, I'm sure not.'

He might have to say it: I still wasn't convinced he meant it.

* * *

We met him on the street during the Saturday after we had exchanged contracts and thus irrevocably committed ourselves to the purchase. We had gone to the house with our builder, to decide what works to have done before we moved in. The current owners had already moved out, and were, unusually, permitting us access for works before completion so we'd be able to live in the house without being surrounded by plaster, paint and the smell of turpentine.

He was with Frankie. They were walking back from Sainsbury, guiding a supermarket trolley, each of them pushing with one hand. I saw others who lived on the street also pushing their loaded trolleys home, or returning empty ones to the store car-park facing Cloudesley Road across Tolpuddle Street and which, because it was a flat, open car-park, contributed to the street's atmosphere of light and space. Soon, we'd be doing the same.

'Frankie. You remember Dave, don't you? And this is his friend, Sandy. And, uh, er . . .'

'Alton.'

'You're serious about the house, then?' he asked.

Frankie was much taken with our child; but he was asleep and didn't care enough to wake up to talk to her.

'We exchanged on it this week,' Sandy said. I'd never heard an announcement of a house-purchase spoken with such defiance before.

'Well, well,' he wasn't going to pretend he took easily to the idea of us as neighbours. But he knew how to be a gracious loser even if he didn't like it. 'Would you like to come in and have, uh, a drink?'

'Sure. Why not?' I accepted before Sandy could plead want of time.

We walked the remaining hundred yards to his house and followed him in. He put the food away, and Frankie was bribed to return the trolley on promise of keeping the one-pound coin refund. We chattered idly until she came back and, not without considerable hesitation, allowed her to carry Alton up to her room and even, as a part of the game, to take up the carry-bag of Pampers, powder, juice and the remainder of the paraphernalia he insisted we take with us everywhere we went.

'I saw an old acquaintance of yours the other day,' I said as if still merely making pleasant conversation: 'Alex Keenan.'

His face clouded like a sudden summer storm. It looked the way I saw it in the kitchen last time I was there, just before he realised I had come in. Then it passed.

'You never forgive, do you, Russel? Doesn't it get tiring?'

He brought us our drinks without mishap or tantrum and sat down opposite us in the same leather armchair in which he used to sit, staring out of the french-windows of his Highgate flat, looking at the trees and the sky, at an angle that brought no other houses or people into the line of his vision. He took the question seriously.

'Perhaps, but it's always safer not to forget, don't you think?'

'Forewarned and all that? Who do you think still wants to hurt you, Russel? Hell, who ever really wanted to?'

'You know better than that, Dave.'

'Perhaps. But which came first, the chicken or the egg?'

'Yes, I know,' he conceded the point Keenan had made: he had provoked much of the animosity that had been directed against him. 'Then let me put it a different way: why give people a chance?'

'You've got such a pessimistic view of the world,' Sandy interrupted. 'You think that everyone's bad, everyone's selfish, everyone'll do you harm if they can. People aren't like that, Russel.'

'Aren't they?' He treated the question as seriously as if he had been asked for his legal opinion on a subject. 'I think most people are capable of doing some pretty bad things. Once bad things start to happen, they go on. That's been my experience. I agree people aren't basically good – or basically bad. They're both. But they remain capable of being bad, and they remain capable of being made to behave badly: it's only a question of knowing which you want from them.' He dismissed free will as an irrelevance. 'If I don't suffer from it, it's only because I'm ready for them, I'm ready,' he added grimly. 'And I win.' He challenged either of us to deny it.

Daring life and limb, Sandy asked, 'Is it, well, the best way – the best atmosphere – to bring a child up in?'

He shot her down.

'You mean, instead of addicting her to cigarettes, Southern Comfort, lying in bed until midday and, as I recollect, spending a small fortune on cocaine.'

I laughed hollowly. I didn't know what else to do; it was all too true.

Suddenly, unprecedentedly, before Sandy could come to my defence, he abandoned the attack.

'It's too late. I won't change. I'm fixed now.' His massive mind had been brooding on the dark side for far too long. 'I can't compromise,' he added, without explaining what he meant. 'I'll stay on the bench until Frankie's left school and college and doesn't need me anymore. Then I'll retire.'

'And do what?' I asked before Sandy decided to throw the apparent olive branch back in his face.

'I'm not sure. Go abroad to live, I should think.'

'Where would you go?'

'It doesn't matter. Norway, perhaps.' Where he had his friends. 'Or Switzerland. I'll want still to be accessible to Frankie. If she wants . . .' He didn't want to think of a time ahead when she was so independent she might choose to keep as far away from him as possible. The way everyone else had done.

'Is that why you don't want anyone living in, to help you with her I mean?' Sandy asked in a neutral tone.

I'm not sure I understood the logic of her question, but he did. He looked at her thoughtfully:

'You mean so that no one takes her attention – affection – away from me? Perhaps. But she's increasingly close to her sister; I don't discourage it. On the contrary, I encourage it. Family's important. If you've got it.'

'Why did they choose you?'

'You asked me that before, the first time you were here.'

'So I did.' But then I had been working for him so I hadn't really listened to the answer. 'What did you tell me?'

'I can't remember,' he laughed almost pleasantly. 'We were friends. He was my best friend. I was close to Eartha too. It wasn't her first marriage. Well, of course you know that. You know, when a friend gets married, it's not uncommon to lose him. But there was never any jealousy on Eartha's part; she accepted me as his friend, and encouraged us to keep up our friendship. She became my friend too. I don't think she and I ever had a cross word or an uncomfortable exchange.'

He didn't know, then, how she had felt about his visit. He continued:

'I think I was the only one of his friends who stayed close after their marriage. She had friends, who stayed friends, and family but most of them weren't that well-off, and I think most of them, perhaps all of them, had their own children. By then, I was, well, successful, financially too. Besides, you know, you never really think these things are ever going to happen. People don't care as much what they arrange for after their deaths. They think they do, but because one's own death is really so unimaginable – I don't mean the fact of it, but what it means as a state of mind – they don't apply the same criteria they'd apply to a decision while alive.'

'Sometimes they use it to do things they couldn't do when they're alive,' Sandy observed. 'Revenge wills, and the like.'

'Yes. I think I'll leave all my money to my good friends and colleagues at the bar,' Orbach said in what was for him a rare moment of self-deprecating humour.

Frankie brought Alton back down.

'I changed him,' she announced proudly.

I had to restrain Sandy from grabbing Alton out of her arms to see how much damage she'd done. She said tersely:

'Shall we go and see if you've done it right?'

'I've done it right,' she insisted.

Orbach beamed. Of course she had; she was his girl.

While Sandy and Frankie were out of the room, I asked if he still flew.

'I didn't for a while but funnily enough I missed it so I started the lessons again when I had more time.' When he went on the bench. 'I don't want Frankie to grow up with a phobia about it.'

'Fear of Flying?'

He didn't get it and it wasn't worth explaining.

\* \* \*

It only took Battle a couple of days to ring in and confirm, as instinct had told me, that Orbach had sat as an Assistant Recorder in Southend, and that he had done so during the period that mattered.

'Sentencing him, Assistant Recorder Orbach said . . .' was how he found it: Assistant Recorder Orbach and Assistant Recorder Llewellyn Evans and Assistant Recorder Smith and Assistant Recorder Papworth and Assistant Recorder Uncle Tom Cobley and all.

He had sat for a two week period, during which he fined members of the local population a total of four thousand two hundred pounds, placed fourteen villains on probation, put two away for six months each and another one for a year but suspended, and made a dozen or more community service orders.

'What else do you want me to do while I'm down here?'

'Nothing for now. Thanks. That's very helpful.'

'You sure? It isn't much. A fool could've done it.' I wasn't sure a fool hadn't. 'I mean, I know you don't want to tell me what this is about, but we both work on the same team, you know. I could be a lot more help.'

'Yes, sure. But I need to talk to Nigel Morris first.' I was stalling – talking to Morris was a great way to stall. 'That'll take forever. Suppose I give you a ring back in London, what, tomorrow?'

'Fine. I'll come back now.'

But he didn't.

After he hung up on me – although Carson didn't know to whom he'd been speaking – she followed him back to his hotel. He didn't check out. It was already too late in the day for any other kind of office-hours' investigation. She was staying in the same hotel. She didn't think he'd connected her: there was no reason why; he hadn't seen her in the club; she was reaping the rewards of her post-Australia, less flamboyant style. He spent an hour in his room then emerged and strolled down to the front. He seemed to be wandering aimlessly, popping into pubs, drinking alone, only a pint in each.

At about half-past eight, it seemed like he found who he was looking for. He sat down in a booth.

'Mind if I join you?' He asked its solitary occupant, a greasy-haired, sour-faced, sallow, middle-aged man in a crumpled, polyester suit who was nursing a pint of lager in a tall glass.

Carson couldn't overhear anything more. She stayed at the bar, chug-a-lugging Fosters Fermented Fly-piss or some similar Aussie brew that she had felt since her return chauvinistically bound to buy even though she liked it about as little as did I. But she could see. And she saw when he passed something under the table that looked suspiciously like a bundle of brown notes.

'More than you pay me,' she added when she reported.

Battle left soon after the exchange. His companion stayed where he was, looking furtively around until he was confident no one he knew had seen him. He came up to the bar to get himself another pint. As he picked it up, Carson bounced into his back, apologising almost before his drink was spilled. She insisted on buying him another; unaccustomed to being accosted by a woman, he stayed up at the bar to drink it with her. It cost her two more rounds, and more patience than she used to have, to find out that he worked in the local Crown Court.

'Nothing fancy. Just a clerk. Just a job.'

'We've all got to live,' she'd said profoundly.

'That's life. Would you like another drink?'

She was learning patience. She made a choice. If she pushed further, there was a risk she'd scare him out of doing whatever Battle was paying him for. If she left it until it had gone down, she could scare him into giving her the same information – and for free.

She went back to the hotel and ate there, her back to the table at which Battle was sitting, now in company with a travelling saleslady he was regaling with tales from the Fleet Street front to what, from her sarcastic interjections, Carson guessed was little effect. Nonetheless, the woman went with him into the bar and subsequently they went upstairs at the same time though she neither knew nor cared whether to one, other or separate bedrooms.

I didn't ask what Carson'd done – she didn't tell me, so it wasn't my business.

The next day, she was up before him but not before his prior night's companion. The latter looked in worse condition than the evening before, but as, according to Carson, the beds in the hotel were less comfortable than the bunks at Chelsea Police Station, that didn't give her any additional information. By the time Battle came down, Carson had packed, loaded her bag in the car I'd let her rent and checked out.

She didn't leave town. She followed him again, on foot, this time into the town centre. In a coffee bar near to one of the local newspaper offices, he was joined by a young woman Carson recognised from inside it. She in her turn was the beneficiary of a handful of notes –

'But only fivers.'

I waited for another crack, maybe how it was more my scale, but she knew how to let me down, and let it pass. Instead, confusingly, she asked, 'Journalists don't share sources, do they?'

'Not if they can help it. No more than a copper shares a snitch. What're you thinking?'

'My guess is, she's a secretary or maybe works in the cuttings library or something like that. He got the name of someone else's source out of her, and whereabouts he might be found. This was the pay-off. It's a small enough town; I doubt there are a lot of real secrets; just things people think are secret.'

At lunch time, Battle had met up with his and Carson's drinking companion, and a buff envelope changed hands the opposite direction the notes had gone the night before. She followed our man back to the Law Courts on Victoria Avenue and, with a little bit of disingenuity, to his office. He did a double-take when he saw her, but his first – extravagantly vain – reaction was that she'd come back to chat him up.

'I came to apologise to you for last night,' she said softly.

'That's alright. You don't need to apologise. I mean, that's life.'

'What I mean is, I'm apologising for lying to you.'

He slouched back in his chair, confused more than frightened. But fear was beginning to rise; he'd left Battle only a little while before; he was still feeling guilty.

'I told you I was on holiday. I'm not. I'm working down here. Carrying out an investigation.'

She had his full, bated-breath attention. She said:

'Whatever you gave him, I want copies of. All of it. I'll get my hands on his copies, soon enough. And I'll know if you've left anything out.' I know how intimidating Carson can be. I still commonly feel intimidated by her, and she's supposed to be my friend. I could imagine how he felt.

He didn't argue. He hardly spoke. He was sweating so badly, Carson was positively relieved when he told her he couldn't get the material until later in the day and that there'd be trouble if she stayed in his room. She couldn't wait to get away. Before she left, she leaned across the desk, snorting into his face, trying not to breathe, telling him how long the last person to cross her had spent in hospital. He probably thought she didn't mean it. I knew she was telling the truth.

She spent an uncomfortable afternoon moving around town, not looking for Battle for any reason other than something to do, nor finding him: as we later learned, he'd come straight back to London. She thought every policeman she saw was after her, whatever the clerk had done wrong for Battle didn't make what she was doing any better. But he showed up on schedule, at the pub they'd met in the night before, with an envelope that looked no less full than the one he'd given the journalist. Oddly enough, once he'd handed it over, he refused her offer of a drink. She had a feeling he wouldn't be drinking in that pub – or the two or three Battle had looked in first – for a while to come.

I had been wrong. Battle was not a fool. He knew we were looking at the activities of a judge. He'd known enough to ask about Pulleyne even if I hadn't given him any answers. What he'd paid for was a full set of charge sheets and court records for the cases Orbach had sat on during his stint in Southend, whether or not they had been reported in the local papers. The court records included, where relevant, the previous convictions of the accused – whether or not on this occasion found guilty.

There was one case that hadn't made the papers. The court had sat unusually early, and a plea of guilty had been entered to a charge of indecent assault involving a couple of local youths. The assaults had not involved violence – the boys were willing hands. But it was assault because they were under age. It should have merited prison time, because there had been a similar previous offence some years before, albeit in a different town. Orbach had, however, suspended the sentence and let the man go.

The man's name was Walker. He was twenty-eight, married, and his occupation was aircraft mechanic.

# CHAPTER FIVE

'You could have knocked me over with a feather when I saw who he was. I didn't know if I should have said something. But he didn't and I thought, well, it's his court, he's the judge, you know?'

Stephen Walker was not so open when first we approached him. To the contrary, he denied he was Stephen Walker, denied he'd ever worked at Southend Rochford and even denied he cared that it would be a criminal offence if he hit me with the wrench he was hefting from one of his grease-blackened hands to the other throughout the first five minutes of what may sardonically be described as our conversation.

We didn't get back to Southend for a few days after Carson's return to civilisation. There were other jobs to keep up with at the office and then the weekend intervened. I know private investigators aren't supposed to take weekends off, but Carson had already arranged to go out of town to catch up on some friends and I couldn't persuade Sandy that the way she most wanted to spend it was to pay a visit to the seaside in the early spring, cold enough not to be sure we weren't still in winter.

There was a surprising number of Walkers in Southend-on-Sea and its surrounding area. He had moved from his old address, which was a council tenancy so the new occupier didn't have a clue where he now lived. She directed us to a neighbour who'd lived in the area for enough years, but in turn she could only tell us that Walker had moved elsewhere in the town. She thought he'd changed his job at about the same time and perhaps that was why he'd moved. She wasn't too precise about dates, but give or take a decade, it fit.

I wasn't too bothered. The weather had improved. It was even a little sunny. It was better than being stuck in the office in London. Carson insisted I buy her an ice-cream cone with all the trimmings and we sat on the front looking across the water at Canvey Island while it dribbled down her fingers. We'd had no joy out of Battle. When we rang the paper, they told us he was on leave. When Morris rang his editor, he confirmed that Battle had taken some time off, long overdue, but was cagey about when he had booked himself out. I had learned a new rule of detection: when a gift horse looks you in the mouth, rip his open by the teeth, wrestle him to the ground and break his legs.

We had also gone out to the airport, just north of Southend, off the A127. Walker had never been employed by the airport; it had been possible that he was, but equally possible – and in context probable – that he had worked for one of the aircraft maintenance companies who serviced the clubs; the airport carried no employee records on the private companies. We strolled around, pretending with difficulty to be interested in joining a flying club and learning to fly, but our access was limited and we met no one who remembered him. There were other Walkers, we were told, but none who matched in age.

There were not, however, too many Walkers with an initial 'S' to be found in the phone book for resort to the oldest, most tedious routine of all.

'Hallo, is Stephen there?'

'Who?'

'You got the wrong number, mate.'

'Fuck off.'

'You've got a nice voice. How about meeting for a drink?'

'What number do you want?'

'Why don't you learn how to dial.'

'. . .'

Click.

'He doesn't come home for lunch. You'll find him at the garage,' a woman's voice told me. I could hear a child

crying in the background. It was still only a long-shot, but
I asked nonetheless:

'Have you got the number?'

'Who is this?'

'An old friend.'

Click.

Carson helpfully pointed with an ice-cream sticky finger
to an entry for Walker's Classic Car Repairs. It was worth a
try. Using our brand new town map, we found the address.
I was surprised it was listed in the phone book. I was
surprised the phone company had lines running down the
long and unpaved alley that led to what looked like an
abandoned Nissen hut until we turned the corner, cursing
the damage to the suspension of Sandy's Peugeot and our
own backsides, to find there was a door on the other side,
facing the wrong way but open.

Inside was the man we eventually established was
Walker, working on a Morris Minor in the best condition
I'd seen since I hopped up to the window of my mother's
car and kissed her good-bye when she went off to have her
hair done and, I for the first time in my life, was left alone
in the house for a full hour, aged nine or ten.

'You Walker?' I asked.

He unfolded himself from beneath the bonnet and
scowled. He was a big, beefy man, with a weak face
and too many chins to count, wearing what had once
been white overalls but now couldn't be seen in the dark
and with thick, hobnailed boots on his ample feet. He had
a wrench in his hand. I waited patiently and politely for his
answer and for him to put it down.

'Who're you?' He flipped his head at the car: 'I don't do
modern.'

'It's beautiful,' I gestured to the Morris Minor. 'We live
in London so there's no point: it'd get ripped off in ten
minutes. How'd they manage to keep it in such good nick?'

My friendly interest provoked exactly the response you
would expect from someone who had already received a
warning call from his house:

'Go away. Go on, go away.'

Carson tried next.

'Listen, we just want to talk to you, Mr Walker. We just want to ask a few questions.' He responded to her own tentative foot forward with a step towards us of his own, considerably less tentative.

'I've got nothing to say. Go on, go away, this's my property.'

'Uh, no, it isn't actually.' I was guessing – but it was an educated guess. 'Your lease is only of the hut.'

He relaxed for a second:

'You from the landlords?'

'Uh, yes, right.' This time I took a pace towards him. 'We've been asked to pop down and have a chat with you.'

He bristled at my movement.

'You got identification? Who are the landlords?'

'Ah.' One step forward, one step back.

I took a deep breath.

'You're Stephen Walker. You used to be an aircraft mechanic working at Southend . . .' And I claim my five pound reward for spotting the newspaper's mystery man on the sea-front.

'You've got the wrong bloke. You want to watch what you're saying.' He raised the wrench. 'Why can't you people leave me alone?'

'You've already got one criminal conviction you don't want anyone to know about. You don't want another . . .' I cautioned him.

'I don't bloody care . . .'

'Least of all your wife and children.' I took another educated guess: 'We don't . . .'

Wife and children were the wrong references. He roared like a bull and charged at me with about as much grace. He might have been a midnight gay but during the day he was as sexist as the next man and forgot about Carson until she stuck a sneakered foot into his path and as he went down jumped him from behind, twisting his wrench arm up around his back.

'Get off, get off . . .' he pleaded.

'Drop the wrench,' she suggested pleasantly.

He did as bid, so she did too. He got to his feet slowly and awkwardly, looking sheepish as he did so:

'I'm not a violent bloke, really.'

He could've fooled me.

'It's OK,' Carson said.

He turned to examine her with curiosity. 'Where'd you learn to handle yourself like that?'

'Dave – that's Dave, he's my boss – he's useless; one of us had to learn.'

Thanks, Carson. It wasn't strictly true, either. I'm not great with my fists, or with my feet except for running away. But give me a big enough human target less than a couple yards directly in front of me, and a gun that someone else has loaded, I can usually do enough damage. Also, I'm not bad with medieval weaponry.

'Can we talk now?' I asked gently.

He nodded.

'How about closing up the shop and coming for a drink?'

'I'll close up and come with you, but I don't drink, not anymore. Not since . . .'

I got the point. It's not news anymore, but I can remember a time when each day's papers, especially the local papers, carried an account of how this or that reputable, often middle-aged man, usually married and/or a vicar, had been arrested in a public lavatory, drunk as a skunk and down on his knees chewing gristle. 'But officer, I thought it was wafer.'

He slipped out of his overalls, locked the door of the Nissen and got into the back of our car, directing us to a pub where we would be able also to get a bite to eat. As we bounced back down the alley to a real road, I said: 'I'm surprised you get any business down there.'

'I get enough. It's just me and a part-timer. Mostly it's word of mouth. The classic car owners know each other.'

'Do you ever do any of the really old stuff, antique cars?'

'No. I haven't got the equipment.'

'It isn't exactly the safest spot I've ever seen,' Carson contributed to keeping the conversation casual.

'I've got it wired up well. I'm good with electricals. That's what I mostly did on the planes. It's safer than you think.'

74

We pulled into the pub car park and piled out of the car. He took my arm and held me back as Carson led the way in.

'Do we have to talk in front of her?'

' 'Cos she's a woman?'

He nodded miserably.

I shrugged. 'We don't have to. But she's, uh, pretty broad-minded and, look, Steve . . . Can I call you Steve?'

'Stephen.'

Diminutives had gone out of style.

'Stephen, then. I don't want to know about what happened. Not why you were in court. OK?'

Reluctantly, he agreed that I didn't need to send Carson to eat at another table. If he'd ever seen her gobble a ploughman's while slurping lager, he might not have given in so easily. When we were settled at the table, I summarised:

'You used to work at Southend Airport. You were a mechanic. You had a conviction, some years before, for, uh, the same thing you got caught for again. You were married?'

'Not when . . . Not the first time.'

'Right.' It added up. 'You worked for one of the private maintenance firms, on private planes, usually through the clubs, right?'

'Yes,' he sipped his St Clements: orange juice and bitter lemon. Then he swallowed whole a quarter of a cheese and onion sandwich. I wouldn't like to be the engine he was breathing into that afternoon.

'Then you got picked up again. The case went to the magistrates' court first?' It would have had to.

'Yes. But it was all very quick. Over and done with. I pleaded guilty. I mean, I was guilty, wasn't I. Because of the time before, I was sent up to Crown Court for sentencing.'

'OK. Was there any publicity at the magistrates' court?'

'No. I was lucky. It was the same as when I was in front of him; it came on before the court really started.'

'Why? How?'

He shrugged. It was an ambiguous shrug that could've meant he didn't know, or that he wasn't going to tell us.

'So what happened at Crown Court?'

'Like I said. It came on the same way, early. We all stood up. He came in. I didn't recognise him for a bit, because, you know, he had his wig on and one of those funny collars . . .' Wing collar; barristers' bands. 'Then I recognised him and he looked straight at me and I know he recognised me too so I thought it's up to him to say anything. He just said he'd read the reports and he was going to give me a year but suspend it for two years and did my solicitor want to say anything. Then I was told if I got into trouble again in the next two years I'd go to prison and that was it and I was free to go. It took less than five minutes.'

'Tell me about the Mellors.'

'Who are they?'

'Orbach – the judge – he was learning to fly at Southend, right?'

'Yes. He had a plane. A Cessna. It was a six-seater . . .'

'Single span turboprop. Yes, I know.' I knew it off by heart, even if I didn't know what it meant. 'He owned it with some other people. A man and his wife. She was black, does that help you remember?' I shouldn't think, to this day, that it's a common combination: white man, black woman, learning to fly.

'Yes, I remember,' he said excitedly: 'She was a decent sort.' As if it was a surprise. 'I remember. What about it?'

'What do you know about the crash?'

He frowned:

'What crash? Did the plane crash? When? How?'

If I could've answered the latter, I would've been out of a job.

I remembered what his former neighbour had said:

'You left your house about the time of your case? And your job?' If so, he would no longer have been employed at the airport.

He nodded: 'My dad thought it was the best thing to do. You see, my wife knew about the first time, the old one, I'd told her. My dad was mad at me, he said I shouldn't tell anyone. But I couldn't do it, you know, I couldn't marry her without telling her. But, well, when it happened again . . .' He paused to try and find the distinction between needing to tell his wife before they were married and not telling her when it happened afterwards.

He couldn't put it into words and I didn't push him. It wasn't relevant, and besides I understood all too well: the past is past; the past isn't an infidelity; the past didn't reflect on her. He continued: 'I didn't say anything. I knew, well, I knew I could go to prison, but my dad told me not to worry, I wasn't going to.'

By then, I knew better than to ask whether he in his turn had asked how his father could be so sure; Stephen – even now, in his mid-thirties I guessed – took for granted that his father could fix anything.

'My dad bought me the lease on the hut. He wanted us to leave Southend, but Gina – that's my wife – she wouldn't go. Her family's all here. But he put me off the job and he lent me some money and he got us a transfer to another house, in Raleigh.' Raleigh and Southend ran into one another. To a stranger, and to the phone book, they were one and the same town. 'I always wanted to do this anyway: it was always a hobby. I've made a go of it, you know. You'd be surprised. Next year I'm going to get a proper building. And we're buying our house from the council.' The Law required local authorities to sell their houses and flats to sitting tenants, at a substantial discount.

'You said your father "put you off the job" What do you mean?'

'Where I worked, it was his firm see.'

I saw.

* * *

There was something else I asked Walker about before we left him alone.

'Why was your wife so suspicious on the phone this morning? Why did she ring you to say I'd called?'

I merely wanted confirmation.

'There was someone else came around a couple of days ago. She knew I'd had a stranger visit; she thinks it's

77

something to do with the business; she knew it'd worried me.'

'Tall bloke?'

'Yes. Brian Battle. He was from the papers. He threatened . . .' He choked up on the memory. 'He threatened he'd write about my conviction.'

There was no way he could get a word into a national newspaper, or probably even the local paper, about a four-or-more-year-old conviction of a nonentity for indecent assault, but Walker wasn't to know it.

'What did you tell him?'

'I didn't know what to do. I rang my dad. He told me to send him to his office.'

'Did you ring your father about us?'

He shook his head.

'I didn't know what you wanted. I would have.'

Carson asked:

'Are you going to ring him now?'

His shoulders slumped.

'Well, I've got to, haven't I?'

She said, 'Stephen, we want to help you. Really we do. Battle's trouble; we can take care of him. We can shut him up. But if you bring your father into it, I don't know if we can.' I could count three lies and one non-sequitur in her statement.

'What do you want?' He asked dully. 'What's all this about?'

I had to give him something:

'It's about the plane crash, the Mellors, you see.'

'I don't know anything about that. I told you. I never even heard of it till you told me. What's it got to do with me?'

'We think . . . Look, we'll trust you . . . But if we trust you, you've got to trust us. OK?'

It was a deal simple enough for him to understand. He nodded quickly. He'd grab at anything that left him out.

'We need to find out, well, how honest a man Orbach is. We think he may have had something to do with the crash. We think what you've told us, well, you must have thought – your father – Orbach – the way everything was handled – you know what I'm saying?'

He was on the verge of tears: 'I never asked him to . . .'

I went on quickly, 'It's alright. You see, we're not interested in that at all. We've got what we need now. But if your father knows we're, well, snooping around, he's going . . . he's bound to think we're, uh, after, I mean interested in him, isn't he?'

'But you're not? You're saying you're not?'

'That's right. We can leave him out too.' It paled Carson's lies into insignificance: but I'm a qualified lawyer while she only trained as a para-legal. 'Do you see what I'm saying?'

'I think so.' He was blinded by how badly he wanted to believe us. 'What about Battle?'

'I told you. We'll take care of that. How long ago did he come round?'

'Before the weekend.'

'What happened between him and your father?'

'I don't know. Dad rang me later and told me not to worry, he'd seen to it.' His eyes shone, 'He always does.'

'Are you an only child?'

'I've got a sister. Why?'

'Just curious. What about your mother? Is she still alive?' The curiosity was genuine, but probably not enough to have bothered asking if I hadn't wanted to distract him from his father-idolatry.

'I don't know.' His eyes clouded over. 'She left us, a long time ago, when we was kids. It's always been Dad and us.' So much for my distraction. It hadn't been a total failure though: 'I won't tell him you came round. I want, I need, I ought . . .' To make up his mind what he wanted to say? 'I don't want to keep going running to him. In a way, what you're saying, it'd be doing something for Carson, wouldn't it?'

'For sure.' I restrained myself from patting him on the head and telling him he was a good boy.

We drove back to London, less chatty than on the way down. Things about parents have that effect on both of us. I never got along with mine, and Carson's strained

79

relationship with her father had taken a plunge between the time she'd saved his life and – soon after – when he had himself finally let slip away what little was left of his broken spirit. He'd felt humiliated that his daughter, still a child in everyone's eyes but her own, had to save him. Her mother, too, had abandoned them when Carson was a kid, which was another point of identification with Stephen she could've done without.

Sandy on the other hand hadn't had a day's trouble with her parents in the whole of her life, except when they were still bullying her to get married and settle down. They'd accepted half the cake: settling down with me; she still spoke most days with her mother, and there were few weeks that went by without some gift or other for Alton arriving on our doorstep or notified by this savings institution, that broker or the Premium Bond people. To be fair to my father, he'd also sent a present when Alton was born: a cheque for twenty-five pounds. It contrasted well with the ten thousand Lewis had left him in his will.

'What're we going to do about Papa Walker?' His son had given us his proper name, Nicholas R, known as Nick.

'I'm not sure. I think a little bit of company research first, just for form.' Stephen had told us which was his father's firm. 'Check out the local government year-books, see if he was a councillor.' I had forgotten to ask when Stephen said his father had arranged his tenancy transfer; it's less easy to do than many people believe and suggested considerable local influence. 'Maybe he's a magistrate himself – they've got books'll tell you that too. I want to know more about him before we beard him.'

Especially now Battle'd queered our pitch. I was going to have to catch up with Battle before long. He might be aiming for the British equivalent of a Pullitzer, but unless he got out of my way he was going to be out of a job.

\* \* \*

It wasn't a good time for me to have to spend so much time away from the office. Sandy was hardly ever in. She was organising the move, supervising the builders, looking at

80

one and the same time for live-in help or else new child-minding facilities in the area, showing people around the old house and pretending she was taking it all in her stride.

She wasn't; though she was, unusually, not taking it out on me, it was making her headaches worse and I was worried about her, although there was little I could do to help apart from take as much strain at the office as the case allowed me and occasionally suggest that she go in for a medical check-up.

We went out to dinner that night, just to get away from it all. Carson babysat. For some bizarre reason, Alton had taken to her like I felt about Southern Comfort. It was mutual: Carson had fallen in love with him too. Sandy wasted an extra half-hour fussing and telling her ten times over where everything was – much of it already boxed for the move – and where we could be found. Just in case.

We had a drink at the club and I caught up on business with Natalie, then went to a restaurant off the King's Road we hadn't been to for a long time – not since I lived in Earl's Court – that we were pleasantly surprised to find was still in the same hands. Restaurants in the area change owners, theme, cooking ethnicity and price-range more often than the cooks change boyfriends.

'How're you doing?' I asked once we'd settled back and ordered. I like going out with Sandy. She doesn't drink too much. There's no dispute over who's driving home. It means that one time in twenty I'm not gambling with my licence.

'It's OK. I feel less, well, out of control than I expected.' This I had already appreciated. Sandy out of control makes Woody Allen look laid back. 'How do you feel?'

'Strange.' It's not every lawyer who can reach his forties with a newborn child, an overdraft, not even the smallest share in a house but the owner of a drinking club instead. 'It's easier than I thought it'd be. To settle down. 'Course, it's different at the moment.'

They brought our starters. We are unimaginative eaters. Exotic dishes terrify us. She had deep fried slirts; I had stuffed pettifer. We'd crossed town for a meal we could have bought at any half-decent restaurant within a ten minute walk.

'But I can't deny I'm pleased. I never thought, you know, all those years, well, maybe the reason I kept on like I did . . .'

'Like an asshole?'

'Yeah, right.' She has a charming tongue. 'You know, I couldn't see anything that far ahead in the future. I mean, when you're young, you can't be that excited about something as conventional as . . . well . . . having children, buying a house, you know, stuff; even making money.' Sandy hadn't had that problem, she'd always lusted after material security. 'But if there's nothing else that excites you instead, it adds up to not a whole lot of things to live for. You know?' For once, she didn't want to take over the conversation so I went on: 'It's sort of touch-and-go. Which comes first – blowing yourself out or finding something worth keeping going for?'

I was talking about myself, though there was a moment I wasn't sure if I was also talking about Orbach.

'Just luck you made it, huh, kid.'

I grinned and took her hand and, unexpectedly and entirely possibly unprecedentedly, brought it to my lips to kiss her fingertips. After letting them linger for a bit, she snatched them away ostentatiously, with a phoney drawl:

'Husht, honey, someone might see.'

I poured us both more wine. We held our glasses up.

'Cheers.'

Someone had seen us. The manager came over to welcome us back. He joined us for a glass of wine. I liked him. He was a Spaniard whose English was not much clearer now than when he came over, long before we first met him; his children, about whom we'd heard over the years, were growing up; his daughter was qualifying as an accountant. I'm sentimental. I found the idea appealing that the daughter of a Spanish waiter could become an English accountant.

The moment had passed. She asked: 'What do you think really happened, Dave?'

I knew what she was asking about.

'I don't know. If I'm honest, I admit I still don't know, and I still have difficulty believing it – even of him. But I can see how it might have happened.' I gathered my thoughts. 'I know we always see Orbach as a great planner and manipulator, but I'm not sure it's all that true. I think it's more a case of finding a use for everything that comes his way. The way I see him – he wants something, and he can't stand it when he can't have it, so he pushes and shoves and doesn't give up and doesn't take no for an answer and somewhere along the line someone or something gives . . . and that's why and when what he wants happens.'

'When he visited the mother . . . What's her name? Eartha. You don't think he had anything planned?'

'No. I'm certain of it. Otherwise, why would he still be trying to talk them out of emigrating? I don't think . . . I can't see him working out how to do it, and then trying to change their minds to save him from having to carry it out. Anyway, I don't think he could have set it up that early. No. At that point, he just wanted them not to take Frankie away from him . . .'

'Frankie – not to keep them from going away themselves?'

'Obviously just Frankie.' As usual, it took a moment to sink in that she might have a point. 'Well, maybe not so obviously, maybe he would've liked it best if they'd all stayed, though of course she'd never have come to live with him. But you're right; he didn't necessarily want that much.'

'And then he gets his main chance?'

'Only chance, it would've seemed.'

'And Daddy was willing to pay the price, just for seeing sonny boy walk free? It's a hell of a price. Couldn't he have cut a deal with the prosecution on the basis of what Orbach asked him to do?'

'I doubt he'd think of it; I doubt he'd be sure they'd keep his son's name out of it. I doubt Orbach would have told him outright what he wanted back, or even necessarily that he'd want anything back, though a man like Walker must know that nothing comes free. A lot of corruption's like that. It isn't a straight swap. It's scratch my back 'cos I itch now, and I'll scratch yours when you start to itch.'

'I would've thought . . . the scratches had to match.' She can mix a good metaphor.

They brought our main course. Alsacian turwell with pietfrau slowly poached over charcoal; pressed ly-flower salad; another bottle of sparkling Andalusian charantz rosé.

'Yeah, but you're running ahead of yourself. By the time it came to it – to the "favour" – it wouldn't've been that straightforward anymore. First of all, Orbach could still leak about the boy: it was recent enough then to be a story in its own right. Secondly, the fix had been in at the magistrates' court and someone at the Crown Court also had to rig the early hearing; the police had to be involved; maybe Orbach knew about the house transfer; he would've been in a position now to bring down father as well as son for a hell of a lot of local fixing. Finally, it'd be difficult to prove Orbach himself actually did anything wrong; there were reports; he made a lenient decision; that's all. That's how it could've worked: he let Walker build it up until it was a much bigger debt available to call in.'

'What are you going to do about Battle?' We'd arrived back in town too late for me to catch Morris.

'Sell him to Colonel Sanders?'

'What's he up to?' A bone got stuck between two side teeth and she couldn't get it out. I reached over and extracted it for her. No greater love hath man. Then I replied: 'He thinks there's a good story in it; he's taking a hell of a risk with his job. At least,' the thought occurred for the first time, 'maybe he is. It's possible his editor knows what he's up to, in which case they're both about to be deep-fried.'

We were silent while we considered dessert. After we'd ordered, she shook her head:

'I don't think he could've done it. I mean, I know him. I just don't see how he could kill his own friends, his best friend, his godchild's parents, too. Mind you, I've never understood how anyone could kill someone else.' She caught the look on my face and remembered it was a subject I was still sensitive about. 'I'm sorry, Dave.'

'It's OK. Mine were when there weren't a lot of choices.' It was true of those I'd killed. But was it also true of others whose deaths could be laid at my door? There was one in particular at whom I had knowingly and coldly pointed someone else's trigger finger. Was that the point Keenan had been making? Was it why Dowell kept telling me I was too like Orbach for my own comfort? Was it why, according to Sandy, I had to satisfy myself about it? Or was it why she accused me of thinking he was God?

I shrugged.

'Hell, I don't know. You say we know him; do we? Would you have said he was capable of other things we know he's done, before he did them? How many times do you read about people – or have we acted for people – who those who've known them best would've said, or did say, it isn't possible? Who knows the depths of anyone else's dark side, or even their own? Maybe there simply is no bottom to it – it's a question of cross the line once, find out what you can do that isn't as unthinkable as you believed it to be, then keep going.' It wasn't what Orbach had said, but maybe what he meant.

She said: 'This is different, it's so much worse.'

The manager came back over.

'Mr Woolf. There's a phone call for you.'

We nearly knocked each other over as we scrambled to find out what disaster had overtaken Alton; we did knock over both the manager and the table. Sandy got to the desk first and grabbed the phone.

'What? Carson? What is it?'

There was a prolonged silence while, I could tell from the glow in Sandy's eyes, Carson reassured her. Then said, 'Here he is.'

To me she just said, 'He's fine.'

'Yup, Carson?'

'Boss?' She sounded shaky, Sandy hadn't noticed, in her anxiety about Alton. 'We got problems, boss. I got problems.' Shaky, hell – more like on the verge of tears.

'What is it, kid?'

'It was on the news, just now: the local news.' I glanced at my watch: it was ten thirty-five. The Regional News would have just finished on ITV. 'They found a body; like, a clerk from the local court, y'know.'

'Cool it, Carson. It could be coincidence; might not be the same one.'

'Yeah? Well, seems like it didn't take them any time to i.d. him: the bobby who found him recognised him from the court. And they showed his picture. Oh yeah, and something else . . .'

'What?'

'They're looking for a woman in her late twenties or early thirties, sort of a big, economy size woman, seen in his office with him the other day having some kind of an argument; seen in town with him, y'know. They showed a photofit: it's not a bad likeness, boss.'

# CHAPTER SIX

When we got home from the restaurant, we found Carson sitting in the living-room, without any lights on, but wearing a pair of my sunglasses, a scarf of Sandy's and one of Alton's (clean) potties on her head.

'Waddaya think? Think anyone'll recognise me?'

Sandy didn't let us stay at the restaurant for coffee, so as soon as she had been up to see Alton was unaffected by an evening in the hands of a murderess, she went to make up a jug while Carson and I went over what we knew.

There was not much to add to what she'd already told me. The body had been found in the early hours of Sunday morning. He was found on the beach on a strip the gays cruised and it had at first been taken for a fag-bashing: 'homosexual killing', the newsreader had said marginally more politely. Enquiries during Sunday and Monday had apparently convinced the police it was something more though there had been no explanation why. And those enquiries had thrown up a mystery woman, whose visit to his office at the court had apparently caused him some consternation.

Also, she had his name – Arnold Waterbottom.

'Jesus, someone did him a favour. Maybe it was suicide?'

'Maybe that's where they got the fag-killing from. Actually, I didn't think he was a fag, either. Not the way he was looking at me in the pub.'

'What does that mean? Sexy Stevie's got two kids. I don't suppose he found them in the back of a Morris Minor.'

She shrugged:

'I just don't think so, is all. Which means the police're going to go on looking for me until I show up.'

'Let's be calm about this,' I poured us each a drink to go with coffee when it arrived. 'I figure, plead guilty to manslaughter, provoked by bad breath and dandruff, you'll probably be out in ten years, with good behaviour – so, OK, twenty,' I corrected myself: it was unlikely Carson would behave herself for ten days let alone ten years in Holloway. 'Look on the bright side: we'll be living within walking distance; I can come sing to you outside your window some moonlit night.'

The coffee arrived accompanied coincidentally by Sandy. She heard my last remark and grimaced: 'Ask for an inside cell.'

Singing is a misleading description of what I do in the shower. In hotels, people've been known to call the manager and, once, a doctor.

I said two words people don't like to hear, the second one of which was 'in'.

Sandy said:

'You know what I'm thinking, kids?'

No one knows exactly what Sandy is thinking so the question had to be rhetorical.

Carson guessed: 'He's had too much to drink?' Meaning me. A safe guess.

I guessed:

'Carson didn't do it? Nah. The police never look for someone if they haven't done something wrong.'

'I'm thinking . . . How many deaths were involved in Disraeli Chambers, Dave?' I had to think for a moment before I could tell her. 'And at Mather's?' That one was harder: exactly how many to include was an open question. I erred on the side of modesty and gave her the lowest possible figure. 'And last time?' Carson totted it up out loud for her.

'That's one hell of a lot of dead bodies, Dave. Now there's one more.'

'You're thinking it ain't gonna be the last?'

'Right.'

'So you're thinking,' I knew her this well, 'I gotta talk to Tim before it gets any worse?' She had an image of Tim as my guardian angel that accorded not at all with my own perception of his role.

'That's one option: the other is to get out.'

'Hey,' Carson protested. 'What about me? You want I should go back to Australia?' She spent her days with me, with Sandy, with Natalie: you should be surprised she was beginning to sound Jewish?

'You've got an alibi,' Sandy answered calmly. She's a lawyer, too, and a better one than I. 'You were with friends at the weekend. It isn't about whether you did it or not; it's just a question whether and when you go in and give yourself up to clear yourself.' Which would still call for explanation about her connection with Waterbottom and was therefore no different than if we decided to tell Dowell directly.

'I offered Tim in. He didn't want to know. I go talk to him now, or Carson walks into Southend nick, we've got to give up Battle, the Walkers, and what do we get out of it?' One of my greatest failings in life is my tendency to ask questions which I intend to be rhetorical but others expect an answer to.

I continued, as if I'd always meant to do so: 'First, maybe it's coincidence, so we blew it for nothing.' I paused to let them snort their derision in harmony. 'Secondly, one of 'em's got something to hide about Waterbottom. You sure that was his name? Maybe you misheard? Maybe you made it up?' She didn't dignify either alternative with an answer. 'If it's Walker, what it does is put him out of our reach which correspondingly means we don't get to find out anything more about Orbach. If it's Battle . . .' I shook my head, unless he was a psychopath there was nothing in it for him; he might be bad news, but he wasn't a baddie.

'I'd say that made three possibles.' Carson contributed: 'Or back to two if you acquit Battle.'

It was a thought, but: 'Orbach doesn't get his hands dirty; that's not his style.'

'I think what Carson's saying,' Sandy translated, 'maybe you'd get Walker acting on Orbach's instructions. That'd be enough, wouldn't it?'

'Nah. It's the same deal. To get Orbach, you'd have to

get cast-iron evidence; hell, even in the case of an ordinary villain, the uncorroborated evidence of an accomplice doesn't count for much, you know that.' A jury can convict on it, but the trial judge has to warn them that it's risky. 'Waddaya think it'd count against the word of a High Court judge?'

'Then what sort of evidence are you looking for, Dave? What sort of evidence will be sufficient?'

'You're forgetting. I ain't trying to find enough to convict him; just enough to justify them publishing the story.' As of tonight, the story's value to my clients would have doubled. 'What I'm saying is, as soon as I give Walker to Dowell, he's out of my hands, off the street, out of touch. Then you've either got to talk criminal conviction or nothing. That's so whether it's just Waterbottom or the Mellors as well. And criminal conviction – of Orbach – you ain't gonna get; not even prosecution. Nope, I need Walker outside.'

'Where you think, maybe, he'll write it all down for you and have it notarised?'

'You know me better than that, Sandy. I can't think that far ahead. I'm only thinking a step at a time; let me get Walker into a corner; then we'll work something out.' But she had an idea: like Walker or Orbach on a wire, or Orbach with his hand in the proverbial till to pay Walker off. I had but one article of faith, and it was Orbach's own – keep on pushing, keep on shoving, something'll give. It was my singular contribution to the philosophy of detection.

'Right now, I'd say your priority's to find Battle,' Sandy said. ''Cos, the way you see it, Battle gave Waterbottom up to Walker – right?'

'You see any other way to spell the story? That's my guess. You got a better?'

Carson shook her head.

'It doesn't add up that way.' She's so contrary, she can't even use my metaphors. 'I know what you're saying – you see Waterbottom as one of the links in the chain.'

She got up to pour herself another drink but when she made as if to pour me one too she caught a scowl from

90

Sandy that sent her scurrying back to the sideboard to put the bottle away.

'But he's not a link in his own right; I don't know, you don't know, if he had anything to do with the original fix; I doubt it, I've met him; he didn't have that sort of clout. His only value was in conjunction with Battle, because of the information he gave him.'

'What you're really saying is, Sandy's right, he's not the last. It's gotta be Waterbottom and Battle or neither?'

'Looks that way,' Sandy agreed with her protégée's reasoning, proud it was a jump ahead of mine, her partner's. It was Sandy's original idea – and, boy, was it original – to bring us together as a team.

'Have a headache,' I snarled. 'You're all so clever, you go solve it.'

'Uhuh, Dave; the difference is, I'd let it go, and I daresay Carson would – if I asked nicely. You're the one so damned determined to pin it on Orbach.'

\* \* \*

Which is why first thing the next morning I drove Carson – well out of my way, but for some reason she wouldn't take the tube or a taxi – to the club, where everyone who could see at all saw double, and then I drove to Southend.

There was one consolation. It meant I had Sandy's car for another day, and she had to make do with my beat-up Beetle. After my Passat had been cruelly and unnecessarily beaten up during my last case, I'd sold it. I gave up on decent wheels. There didn't seem any point. My relationships with cars didn't last as briefly as my relationships with women used to. Carson had her own car before she went back to Australia, but hadn't time to replace it since she returned. I was too mean to let her rent one except on specific occasions I could charge a client for. So on long journeys I took Sandy's.

I couldn't go into Southend with any ostensible connection to Waterbottom. I could with a connection to Battle; the police weren't looking for him, so they had not, at least so far as I was aware, made a link between

91

them. From the club, I rang Morris. I needed another favour. His first effort to bolster my investigative team had proved a disaster so I knew better than to ask for another journalist. But – surmounting the usual linguistic hurdles – I persuaded him to speak to Battle's editor and in turn authorise me to look for Battle on behalf of the paper. I rang in when I arrived at Southend and was sent to a fax-centre to pick up a written letter confirming my commission.

There were three places where Carson had been that counted. Though she'd been seen with Waterbottom in the pub, I figured it for incidental intelligence. She'd been at the court; she'd been at the hotel; she'd been with me when we visited Stephen Walker. I started at the court, arriving before it opened for business – at least, before the time it opened for ordinary mortals without anyone to pull someone else's strings. I was in time to hear the judge deliver a brief oration:

'You will all have heard that over the weekend, our Mr Waterbottom died, and in the most unpleasant circumstances.' I tried to envisage a pleasant circumstance in which to die: I could only think of how Phil Esterhaus went out in *Hill Street*, humping Kate Gardner, and I'm not convinced it didn't too closely resemble strenuous exercise for my comfort. 'Mr Waterbottom had worked in the court system for nearly twenty years. He was a valued member of the court staff. It is a relief that he left no family to mourn him, but we in this court will miss him, and mourn him instead.' I gotta get this judge for my funeral – he'd have everyone who wasn't already in stitches busting their sides.

The judge asked for one minute's silence and everyone else stood, though he remained seated, stroking his sideburns with affection. There were limits; Waterbottom was only a clerk. I didn't see anyone crying; I didn't see a collection hat passed around; I didn't see anyone open a book on who else was next in line to die.

'Next case,' the judge said, to signify both the end of this over-lengthy period of tribute to the dear departed and his wish to get on with playing God himself.

'Police and Everard, for sentence, Your Honour.'

I don't know why. Maybe because I was tired and courts are good places to rest; maybe because I wanted to see a bit more of this joker judge; maybe I still wasn't sure how to handle the next step and needed time to think. I didn't leave. My mind drifted away and was only brought back, just after the judge pronounced sentence, when the prisoner in the dock screamed at him:

'You *cunt*; you fucking cunt.'

The judge was unperturbed. He signalled the police to wait a moment before taking the prisoner down. He said:

'Everard. In a few hours' time, I shall leave this court in my comfortable, three-and-a-half-litre Rover, and be driven to my home in rural Essex. When I arrive, I shall kiss my wife, pour myself a large gin and tonic, and settle down in front of my twenty-six-inch colour television until my dinner is ready. I believe I shall be having a roast tonight: rare roast beef, dripping with blood, microwave crisp vegetables, a bottle of fine wine – I shall spend the journey home deciding exactly which. Later, I shall retire to my custom-made bed, luxuriating in my silk pyjamas, and read until I decide it is time for me to sleep.'

He paused to let others envisage the enjoyable evening ahead of him. Then he continued:

'You, on the other hand, will be going to prison, where you will be strip-searched, given second-hand, rough garb to wear, and fed slops before you're put into your cell, where to toss-and-turn in an uncomfortable bunk, lights out when the warden decides. Now who's the cunt? Take him down.'

He was the sort of judge who used to refer to hanging as a suspended sentence.

\* \* \*

I went out to see Stephen Walker next. As I drove down the dirt track to his workshop, an ancient bronze Jaguar in condition good enough to kill for, its bonnet emblem proud as a ship's prow, passed me going the other way. There was only just enough room, so I slowed to a near-halt to let him squeeze by. Age and beauty. I'm talking cars, not drivers. As our front windows drew parallel, we looked directly at each other. He didn't know who I was, but I was fairly sure I'd just met Nick Walker for the first, but undoubtedly not the last, time.

Walker's part-timer was on the job, so I stood in the doorway until Walker looked up from the engine they were working on. He was startled to see me. I glanced at his colleague, still bent over inside the hood, and he nodded that he would join me outside.

'What do you want?' he hissed. 'You promised you were going to let me alone.'

'Was that your father I passed?'

'Yes.'

'And?'

'And what?'

'And did you tell him about our visit?' I tried to keep the impatience out of my voice.

'No. I said. I said I wouldn't.' He was getting angry. I'd forgotten what a big man he was. I was glad there was someone else within hailing distance; I didn't have Carson to look after me today. At worst I'd only get beaten, not killed. 'Why are you here?'

'Have you read a paper today?' I asked, trying to sound no more than idly curious. He shook his head. 'What about the TV last night?'

'I watched. What?'

He wasn't as thick either as he looked or as he sounded. It began to dawn on him why I'd come back to see him. He looked crafty:

'That was her, wasn't it? That was your girl, your mate. And she knew how to handle herself alright.'

I could see no advantage in lying.

'It was her. But she didn't do anything. She was away at the weekend.'

'Then what are you worried about?' he jeered. He was human enough to enjoy having the boot on the other foot. It was, on him, a very big boot.

I smiled sweetly.

'You're absolutely right, Stevie sweety. We'll just go in and explain what she was talking to him about. We'll tell them we were suspicious of a case a long time ago, a case that got a bit rigged, you know. You see, that's the connection, Stephen: you want that's what we should do? Especially, given where they found him. Yes, you're right: I should clear her and let them go back to their original theory, together with that little bit of extra information, right?'

He shook his head numbly. He wasn't good at being a hard case. It brought him into the middle of it as much as us. Him and his dad. I left him, confident not only that he would not be reaching out to dial 999, but also that he was less likely than before to tell his father about our visit.

\* \* \*

I called next at the hotel where Carson had stayed. I produced my identification from the firm and explained that we were checking up on employee expense claims.

It was routine, I insisted; we did it to all employees every once in a while. I happened to have some work nearby, so it was easier to call in than telephone or write. The receptionist did not take to me: I don't think she appreciated how much in an employee's interest it is to have their integrity occasionally verified; I think she thought I was a suspicious sow-turd. Nonetheless, she sent me through to the manager, who not only thought it was an excellent idea, one he might yet adopt, but also appreciated that I – as an employer – was a better bet for future business than the employee.

'Yes, well, certainly there's a record of her stay,' I confirmed the entry. 'But did you see her yourself? Could you describe her, so that I can know she was here in person?'

'I don't recollect her myself, Mr, er, Woolf. We do have a large number of visitors,' he smirked and stroked his moustache. 'Perhaps one of the girls?'

'Can I ask them?'

'Certainly. Now, let's see; the young lady you saw outside would have been on duty when she checked in

95

and . . . Oh, you're in luck: also when she checked out. She ate here, I see from the account; you could ask the maitre d', but I can't tell from this which of the waiters served her. I'd have to retrieve the original bill. Would you, er, like me to. . . ? I have to say, sir, the restaurant's quite dimly lit in the evenings. It's very unlikely they'd remember.' For which read, it would be a lot of work to dig out the original bill.

I shook my head.

'I'll just ask the girl outside and the maitre d', if you wouldn't mind letting them know.' If God heard me refer to the receptionist as a girl, I hoped she wasn't a feminist: Sandy would've torn my head off and Carson would've done time for me instead of Waterbottom.

It was a risk, because the questions might've prompted someone's memory which hadn't yet, and mightn't otherwise, have clicked to the photofit. It also didn't produce any certainties, because either of the ones I asked might not even, or yet, have seen the picture. But both of them were emphatic they couldn't describe her or remember her face; just that there had been a youngish woman, paying with a firm's credit card; she remembered her bomber-jacket, though.

'That sounds like her alright. Thank you for your help. Have a nice day.' I got it in before she could. It'd only recently caught on in England: I'm sorry to have to tell you your mother just died, have a nice day; I'm afraid the car cost twice as much to repair, have a nice day; we're out of stock at present, have a nice day; gimme your wallet fuckface, have a nice day.

\* \* \*

Finally, a little more secure that Carson had not been identified, and above all secure that she had not been identified back to me, I went to the police station. I produced the fax, and my own i.d., and explained to the desk sergeant that I was, on behalf of the paper, looking for one of its journalists, who had gone strangely absent. He was confused.

'Do you want to post him as missing, sir?' If so, why send a solicitor to Southend to do it?

'Not exactly. No, not at all. He, uh, how shall I put it?' I wished I'd spent more time thinking about how to put it before I'd started. But, as I'd said to Sandy, thinking more than one step ahead at a time was an excessive strain on what I – though few others – like to call my brain. 'He has something, uh, some information, belonging to the paper.'

'Are you reporting a theft, sir?' If so, why aren't you reporting it in London?

'No, I shouldn't say so. Uh, no, definitely not. I'm hoping, well, you see I'm hoping to find him and persuade him to return it. I think, my, uh, clients, would not want to consider charges, not at this stage. I'd say, they've got a lot of time for him. I'm sure it's a question of find him, forgive and forget.'

'The forgive and forget division's down the street and take the third turning on the left, sir,' he said dryly. 'Depending on your denomination, of course.'

'I was hoping, perhaps, a word with one of your detectives – to get some thoughts; perhaps he picked up a parking ticket?'

'Why do you think he's in Southend, sir?'

'Well, he was here for a while; he filed his expenses claim.'

'Did he claim for a ticket, sir?'

'Uh, no.'

'Well, then,' he said triumphantly, as if that explained everything. Which it did – whoever heard of a journalist with a parking ticket not trying to reclaim it?

'So, uh, there's nothing you can do to help?' I asked forlornly.

'I didn't say that, sir,' he sighed. 'If you want to speak to one of our detectives, I can't stop you. They're very busy, though, sir. You may have heard: a matter of murder.'

'Yes, I read about it. In the local paper,' I added quickly. A court clerk doesn't make the nationals; not for a mere bash on the head, however fatal it proves.

'If you'd like to wait there, sir.'

While I waited, I reflected on what I wanted most. If I gave them enough, I could get them looking for Battle. That might help him, but I was certain it wouldn't help me. So either I'd have to tell a few whoppers, which might just land me in trouble later, or else I'd have to tell them the truth, which was exactly what I was there to avoid. If I gave them nothing, nothing was what I could expect in return.

I was shown into an office, where a man sat behind a desk marked D.S. Ambleton. I was surprised; I thought they'd give me to a raw recruit.

'We're short-handed today. Murder.' It was obviously the high-point of the Southend police season. 'How can I help you?' He flicked over the pair of papers which allegedly confirmed my identity and my quest in life as if he never had doubts.

He was not an attractive man. In his early forties, with bouffant hair held in place by too much gel, his fingernails were bitten down but still somehow managed to suggest long-secreted dirt. He was wearing a cheap, black leather jacket to try to keep up with the younger street detectives, most of whom were in their turn trying to keep up with what the public saw on the box. Sergeant was as high as he would ever rise.

I played it like I saw him. Someone else, I might've played differently.

I gave him the same rough outline I'd given the desk sergeant. He gave me the same rough runaround. I asked him where he would start looking for someone like that: he was a detective, wasn't he? He suggested sarcasm wouldn't help me. After I'd apologised, he suggested the local paper, and the bars. I told him both local papers had been rung – which was true, though by Battle's editor in London, not by me – and would he, seeing as how it was lunchtime, care to join me for a drink in the nearest available alternative. He looked at me sceptically, but agreed.

I was relieved. The pubs had been open for an hour and I hadn't put away my first of the day. I treated him to a pint, and – unsolicited – a plate of sandwiches. Comfortably ensconced in a corner, he asked first:

'Why are they really so concerned to find him? I mean, you're a solicitor, you lot cost a packet, it must be something they're desperate about: why not hire a private detective?'

'Well,' I sold out the brethren of my calling without hesitation, 'it is a sensitive matter; they're a crude bunch of buggers. I think, perhaps the best way I can put it, there's a certain amount of internal dispute involved. This isn't news material we're talking about.' I didn't quite tap my nose but I conveyed nonetheless that any intelligent man of the world would understand precisely what it was about. It's a bluff that works ninety nine per cent of the time: people don't like to admit their ignorance.

'Still and all, it's odd. I mean, I know you are a solicitor like you say . . .'

'I showed you my firm's identification,' I reminded him, thinking he was indicating doubt in my *bona fides*.

He sneered: 'Anyone can make identification. No, I checked in the Solicitor's Diary.' All solicitors are listed in it, even me. 'What I was going to say,' he reprimanded me for interrupting him, 'I was wondering if perhaps you did some writing for the paper, whether you were interested in something else.'

'What might that be, sergeant?' I asked quietly, neither admitting nor denying it.

'Well, the only thing it might be is this Waterbottom business,' he munched merrily on the last quarter sandwich, which I'd been saving for myself. 'It's the only thing alive in this whole town.' He was implying he was superior to this provincial backwater.

I chuckled graciously.

'Very good. D'you mind?'

He was so pleased he'd tumbled my true racket he wouldn't've noticed if I told him I'd come into confess. Orbach would have been proud of me. There's nothing like stumbling on the truth, by accident or by skill, to disarm suspicion. If I'd walked in and asked him outright, I'd've been bounced on my buttocks back to Sandy's car.

'Why aren't the regular people doing it? I mean, you must have crime reporters? I don't read your rag, you understand; the Sunday one, isn't it? Bit too highbrow for me.' If that was his idea of highbrow, the Beano comic must've been a strain. 'You do have crime reporters, don't you?'

'Yes and no.' I got up. 'Another?'

'Alright.' He didn't offer to get it. Rounds of drink are the most common, the most acceptable, and possibly the most insidious, form of petty corruption. He hadn't forgotten his question by the time I returned, though: 'What d'you mean, yes and no?'

'Yes, we've got 'em; no, they don't dig deep enough. No offence now – but they do tend to be little more than police mouthpieces. Sometimes, it's more interesting to cover it from another angle. I've done legal writing for the paper,' I could lie my head off now I knew he'd never read it, and so long as nothing I said regenerated his suspicion. 'I thought it'd be interesting to see how the police go at it; never mind the actual crime, if you like; but a meaningless sort of murder like this, how the police work at it.'

The last time I'd posed as a writer, the person I'd been trying to deceive had seen through me in less than a minute: that was Alex Keenan. Ambleton was a D.S. not a Q.C. He shrugged; if it didn't make any sense, he wasn't going to say so. He asked:

'What about this Battle bloke, then?'

'He really has been down here; we really don't know where he's gone; but all I want with him is, if I find him, he's going to work with me on this.'

'You're wasting your time, if you ask me. There's nothing to it.'

'What about the girl? The photofit? What's she about?'

He frowned:

'I don't know. I'm not working on the case, you understand, or I wouldn't talk to you about it. But it's a small department, I've a good idea what's going on.' And an idea that a Fleet Street paper was worth a good sight more than a couple of drinks and a sandwich. 'Waterbottom has – had – a friend who's quite high up in the court system – they played chess together – he saw him with this woman – and he saw her at the office the next day, after which he saw Waterbottom later looking worried. He doesn't like the idea of burying Waterbottom with a bleeding backside. I think,' he hesitated and looked at his glass and sighed.

I did what was expected of me, hoping he wasn't using the excuse for time to change his story. When I came back, he wasn't in his seat and for a moment I thought he'd done a runner until I saw him emerging from the lavatory. I suppressed an audible sigh of relief. After he replenished his now empty bladder, he continued:

'This other guy – I'm not going to say who it is – you needn't try twisting my arm. He's also single; people knew they were friends; I think he feels that if Waterbottom's put down as a fairy, he will be too. And he's got enough clout – well, anyway, he could make things administratively quite difficult for us, you can imagine. That's where it came from.'

'D'you think you'll find her?'

'No way. He said a woman; it'll be a man. He said she was five feet nine or ten; we're looking for a midget. He said she had light brown hair; we're looking for a redhead, a blonde or jet-black. He said she was big-build, we're looking for an anorexic. You're a lawyer; you know how it works. They won't even show the photofit again: it was put out last night to show willing, but that's it and that's all.'

I pressed my luck.

'I presume you don't think he's actually lying?'

'I don't know. I doubt it. It'd be a bit rich; officer of the court wasting police time – like,' he added, as if he hadn't thought of it before, 'like you might be said to have.'

'Drink up, Ambleton. That's never a waste of anyone's time.'

He laughed pleasantly.

'No more it is. But I'll buy this round.'

It was by the book: not generosity or any genuine sense of wanting to show willing. I'd encountered it before. If the mark buys at least one round during a long session, it ceases to be corrupt: 'We each bought rounds; I don't remember who bought how many; I know I bought my share; ask the barman.' You find me a barman can tell exactly who bought how many rounds, I'll show you an undercover cop on the job. I took it Ambleton would know if the barman was an undercover cop.

'So?'

'No, I do think there was a woman; my guess is, he swung each way; he got turned on by her; when she didn't come across, he went out to get the other and bumped into a weirdo instead.'

I grimaced, which fortunately he mistook for a wry look of approval. Suddenly, he swallowed in what looked like one gulp the remainder of his pint.

'I've got to be getting back.'

I was puzzled; he'd bought one to my three – I owed him at least another half dozen.

He was pissed enough to confide.

'See that man over there, the one talking to the manager?'

I nodded. I saw who he meant.

'He's a council member on the Watch.' The Watch was the old name for a local police committee; the committee made up of local council members and local magistrate nominees who oversaw the police of every area except London, where the equivalent polite pleasantries were omitted by the Home Secretary. 'I don't want to be seen.'

He was more scared of being seen over a long, boozy lunch by a council member of his committee than by a magistrate: they saw enough of the seamy side to understand police tensions; politicians only understand their own. He'd saved Carson a trip to the library. 'You staying down?' He still had an eye out for the Fleet Street cheque-book. 'You know the Swan? It's opposite the puppet-theatre on the front. I go there for a jar after work; 'bout seven, seven-thirty. See you later?'

'Right,' I said absent-mindedly, but with no intention of showing.

I wasn't absent-minded because I had recognised Nick Walker. I'd recognised him as soon as Ambleton pointed him out. I was absent-minded because Walker was looking straight back at me – he had recognised me too. I couldn't say who was more concerned about the coincidence: him or me.

# SEVEN

It was moving too fast to observe an ideal caution, or any caution at all.

I knew Margot McAllister from way back when, both as a result of her living with Orbach and otherwise. We'd been at the same occasional parties and the odd campaign meeting. She had been for many years the country's foremost welfare lobbyist, before she went into Parliament, where now she was one of the few responsible and respected members of Her Majesty's otherwise discredited and comprehensively non-credible loyal opposition. As Keenan had told me, she had recently married, another Member of Parliament – they were the only husband and wife team amongst the opposition spokespersons. I was surprised she had married at all: we were all getting old and our dearly-held principles had grown soggy with age.

It was not too difficult to arrange to see her, once I succeeded in getting through on the phone. She was a hard-working, quietly intense, excessively serious and – surprisingly for a politician or indeed for a lobbyist – an essentially shy person, who tended to presume that others did not want to waste their time anymore than she did hers. I said only it was a private matter, I'd be grateful if she could find a space in her diary. She invited me to come to the Commons, where she, as others, frequently had to hang around for long periods, waiting for this or that Division on a matter of underwhelming significance that interested her not at all.

I had to wait in the lobby for her to come down and countersign my day pass. I hadn't often been to the

Houses of Parliament. I was surprised how small it was inside. I expected grandiose halls, sweeping corridors, magnificent arches. Instead, the central lobby couldn't contain an average company's annual dinner-dance, the corridors were long but narrow and several of the arches looked like they were held together with Polymix.

There were a lot of policemen, but they were older than those I was used to seeing on the streets, and less fit. The more serious offences were dealt with by Black Rod or a robed Speaker and punishment comprised 'naming' a member; their hardest task was pouring drunken legislators into taxis. If a trainee guerilla with a water pistol got past the initial security, I'd put my money on him, not them.

When I'd last seen Margot, her nearly-red hair had hung down to her waist; nor did she wear glasses, makeup or jewellery. Now, her hair was styled and barely reached her shoulders; it had been high-lighted. She wore blue-rimmed glasses behind which I saw traces of mascara, and heavy round earrings. Otherwise, she was unchanged. She was still slight and underweight, she had the sweetest smile of anyone I ever knew on those occasions she deigned to display it, but if she and Nigel Morris ever tried to kiss it would take a structural engineer to disentangle their noses.

'We can use my office; it's free at the moment.' This is something M.P.s have in common with another branch of the law, barristers. Except for leading members, or those who have been in Parliament so long they have acquired some elusive and ill-defined rights of passage, they are crammed into tiny offices, which they have to share normally with another member from the same party, though it is not unprecedented for junior back-benchers temporarily to have to put up with someone from another.

'I heard you married. Congratulations,' I offered.

'Thank you,' she accepted my good wishes gracefully. She had a low voice, one that when I'd called her I could've mistaken for that of a man. Her full initials were M and R – though I didn't know what the R stood for – and some of the correspondence which littered her desk was addressed to Mr McAllister. There was no trace of a Scots accent; as

I recollected, the name was an ancient accident of history and she had no connections north of the border. She did, however, have a slight lisp, a hiss on the 's'. 'What was it you wanted to see me about, Dave?'

'Uh, it's delicate. It goes back to when you were living with Russel Orbach.'

She froze. The last vestige of her smile sunk without trace.

'What about him?'

She automatically assumed it was about him; all I'd said was that it related back to that time.

'Look, I'd better put my cards on the table right away.' It was going to be difficult to deceive her; she was by far the brightest of the people I'd had to deal with – Orbach himself excepted. 'Do you remember Mick and Eartha Mellor?'

'Of course. They died. I went to the funeral with Russel.'

'And Frankie?'

'And Frankie.'

'You know of course how they died?'

She nodded, waiting for the promised explanation.

'It's been, uh, suggested, suggested to a client of mine . . . well, that it might not have been an accident.'

She absorbed this information slowly, tasting for all its possible ingredients. I watched her hackles rise. Momentarily, she kept them at bay and, perhaps only playing for time, asked:

'Why have you come to see me, Dave? I'd left Russel well before then. I was no longer involved.'

'I never heard it . . . that you were the one to leave him.'

'It's not important; it was no particular way round; we'd been "just good friends" for a long time beforehand; it was simply a matter of maintaining separate homes instead. You still haven't told me why you wanted to see me,' she added politely but firmly.

'Look, I want to tell you as fully as I can. I want to explain something first, though. You're right, of course, this does concern Russel. But if he knows I'm looking into it, well, you know him, you know how he'll react.'

'I shouldn't blame him,' she said frostily. 'He's a High

Court judge now; any suggestion of scandal would be taken very seriously; besides which, if you're implying that he had anything to do with this . . . this alleged,' she emphasised, 'I repeat, alleged non-accident, he would be entitled to be very angry indeed. It's slander.' She might not have been a lawyer but she knew the distinction between slander and libel. 'It's very serious slander. It is also quite laughable. I don't understand for a moment why you think you could come to me, tell me such a thing, and expect me to remain silent about it – at least, that is, not to tell Russel.'

She half rose in dismissal. I shook my head with enough vigour to propel her back into her seat.

'I haven't said it's true. I said someone hired me to investigate it.' I paused to see if she questioned it as an unusual task for a lawyer. When she didn't, I knew she had remained close enough to Orbach to have followed some of my own activities since last she and I had met. 'Better me than someone who doesn't know him, who doesn't care if the investigation alone is sufficient to hurt him. If Russel finds out, he'll kick up such a fuss he'll bring it into the open even if he's got nothing to hide. As you said, he's a judge now; mud'll stick; a lot of mud.'

A shadow passed across her face so fast I almost missed it; she could believe at least that much of what I'd said.

'I still don't know why you think I can help.'

'I'd say, you probably know him better than anyone else in the world: don't you agree?'

'Possibly. Until Horace . . . my husband . . . until he and I got married I stayed very close to Russel . . . Right up until then we met often, probably once a fortnight; even if it was an odd friendship for a High Court judge.' She meant because of her politics. 'After that . . . ' She didn't complete her sentence.

I read into her remarks not that she would have objected if she'd remained close to Orbach, nor could I imagine her bowing to any jealous pressure on Horace's part, but that Russel hadn't wanted to continue seeing her. She confirmed my guess.

106

'We were sometime lovers, long-time friends. Nothing needed to be read into our continuing as friends so long as we were both unmarried. He was concerned that if he continued to see me, there might be an inference that might be, well, inappropriate for a judge.'

She looked up at a screen hanging from the ceiling which displayed the title of the current debate: the Doggie-doo-dah Bill, Second Sweep Up?

'I'm going to have to leave you shortly. I think, after all, perhaps I can help. You see, Mick – I knew Mick better, for longer; Eartha was his second marriage; Russel and I were already drifting apart by then – Mick was Russel's best friend. Excluding myself, no one understood or tolerated Russel so well. You know Russel; he is difficult; he was always difficult; Mick was perhaps the one person who never found him too much to handle. That's the absurdity in the allegation; it would have been for Russel like cutting off his writing hand. Self-destructive even by his standards.'

I often forgot that, as well as an extensive practice, Orbach had written a number of the leading legal texts on his subjects. For all I knew, many of them were still in use, although as a judge it was a convention that he did not write new books or editions, so as not to give a particular legal argument undue weight when it derived from mere research rather than the heat of adversarial advocacy. I knew Orbach so well, and on such idiosyncratic terms, that it was easy to forget that he was one of the small handful of true stars of the profession – both when he had been a barrister, and now as a judge. As a lawyer, a near-myth in his own life.

She shook her head again, as if to clear it.

'I must be going crazy. I don't know why I'm even discussing this with you, Dave. I hear what you say, I won't tell Russel; but you should lay the idea swiftly to rest if you don't want to do him, or yourself, serious harm. He was fond of you, Dave, in his own way; he'd be very hurt to think . . .'

I held up a hand.

'You said it'd be self-destructive. Of course that's right,

at a lot of levels. Do you say he'd be incapable of it?'

'Of course; that goes without saying.'

She met my gaze and held it for what seemed like several minutes before she flinched.

She was a politician. A Member of Parliament. She had integrity, but she also had her career. Any serious scandal involving Orbach would do her harm too. She nodded permission for me to continue.

'You were around at the time of his break with Disraeli Chambers.'

'Yes. That wasn't why . . . '

'I know. You read about their deaths later.' I remembered that when she was a lobbyist, she used to read all of the newspapers, every day. I imagined she would keep equally abreast as an M.P. 'If I told you,' I selected my words with care, 'if I told you he had more responsibility for what happened to them than any other person, what would you say?'

'I wouldn't believe you,' she snapped. 'This has gone far enough, Dave. I remain very fond of Russel; he was a major part of my life for a long time. If you say another word, I will tell him everything you've said; I'll give evidence that you said it,' she repeated that I could be sued for damages.

'There wouldn't be a case; he'd never sue.' I sounded more confident than I felt. He was proud enough to think he might get away with it. 'I'm not a complete fool, Margot. I'm not without some evidence – about either.'

'Use it, then,' she snapped. 'Don't go around smearing him like this. He's a good man – look at how he's taken care of the child; he looks after her better than if she was his own.'

As when I had canvassed the case with Keenan, I didn't say anything. She went white; she had just seen the one, the solitary, motive Orbach might have to – as she had put it – cut off his writing hand. She got up to show me out, gesturing toward the screen that showed the countdown to a Division. I followed her back to the lobby. As we entered it, I took her arm.

'You'd gone; Mick and Eartha were planning to emigrate; what would he have had left?'

'God save you if you're wrong, Dave.'

'And if I'm right?'

'God save him, then.'

A burly, bull-headed man came up from behind and took her arm.

'Margot . . . '

'Hi,' they pecked at each other's lips. 'Horace, this is Dave. Dave Woolf. He's a solicitor. He's an old . . . friend of Russel's.'

He shook my hand cursorily.

'We'll be late.'

As they disappeared into the chamber, she gave me one, last, backward glance. I couldn't swear to it, but I was sure there were tears behind the blue-rimmed glasses.

\* \* \*

'I want to get a better feel of them,' I justified my wish to see her again.

'You've read my book.' Jada didn't reciprocate.

'It's more about you,' I reminded her. 'There's very little about Mick. You never say anything about why they wanted to emigrate, for example.'

'Him. Not them. It was more his idea.'

'Well, there's something.' Not much, but something.

'We're recording this week. We work late. Call me at home around midnight; I'll see how I feel.' She hung up.

\* \* \*

I used the excuse to go to the club.

It was around eleven o'clock when Dowell walked in.

He didn't waste words.

'What've you got to do with the Southend killing? And where's the Kangaroo Kid?'

'Hi. Nice to see you too. Really nice. Sit down. Have a drink. Have two.'

He sat; I ordered; he waited.

'Why d'you want Carson? How did you know she's back?'

'I didn't till you just confirmed it. What I want her for is to take her down to Southend to stand still in a line-up.' He extracted a folded copy of the photofit they'd shown on the television but that I still hadn't actually seen. Carson was right, it was a good likeness.

'Carson wasn't in Southend at the weekend. She can prove it.'

He shrugged.

'Maybe. That's not my problem, or yours – yet. It's hers.'

Natalie came over:

'Hi, Tim.' Natalie was one of only two women I'd ever known to tempt his fidelity. He groaned inwardly so only his haemorrhoids could hear. 'Thought you two boys weren't playing together anymore?'

'Ha ha. Go get Carson, will you, there's a good . . . ' he caught himself in time, 'uh, soul.'

'Right,' she instantly forgot that Tim was fuzz. 'That was dumb,' she said as she remembered. 'Was it terribly dumb, Dave?'

'Terribly, horribly and awfully – almost as dumb as I was.'

'Shall I get her?' she sighed. 'D'you want another drink?'

'Bring the bottle,' I asserted my rights of proprietorship. The first time I ever said 'bring the bottle', Lewis was still alive, and I was riding as high as a kite because I – wrongly – thought I'd begun to put two and two together on Disraeli Chambers. Only in new maths does it make five.

'We both drink too much,' Tim reflected while we waited.

'I knew a barrister, one of the best, terrific practice, wrote law books, novels on the side, earned a small fortune, beautiful home, everything going for him, drank a half-bottle spirits every night without fail, often with wine or beer beforehand – or both.'

'What happened to him?'

'Oh, he killed himself.'

110

'Cheers,' we held up our glasses. 'See you on the other side,' I added.

'Me too,' our fugitive from Southend joined us. 'Am I in bad trouble?'

'Depends,' I said. 'Don't open your mouth; you'll survive.'

She took off and gave me back my sunglasses:

'But tell Sandy I like the scarf.'

Natalie decided she too needed to put her feet up and sat down uninvited. She said;

'The thing I like about you guys, you've got such a great sense of priorities.'

She clicked her fingers at Tom, behind the bar; she didn't touch hard liquor. Her normal brew was a spritzer. Tom brought it over with a special swish for Dowell but didn't try turning it into a larger party.

'Well, is it you?' Tim demanded.

Lips tightly sealed, Carson nodded firmly.

'And are you alibi'd, like Perry Mason here says?'

'Up to here,' she broke her short-held vows of obedience and silence. 'I went up to Oxfordshire, near Henley, stayed with a solicitor I used to work for and his wife and two kids. He's a mean sod: we went out to dinner on Saturday night and I had to pay half; main courses for six – he ate two; the credit card record'll prove it; he wouldn't take my cheque.'

'Name?'

She gave him the name of the solicitor, and of his firm in Notting Hill Gate. He said:

'I know them.' They did as much crime in their area as we did in ours. 'They're good, but he might be honest anyway. Now it's time for another mean sod of a solicitor to give me some answers.'

I glanced over my shoulder to see who he might be talking to.

'How d'you get it, Tim?'

'One day you're asking me about a plane crash out of Southend; the next day, people start dropping dead in Southend and there's a picture of Tonto on the tube. I'm supposed to be a detective, too, you know.'

'I never said anything about Southend,' I reminded him.
He had, after all, followed up my initial enquiry. 'To get
there, you must've done some work on Orbach; which
means his name's on a file somewhere; which means . . .'

'Crawl before you walk. Of course his name's on a file;
he was part-owner of the plane; how many of his planes
you think crash every day? The man's a judge – not a major
airline. Now,' he reminded me I had yet to give him a clue
what any of it had to do with Waterbottom.

I shook my head and started to say:

'Sorry, Tim; privileged . . .'

As I opened my mouth, he was already adding:

'And don't give me any of the privilege bullshit . . .'

'It is, Tim; really.' In the past, I'd claimed privilege as a
private investigator which, under English law, is altogether
without legal foundation. Orbach had insisted on hiring me
as a lawyer for precisely that reason, so that he could own
outright everything I found.

'Crap. Material's only privileged if it's in contemplation
of litigation,' he was citing someone else's legal opinion,
or a text-book, or maybe something he remembered from
when he did his law degree.

'Who's to say when litigation is contemplated? Didn't
you say, just the other day, I could be working a civil suit
for damages? We could even be talking private criminal
prosecution.'

He shut his eyes to think about it. Natalie was distracting
him. He recited:

'Mellor's only relative was the kid who now lives with
Orbach; hers – well, she had family – but in terms of
damages, that'd have to be the noise.' Jada Jarrynge did
not have a fan in this copper; still, he lived in Ealing where
few people of any taste spend more time than it takes to
drive through without stopping. 'I need to know, Dave,
or I'm going to take Carson in and send her to Southend.
Would you wish that on anyone?'

I exchanged a look with my assistant. She didn't give me
a hint.

'And I need you not to know, Tim. She told you, she's
alibi'd. Unless you can show any connection between what

112

happened to Waterbottom and her meeting with him, you can't hold her, you can't charge her, you've got nothing except a coincidence to be eliminated from your enquiries. Which I happen to know is what they think it is anyway.'

'Yeah, from a loudmouth called Ambleton who thinks – thought – you were writing something for a newspaper. I disabused him; told him you had difficulty writing a shopping list. After I explained to him that if he didn't want to talk to me he could talk to his Superintendent, he told me two things I found interesting.' He didn't bother to list them: that I had i.d. from the paper, and that I was looking for a man called Battle.

'You've got a lot, then.' I pulled the half-empty bottle away from him, not to pour myself another drink but to tell him he'd had everything he was going to get out of me – liquid or solid – for the time being. Carson poured herself one; she was getting as good as me.

She caught the look on my face.

'If I'm going back to Southend, I'm going to need to be pissed.'

'Take the bottle. Hell, it's the least I can do.'

Tim gave it one last try.

'Do you know what you're doing, Dave?'

'Nope,' I admitted with false cheerfulness. 'But as long as I don't, you won't either.'

We waited for Dowell to call our bluff. I don't think any of us expected him to do it. He rose and gestured at Carson.

'Come on, then. I'd like you to assist me in my enquiries, if you're willing to do so, of course.'

And if she wasn't, she'd be busted for interfering with the police in the course of their enquiries into a murder.

\* \* \*

'Mick was a gentle man. A gentle gentleman.' She stirred her herbal tea with a solid silver teaspoon that had a handle in the shape of a microphone. 'Gross, isn't it,' she sighed. 'My agent saw it in a second-hand shop and bought it for me.'

113

I too was drinking tea. This will come as a surprise. The explanation is simple – Jada Jarrynge didn't drink, so neither did anyone else; she kept the first dry house I'd knowingly been inside since I got out of short pants. Nor had she yet extended an invitation to smoke.

She lived in the architect-designed, high, top half of a converted, flat-roofed warehouse on the Isle of Dogs, with a vast expanse of clear glass overlooking the Thames far below. The rooms were on slightly different levels, ascending or descending into the main living area. Along the front of the apartment was a balcony, wide enough to sit out at a table, or sprawl to sunbathe in the unlikely event of a genuinely hot summer.

'My mother had a rough time when she was young. My father wasn't a bad man – he's a good man – and I don't think he was bad with her. But she used him up getting herself straight.' She sipped her tea carefully, cautious not to burn the inside of her mouth, or her solid silver tongue.

'It's funny. She was black; she was born in Dominica; she grew up here mostly; I'm not saying things are easy now, or that there isn't racism, but they're easier than they were; there's many, many more first generation blacks than in her time. When I was at school, it wasn't anything special, different anymore. We were maybe a majority, I don't know. So she should've felt she belonged less than him. But Mick was the restless one; he did his job well; anyway, that's what I knew – he made a lot of money, he got a lot of big contracts, even though his reputation was originally based on small housing cases. So he must have been good?'

'He was good; he was good at the housing cases, and I don't think he knew how to do anything badly.' She wanted the affirmation.

'Yes, I thought he was good. But he didn't belong. He didn't feel he belonged. He didn't belong to the surveying establishment.' She laughed. 'Is there such a thing? I suppose so: there's an establishment for everything.'

'RICS – Royal Institution of Chartered Surveyors. Sure. That's the establishment.'

'Well, whatever it was, he didn't belong within it. I don't mean he wasn't a member. I don't know if he was; but still he didn't "belong". He didn't have a university degree. I think he minded that. I think he felt left out of other sorts of institutions; he worked around lawyers, social agencies, everyone else had been to university. He came from a working-class background: my family, my mother's family, they were – are – working class, black working class of course; he got along well with them, but of course he didn't fit in with them either. I mean, you can't, can you? Not when you do an interesting job, a profession, highly-paid; they're driving cabs, working in the post office, a stall in a market. Do you understand what I'm trying to say?'

'I think so. I never felt – well, part of this country, I suppose. But it's easier in a way. I'm a Jew; I know a lot of black people don't think that's the same; hell, we've been here a lot longer; we're integrated, supposedly; we're white; one time recently, we had five members of the Cabinet – think of that; and at least half the High Court bench is Jewish. Like Orbach. But if you've got something onto which to pin the feeling of not belonging, I think that must be easier than just feeling it on its own, or for a lot of different, unconnected reasons.'

'Yes. That's what I'm saying. That was Mick. He was a handsome man – do you remember? Shall I show you a photograph?'

I remembered, but I told her to show me anyway.

She went to fetch an album. The album was her mother's, because it went back before Mick, and to a time when Jada couldn't have lifted let alone operated a camera. The later pictures included shots of Frankie. There were several in which Orbach featured. I said:

'I'm surprised you keep them.'

She settled back in the peacock chair from which she had been conducting our interview. She was dressed, as the first time I'd met her, casually, with the confidence of a woman who knows she looks good in anything. When I arrived, she had been in the shower; she told me she was going inside to get into something more suitable; she meant it; I didn't even have time to fantasise what she might be wearing before she emerged in jeans so baggy I could have fit into them myself, and a sweater used in winter to keep a family of Catholics warm.

'They're just pictures.'

I pointed to one of her mother.

'Just a picture?'

She looked wistful; for a moment, the child she still – to me – was.

'She was so beautiful, so incredibly beautiful.'

I smiled.

'You ain't no wallflower yourself.'

'I know. But I had all the advantages; she gave them me.' Shelter, food, comfort, care and, above all, protection from the ravages of the social environment.

'Why do you think Mick and Russel were such good friends? People've said to me, because they were both perfectionists, but . . .'

'He puts a hold on people. It's seductive to be around someone who seems to know everything, have all the answers, who's right more often than not, and right more often than others. He's extremely perceptive, and when he wants to, he can use that in a constructive way. I remember conversations with him when I was young – before my mother died, Mick and my mother. I've seen him with Frankie: she is bright, she can do anything she wants – and a lot of that comes from Russel. In our house, he was almost an idol.' She smiled at a memory:

'When Frankie was two or three, just beginning to talk, she used to talk about "Wussel" all the time. The childminder – I don't remember her name – she asked, "Who's Russel?" Frankie couldn't say the word "godfather", so she said "God".'

I, too, had a memory, though not one I shared with her: the way people at Disraeli Chambers used to talk about him – with awe, the sort of fear-based respect that would be more appropriately associated with a mafia godfather; only, they thought he was the devil.

'Do you think,' I began another thought hesitantly, 'do you think Orbach, well, wanted your mother, was in love with her maybe?' Her mother had raised but dismissed the notion in her letter to Mick in Bolivia.

She shrugged; she didn't know.

'Tell me more about Bolivia.' I wasn't sorry to change the subject.

'There's not a lot to tell. It was his dream. She knew, my mother knew he needed it more than she needed to stay here; in a lot of ways, she was much stronger than he was.'

'Have you ever been there?'

'No,' she said gently. 'I wouldn't, would I.' It wasn't a question; she didn't pause to give me time to reply. 'But they talked about it. It's big, and they could have bought land – land like we can't imagine it here – for the money they had. A whole valley, where all you can see is your own; imagine.' She was a sensitive and intelligent, highly artistic woman; she didn't find it inconsistent with a developed sense of material values. 'Do you see the dream?'

I saw the dream and I saw something else. They were chasing their dream. It was only a dream, as transient as any other dream and as expendable as a night's sleep. Once they went they ceased to be who they were before; they could as well simply cease to be. The implications for Orbach, though, were entirely real – a man without his own dreams, he could not respect theirs. Put the other way round, he too was an outsider – why should they be able to escape if he couldn't?

\* \* \*

The same sergeant as before was on the desk. He recognised me and scowled: Dowell of London's attention to the case had not gone unnoticed; the hicks had allowed themselves to be suckered; I needn't expect them to thank me. He didn't.

'What do you want?' He paused, a witticism rising slowly. 'I already told you we don't deal in forgive and forget.'

'This may well be true; but I am a solicitor – as I already told you; and I do have a client in custody, who I'd like to

117

get out.' I gave him Carson's name, as if he didn't already know who I meant.

'I don't know if she's in our custody, sir.' He drew the 'sir' out so far I could've gone for a walk in it. 'I'm afraid you'll have to wait while I find out.' He smiled thickly and pointed to a hard wooden bench.

Once I'd sat down, he waited until he was sure I was watching him before he picked up from the desk the papers he'd been looking at when I arrived and started to study them assiduously, making the odd correction here, sighing, calling out to a constable to fetch him a cup of tea, picking up the phone to tell his wife what time he'd be home for dinner, going to the lavatory for longer than could conceivably be necessary, until I got the message the one thing he wasn't going to do was acknowledge they had Carson in custody.

I'd expected something like it. It was par for the course. As soon as they admitted they had her, they had to let me in to see her, and either charge her or let her go. I doubted they gave a damn about her; it was me they wanted to annoy. I was reassured: once they had finished playing games, I wouldn't have any real difficulty; there wouldn't be any point to the delay otherwise. It was eleven when I arrived, one o'clock before the desk sergeant said:

'Yes, we do have her, sir. I'm told she can go now.'

'Gosh, what a surprise.'

I got up and crossed over to the desk.

He said so softly I could barely hear him: 'You've got some of us into trouble; we'll get you too. Bank on it you bastard.'

'But officer – I'm not a bastard; I saw my parents get married,' I protested. He didn't smile. They didn't study the law of legitimacy at police college.

'Dave?' Carson stood behind me. 'You took long enough.'

'I've been here long enough, too. Come on, let's go.'

She filled me in.

'They brought me down here last night; I rang Alan at home.' He was the solicitor friend with the ambitious appetite. 'He came down first thing. He said 'cos he was

118

a witness, he couldn't represent me, but that was it. They asked a few more questions after, but they had nothing to hold me on. Alan gave me this anyway,' she handed me a bill. 'For his time.'

It had to be a first – a solicitor charging for an alibi that was true.

# CHAPTER EIGHT

I was at the office when I took the call:

'Mr Woolf?' asked a disembodied female voice, a secretary.

'Yes.'

'Just a moment, please. I'll put you through to Mr Schofield.'

I have tried to explain to the receptionist at the office that when a secretary rings for me, she ought to get the caller himself on the line before she connects me. Why should I be left holding on, while only his secretary's time is wasted? It's a game: who's more important than whom? But she seems to think that everyone's more important than me so persists in putting the call through without waiting. Or maybe she justs thinks that she is more important than me? Maybe she's right.

'Mr Woolf?' This time the voice was male. 'Patrick Schofield. I'm an Assistant Secretary.'

'When do I get to speak to the real thing?'

'Excuse me?'

'Oh, never mind. What's this about? What can I do for you?'

'We, uh, have a common acquaintance: Detective Inspector Dowell.' He got that right – common as muck. 'He, uh, thought it might be a good idea if we, that is you and I, were to have a little chat.' I waited. After a moment, he said: 'Mr Woolf?'

'Uh? I'm still here. Chat on.'

'Well, I was rather hoping, if we could perhaps meet . . .'

'Are you looking for legal advice, Mr Schofield?' A

client-referral from Tim Dowell would be a first; it must be his worst enemy.

'Oh, good Lord no. I am a lawyer myself. I work, well, with the Lord Chancellor's Department.'

'Well, that's alright, isn't it.'

'I was, uh, rather hoping, well, that you wouldn't mind popping in for a little chat. Uh, here.' When I still didn't say anything, he continued, somewhat more firmly: 'I'm quite sure it would be in your interest, Mr Woolf. Quite sure.'

'Yeah, well, if Tim Dowell suggested you ring, it could hardly be otherwise,' I replied.

The sarcasm was entirely lost on him. He said:

'Oh, good, I'm pleased you see it that way. Would it be possible . . . say this afternoon? Say five thirty?'

\* \* \*

'Put me down at Chancellor's Gate,' I told the taxi driver.

Chancellor's Gate is an archway into the House of Lords, where the Lord Chancellor's Department works. The end of the archway is barred to pedestrians save for access to an incongruous, prefabricated security building. I had to wait on line to pass through the metal detector, then again to talk to one of the two uniformed police officers behind the desk. Unlike those I had seen posted within the House of Commons, these were burly and intimidating. He seemed surprised to find my name on his list. I had to produce identification: he seemed surprised I had any. Then I was issued with a day-pass and told to wait in a tiny cubbyhole for someone to collect me.

'Mr Woolf? Would you like to come with me?' If I was a piece of paper, she'd have held me by a corner, at a distance from her body. She was middle-aged, blue-rinsed, bespectacled and nothing like what I expected of an Assistant Secretary. This was not a surprise. She was the real secretary, to whom I had spoken earlier. She dumped me in a waiting-room with copies of *Punch*, *London Life*, the *Lawyer* and the *Law Society's Gazette* just like at the dentist's.

121

After another delay we went on a wander through wonderland. I wasn't sure whether we were still in the House of Lords or the Commons. One of the corridors looked familiar from my recent visit to Margot McAllister.

'Come along in, Mr Woolf,' a thin man with a hawk-like face offered me a seat. 'We're pleased to meet you.'

I raised my eyebrows. He was the only one I could see.

'Is that the royal "we" or is there a midget in one of your drawers?'

He chuckled appreciatively, with the wholehearted comfort of a man in perfect control.

'Yes, I've been told you're something of a wag. Jolly good. No, I'm afraid it's just me.'

'I thought – I read somewhere – there's always at least two of you?'

'Oh, well, usually, but I'm sure you're not going to offer me a bribe. Are you? I'm dying for a couple of seats to *Aida* – you wouldn't have any ideas, would you?'

'Chuckle, chuckle.'

He frowned. Sarcasm was a low form of wit. Too low for a senior civil servant.

There was only one of him because he didn't want a witness.

'Cigarette?' He pushed an onyx box across the desk towards me. 'They're our own brand, you know.' Houses of Parliament cigarettes, to help our legislators die of something other than boredom. I wondered if the original package carried a government health warning but refused his offer and lit up a Camel. 'Sherry?'

I shook my head.

'Scotch? We've all become rather fond of Scotch recently.'

Since they appointed the first ever Scottish Lord Chancellor, even though he did not himself drink any alcohol. His relations with the Bar since his appointment had been abysmal: they shared neither a legal tradition nor a social.

'Southern Comfort?'

'Who? Sherry or Scotch. Or tea?'

'Yes, alright, tea.' He buzzed and within minutes

another secretary brought in a pot. I waited until he'd finished playing mother before asking: 'You wanted to see me. Why?'

'I thought it was time I met you. I'm, uh, rather familiar with some of your, uh, work, Mr Woolf.' He made it sound like he found it difficult to dignify my activities as 'work'.

'As in – Tim Dowell – Martyn Pulleyne?'

Pulleyne was the focal point of my last case, the one I had worked for Orbach. I knew that at some point Tim Dowell had gone to the professional authorities, or else they had come to him. I also knew from a couple of casual remarks – if anything Dowell says can ever be treated as casual – that his contact had not been technically a member of the Lord Chancellor's Department itself, but some sort of liaison group. It tallied with Schofield's description of himself on the telephone as working 'with' the Lord Chancellor's Department.

'Something like that, Mr Woolf,' he confirmed. 'I thought it would be interesting to, uh, explore with you, uh, anything you might have to say in the same sort of area.'

I smiled. He had style.

'You mean Dowell thought I might tell you something I wouldn't tell him?'

He smiled too.

'I think we understand each other, Mr Woolf. And are you going to do so?'

I had never witnessed such a quick-step from polite dissembling to the point.

'No chance.'

'Then I wonder if you'd be willing to listen to me, instead?'

'Listening's what I do.'

'Really, Mr Woolf? I thought you were quite an active sort. I mean, you were quite active at Disraeli Chambers. And then again at Mathers.' I presumed he wasn't telling me how much he knew just for the hell of it. I wasn't surprised at what he knew; I would have been more surprised if he didn't.

'Why don't we talk about Pulleyne?'

'Pulleyne?' He repeated, as if he had difficulty remembering. 'Sad loss to the bench, eh?'

I shook my head in awe.

'You said that with a straight face. I wonder how it worked. Did you make him a deal or what?'

'Golly gosh, no. Nothing like that. More a question of helping him do the right thing, wouldn't'cha say?'

'For what?' I asked, suddenly serious. 'What was his offence?' I wanted to hear how he put it.

'Well, you know, being a bit too close, to, well, a couple of chaps, sort of, wrong type of friends. D'you know what I mean?'

I shook my head.

'Wrong. Pulleyne told me so. That was no crime. The crime was being found out.'

Schofield shrugged.

'Perhaps he meant the same thing as I did.'

His smug self-satisfaction began to irritate me.

'What about everyone else who got hurt?' There were many – Lewis, Malcolm, a couple of lawyers. 'What about his family?'

'I'm sorry, I'm not concerned with that. His family, well, if they were upset by what happened, of course it's always unfortunate for the family. But I'm a civil servant, Mr Woolf, and you have to understand that what concerned me was the welfare of the nation. Oh dear, that sounds more pompous than I meant it to. But it is my job, all our jobs as civil servants; be we ever so humble or ever so grand.'

I felt like screaming. I could see how for centuries they had managed to rule the world. Complacent calm confidence. There's no more powerful weapon.

'Pulleyne read me a bit out of a judgment. It was all about how one bent judge in a thousand is worth covering up for, for the sake of the other nine hundred and ninety-nine. What I want to ask you is – what about when we're talking two in a thousand, then ten, then a hundred like in the United States? At what point does it cease to be worth covering up or, rather, at what point does it become more important to sacrifice the judge for the sake of the office? Can you tell me that?'

'More tea, Mr Woolf?'

Despite myself, as if hypnotised, I saw my hand move cup and saucer across the desk. In penance, I piled into it several teaspoons of sugar from the silver bowl, sufficient to cause him to wince.

'I can't answer all these questions, Mr Woolf, they're for finer minds than mine.' I wondered if that was how he spoke to his wife when she asked how he would like the chicken cooked for dinner: 'That's a question for a finer mind than mine, dear.' 'I'd be interested to know why this, uh, old history should concern you at the present time, though.'

I sipped my tea. He was right: it was disgusting. I pushed it away from me while I pulled my thoughts into order.

'I'm curious to know just how far you'd go to prevent a similar scandal – or one that was worse?'

'There could be no worse,' he said flatly. 'It couldn't happen; it wouldn't happen.' He watched my face to see if I flinched. When I didn't he sighed. You don't get to be an Assistant Secretary by being extremely thick. He explained. 'As there was no Pulleyne scandal, as you call it, so also would and could there be no similar scandal, let alone one that was worse.' Five times nothing is nothing.

'In any circumstances?'

I waited.

He waited.

I said: 'Well? What's your answer?'

'I thought I'd already given it, Mr Woolf.'

'Is this what you wanted to tell me? Why you called me in here?'

'I wanted to be quite sure that you understood, Mr Woolf. I can be sure, can't I, Mr Woolf?'

I smiled and got up to leave.

He showed no sign of concern.

'Good day, Mr Woolf. More tea before you leave, Mr Woolf? A Houses of Parliament cigarette, Mr Woolf?'

125

I pulled the door shut behind me quietly as he picked up a telephone. I had a good idea who he was calling.

\* \* \*

No sooner was I in the door than Sandy said: 'You had a phone call.'

'Another! I'm getting popular.' I presumed it would be Tim, reacting to the call from Schofield, ranting and raving because of my failure either to give up my information or to give up the case.

'I'm not sure that's how you'll feel. Russel rang. He wants you to call him.'

Which I did.

'Ah, Dave, good. Wondered how you'd like to come for a little trip tonight. Little flying trip.'

'Flying? Tonight?' The case was over. He'd finally flipped.

'That's right. Night-flying. Wonderful experience. Do it quite often when there's something on my mind; it's the best place I know to get my thoughts sorted out.'

'I hate flying, Russel,' I said firmly.

'No, no, you'll have a marvellous time.' When I didn't respond, he said, in a different tone of voice: 'Interesting, anyway. You'll find it interesting. I promise.'

I didn't have a lot of choice. There was no way it was coincidental. There was no way I could turn down the opportunity and continue with the case. Sure I was scared, but only at the prospect of flying; it never occurred to me to be physically frightened of Orbach. Weakly, I agreed. He wanted me to meet him at Southend, at the airport. He gave me precise, detailed instructions how to get to the private club area, where to park, even what to wear:

'It's cold up there; wear something warm.'

I called Carson, she was out; Natalie offered to come with me; Sandy offered to come with me; Alton offered to come with me. I went – as invited – alone.

\* \* \*

Though only a small airport, Southend Rochford was staffed twenty-four hours a day; even when there weren't any scheduled flights, private planes might want – or need – to land. Orbach had directed me not to the main building but to a side-gate to the airfield itself that would be open, near to which I could park. Over to my right I would be able to see a line of small aircraft. That was where Russel's plane was supposed to be waiting.

I pulled off the A127 onto a slip road, then as instructed onto a narrow lane, an external service road parallel to an unlit, internal strip. The warm weather had been deceptive: it was a cold night; it was dark. I could see the airport building in the distance, maybe a mile or more away. It was dimly lit, throwing off a hazy shimmer; signs of life were most noticeable for their absence. All but one of the runways were pitch black, with low night-lights picking out what I took to be the solitary, permanent, emergency landing-strip, designed to cast the minimum possible light into the surrounding area.

I could only just make out the line of planes Orbach had told me about. I was beginning to wonder if it was all a practical joke when he stepped out from between two planes and waved me towards him. I felt like I was walking through a minefield. I nearly tripped as I crossed the concrete of the first, unlit strip, that which was parallel to the mesh-fence. As he ushered me onto his plane, I looked around and noticed a light flicker briefly in the cockpit of the next plane in line but then go out. I asked him about it. He told me to get into the plane and made his point with a little shove, sliding the door shut behind me and leading me forward to the pilot cabin with a tight grip on my upper arm.

'Don't be frightened, Dave; trust me; there's nothing to it. Just pretend you're at the fairground.'

'Fairs scare me too, Russel.'

He chortled delightedly. He switched on the engine: it was just like a car in this respect, but there were far more knobs and dials and so far no sexy stewardess had offered me a drink.

He spoke into the microphone.

'This is Sir Russel Orbach.'

The control tower acknowledged and asked for his formal call-sign and confirmation of flight-plan. A few moments later, the lights of a small runway, connecting to the emergency runway that was already lit up, came on. I gritted my teeth and strapped on the seat-belt.

He drove the plane slowly and evenly onto the runway. Twisting my head, I could see that behind us the other plane was reversing in the opposite direction, onto the unlit strip. We were between it and the airport building. Our cabin was lit up, and so were our wing-lights, red and green for port and starboard like a ship or a pair of Kickers shoes. No lights at all showed from the other craft. It took me a while to realise what was happening. Our plane was the shill – the magician's way of distracting the attention of his audience – for the control tower, to cover the noise of its take-off and its movement.

I asked:

'What about radar?'

He shook his head:

'Not at this height. By the time they pick it up – if, that is, anyone's watching at this time of night – we could have come from anywhere.'

'So what's it all about, Russel? Why the Red Baron act? Who's in the other plane? Snoopy?'

'What other plane?' He asked, as if he had not just a moment before acknowledged its existence. 'Where's your assistant?'

'Who?'

'The Australian.' She had first worked with me on the case I had worked for him.

'Went back to Australia,' I said gallantly. He didn't argue so I figured he didn't know I was lying.

I was less scared being up in the air in a small plane than I had expected. If it hadn't been for the circumstances, it would have been an exciting experience, exhilarating, even enjoyable. I was surprised how much I could see of the ground below. The accumulated lights of the towns extended from above to the fields around them; there were lines of road-lights well out into the undeveloped countryside.

The other plane came alongside us. My eyes had adjusted to the dark and I could now see the pilot, though not clearly enough to make out his face or any features. I had a fair idea who it was:

'That's Walker, I take it.'

'Who's Walker?'

'I suppose you never heard of Waterbottom, either.'

'Who's Waterbottom?'

'And Battle?'

He didn't say anything. I got the point. He would talk about anything other than what this was all about. Not yet. Not until he was fully settled into the pilot's role.

'Who's babysitting Frankie?'

'Jada. That's . . .'

'Yeah, I know. I just wondered if you might ask me who Frankie was too.' I don't know why but I found it reassuring to think that Jada was with Frankie.

He chortled again; it was out of character; it was the most frightening aspect of the adventure.

We were heading out over the sea. It grew darker. We flew through low wispy clouds of our own, then as we emerged we could watch the stars flicker between higher levels of thicker cloud. It was eerie, but not unpleasantly so. It was vaguely like I imagined might be the thrill of sitting beside a camp-fire in the middle of an otherwise dark forest. I could only imagine it; I'd never been camping: tents don't have TV. Notwithstanding my sweater, I realised it was getting cold.

'You wanna turn on the heating?'

'It's not the same sensation,' he declined my invitation. I'd discovered what he did for – or instead of – sex. I flashed an image into my mind of Orbach jacking off while flying: it was suitably grotesque.

We flew in silence for a few more minutes until at last he said quietly:

'I want your help, Dave.'

'Sorry, Russel, only one client at a time.'

'Who's your client?'

'What client?'

He caught the crack and smiled thinly.

'Same old Dave. You're the one constant in my life.'

'I don't mean to be any part of your life, Russel; it's the last thing I want.'

'But you are, Dave. I don't seem to be able to shake you out of it.'

I looked down at the sky; I felt pretty shaken just then.

'What do you want, Russel?'

'I suppose, just for you to listen. Well, listen and think.'

Suddenly everyone wants me to listen.

'I didn't kill Mick and Eartha.'

'Did I say you did?'

I cursed Stephen Walker under my breath. Then I cursed my own stupidity, thinking I was clever enough to prevent him telling his father about our visit. Then I cursed Carson's stupidity for not coming up with a better way to keep him quiet. Couldn't she have done something? Maybe she could have seduced him. Maybe not.

'You've been investigating me,' he said flatly. 'I realised it the moment you turned up at my house. How did that happen? Coincidence or contrivance?'

'A bit of both. Started out as contrivance, ended up as coincidence when Sandy took an untarnishable shine to the house.' I laughed a lot more heartily than I felt. 'We're going to be such close neighbours you'll wonder how you ever got along without us. Maybe we can babysit for each other – waddaya think?'

'No, I don't think so,' he said sadly as if he truly regretted that we now could never be friends. 'I don't think moving in is that good an idea.'

'You know we've exchanged contracts. The builders are already in. You know Sandy. You tell her. I'd rather jump out of this plane without a parachute. It'd be safer.'

He didn't smile. He turned to stare at me, puzzled until he realised it was only another of my so-called gags.

'So what made you think I was investigating Mick and Eartha?'

'I didn't think it to begin with. I didn't know what to think. Just that you had to be up to something.' It was a back-handed compliment. 'But when you turned up in Southend, looking at the Walkers . . .'

'I thought you said you didn't know anyone called Walker?'

'I've just remembered,' he said dryly. 'There's a man called Walker who runs the maintenance company that services this plane. Nick Walker. Is that the one you mean?'

'Right. That Walker,' I tossed my head in the direction of the other plane. 'The Walker with the son who has trouble keeping his fly done up. The son you let – pardon the pun – walk. Gee, Russel, I'll never cease to be amazed by your powers of recall. Got any more tricks like it?'

'Well,' he said, 'I don't think that can be Mr Walker. I don't even know if he can fly. So far as I'm aware, he doesn't own an airplane, and he certainly doesn't own that one. It belongs to a local travel company. They don't use it in connection with their tours, at least not so far as I'm aware. It's more a promotion and hospitality job. Tax-free perk for the managing director, I daresay.'

'What sort of promotion are they doing out here now? Exploration of hotels on the moon?' That's how it felt; nothing between the earth and the moon – just us.

'What's out here now?' He contradicted himself inconsequentially. 'That plane can't fly; it's scheduled for a service tomorrow morning. Planes are well-documented. There are paper records, flight plans, logs, that sort of thing, and mechanical records too of course, and other ways of telling whether a plane has been in the air. My guess is, that plane you think you see out there is firmly on the ground – probably where you wish you were – and it will show no signs of having been airborne since it was last taken up by its owners.'

Walker would spend the rest of the night and its scheduled service in the morning personally stripping down the parts and cleaning them, turning the meters back, refuelling to precisely the correct level and eliminating every means of proving it had been up and out.

'You said you wanted me to listen,' I reminded him. 'To what? To how clever you are? How you can make me think

131

there's another plane up in the air with us and prove there isn't?'

'No. I hope that question won't ever arise.'

'What then?'

'You're quite right that I let Stephen Walker off with a soft sentence. You're quite right that I did it for Nick Walker. I'm not going to deny it: not to you, anyway. I won't take you for that big a fool. I won't be the first and I won't be the last judge who allowed a personal consideration to affect a sentencing decision. After all, most judges do, even if they don't realise it; the things that judges are soft on are the things they don't personally believe are that bad, and vice versa. I don't believe that what Stephen Walker did was that bad. The boys were only just under age, not little children. They knew what they were doing. For God's sake, Dave, don't be such a prude,' as if I had started to argue. 'Masturbation in a public lavatory is all we're talking about.'

I decided unusually in favour of silence. Let him talk it around for himself.

'But I sought no favour from Walker in return, let alone something as awful as what happened to Mick and Eartha. For God's sake,' he was invoking the Almighty a suspicious amount of the time – also uncharacteristically. 'They were my best friends. I was the godfather of their daughter. I had to take her in because of their deaths.'

'It was an accident, huh? Just an accident?'

'That's what I thought until recently. You see, well, I did have a little suspicion at the time; it is true Walker knew how unhappy I was at the idea of them leaving the country. Just from chatting, while we were waiting around in the hangar or what have you; I mean, not only from me but from them.'

'So he decides to return your favour by wacking them out? Come on, Russel. You said you weren't going to take me for a fool.'

'Walker knew about that, Walker knew about Frankie,' he recited the facts as if he was presenting a case in court. 'The thought occurred to me that he might have believed I wanted them dead. But I brushed it aside: it was too wild;

people don't do that sort of thing; the CAA concluded it was an accident; the insurance paid out; at the time, I think I felt guilty – one often does when someone close has died – especially if something comes out of it that is, well, good, and you know how I feel about Frankie and my life with her. People feel the same way when they get an inheritance: well, in a way, I did get an inheritance, and I realised I was feeling guilty and that came out as the idea that Walker might have fixed the plane. But,' he hesitated, as if struggling at such intimacy, 'you have to appreciate, I'm talking about something I thought once or twice – a few minutes over a few weeks. That's all.'

'Until recently,' I reminded him.

'Until yesterday,' he announced.

'What happened yesterday?'

'Walker came to see me.' He half-turned his head, to see how much of it I believed. I tried to look expressionless. I don't know if I succeeded. I doubt it. 'You mentioned Waterbottom. And Battle. That's what he came to see me about.'

I tried to stay ahead of him so as to be able to pick holes as they appeared. He was clever. It was a neat fit. Walker comes to him and says he whacked Waterbottom. If Orbach goes to the police, he'll spill both the Mellors and what Orbach had done for his son. It would not be enough to convict Orbach, but enough to make him keep silent. Walker could – as Carson had guessed – only have wanted Waterbottom out of the way if he knew about Battle. Absent divine intervention, Battle had to be how he knew about Waterbottom. Which left the question:

'Where is Battle? Is he dead too?'

'Ah, there's the rub. Walker didn't mean to kill Waterbottom. So he says. Battle came to see him – Walker. He, uh, got Battle's source out of him . . . .'

'How?'

Orbach grimaced.

'Walker plays rough. Well, that's obvious. He's still got Battle, as a matter of fact. He belongs to a gun club – it seems that a lot of people in Essex do. It has one of the highest per capita licence ratios.'

133

'Fascinating,' I said dryly. 'Let's say I go along with you for the moment. Walker beats up Battle, gets Waterbottom from him. What did he want from Waterbottom?'

'I imagine, to make sure he had told no one else.'

'Which he had,' I completed. Me. Through Carson. Hence his question about her. In answer to which I had lied. Which he knew. I was beginning to get very frightened indeed. He repeated his earlier question.

'Who's your client, Dave?'

'I told you. I don't have one.'

He snorted derisively.

'Ah, I see.'

'What do you "ah, I see"?' Even now, he had the most sarcastic tongue I knew, even including Sandy's.

'Ah, I see now why you had to get me down here, or perhaps I should say up here. All you've managed to get is a connection back to me.'

He banked slightly, following the other plane further out over the North Sea. I had been studying the dials, and I thought I'd worked out we were now flying at about fifty-five hundred feet. I asked him and he told me I was right.

'So what do you want from me, Russel?'

'I want you to understand. I want you to believe my account of what happened. I want you to accept that I am not responsible for Mick and Eartha – or for that matter for Waterbottom. I'd like to know who your client is, but it doesn't matter that much if you won't tell me. I'll find out. I always do.' It wasn't an idle boast.

Nonetheless, I derived some comfort from his ignorance. He was assuming that whoever had hired me was only concerned with getting Orbach rather than the truth of the plane crash.

'You want me to tell my client it wasn't your fault?'

'I want you to tell your client I had nothing whatsoever to do with it.'

'And Walker? What about Walker?'

'What about him?'

'What am I supposed to tell my client about Walker? Why wouldn't that bring you down anyway – if he's prosecuted for Waterbottom, even if they don't now prosecute for the Mellors.'

'How will they know about Waterbottom? Unless you tell them.'

'Which you don't want me to do. Right?'

'Right.'

I shook my head in disgust.

'You're a High Court judge, Russel. You're asking me to cover up three murders, for Christ's sake. Doesn't that mean anything to you?'

He shrugged.

'What can I do? It won't bring them back to life. If Walker is sure things will go no further, it's all at an end.'

'What about Battle?'

'Yes, that is a problem,' he said sadly.

Throughout this discussion, the other plane had been flying within our sight. Suddenly, it wiggled its wings in what I understood to be a signal to Orbach. Orbach hesitated.

'Do you believe me?' he asked.

'Does it matter? You're telling me what you'll say – if it ever arose – aren't you?' It was as close to denying him as I dared.

He sighed.

'I didn't think so.'

He wiggled our own wings in reply and pulled the plane into a climb, crossing over above Walker's and coming back down on the other side just as the passenger door slid back. The cabin was fully lit up. We were very close. There was a body within – a man's body – naked, stretched out along the deck, one leg at an angle that meant it had been broken, wrists tied to the seat-struts. Walker knelt down within to untie him. I think I saw it happen in my mind's eye a split second beforehand. Stupidly, futilely, I lashed out at the window as if there was anything I could do. Orbach jerked me roughly back into my seat.

I watched, then, as Battle's body – I didn't know at the time whether or not still alive – flew out of the plane. He fell, turning over and over, faster and faster, arms and legs flapping wide, until we lost sight of him beneath us

135

in the dark, descending like a bomb that would explode on impact with the water.

By apparent design, the two planes now parted company. My mouth was as dry as my eyes were wet. There was a soggy sensation in my underpants and I realised that, if I had not quite proverbially pissed myself, I had permitted a literal leak. I wanted to claw off my clothes. I wanted to follow Battle to his watery grave. I didn't want to live with the memory of it.

Strangely, it never occurred to me that Orbach might be about to extend to me the same opportunity to re-establish that only birds, not men, can fly. I was shaken more through horror than fear for my own life. For the first time since the flight began I lit a cigarette, my hand quaking; it took the silver Dunhill Sandy had bought me for my birthday and that I hadn't yet managed to mislay, an unprecedented half-dozen strokes to catch. I placed the cold metal against my hot forehead with one hand while I dragged deeply on my cigarette held in the other.

Orbach was leaving me to work it out for myself. I wasn't doing very well. I was supposed to be investigating him for a past crime, one that at best would be hard to prove and that, hitherto, would be likely to have led to nothing worse than his resignation in disgrace. The odds were overwhelming against being able to tie him into Waterbottom, whatever the truth of his involvement in it might be. Nonetheless, he had now handed me the first-hand evidence of his complicity in a whole new murder.

I felt guilty; I felt responsible for Battle's death; if I'd confided in him, trusted him, perhaps he would never have gone off on his own, or at least he would have understood the nature of the beast he was tracking. I'd witnessed his death. His death had been orchestrated for my entertainment.

'For your education,' Orbach broke in, as if he could read my thoughts. For all I know, in the state I was in, I might well have been babbling out loud. 'Listen to me, Dave. You will give up this investigation. You will never suggest to anyone that Mick and Eartha's death was anything but an accident. You would do best never to mention them ever again. You will never say a word about what happened tonight; you can't prove it, but you won't even try. Am I making myself clear? Do you understand me?'

I understood alright, but I was damned if I'd let him off the hook of spelling it out. I looked blankly back at him as if I didn't know what he was trying to tell me.

He frowned:

'Alright, Dave, we'll do it your way. If you ever give me the slightest cause to think that you are doing anything about any of these matters – Mick and Eartha or Waterbottom or Battle – if you ever give me the slightest cause to think that you are investigating me, interested in me, writing about me, suing me, even thinking about me, the next person you see falling from a plane will be you or Sandy or your son.' And if not a plane, then a car, a mugger, a fire in the new house or ten hours locked up listening to Nigel Morris. 'You've threatened the life I lead with my child; I'm threatening yours,' he added flatly. 'You see, it wasn't that funny a joke after all, was it?' My earlier unfortunate crack about what I'd rather do than tell Sandy we weren't moving into Cloudesley Road.

I asked:

'Why, Russel? Why not simply kill me too?'

'Are you complaining, Dave?' He didn't wait for an answer. 'I like you, Dave; I've always liked you.' Margot McAllister had said something similar. 'I like Sandy, too. I don't think you've ever set out to harm me, not in the way that others have done; not until now. I don't want to have to harm you, so long as you don't make me.' I didn't believe his reason for a second, but it wasn't the time to tell him so.

We neither of us spoke to the other until we were back on the ground, though Orbach told traffic control we were coming back in. I guessed that Walker was flying the other plane the same way he'd gone out, but I didn't see it come down and it didn't come back to its parking space beside us, at least while I was there. Possibly, it was taken elsewhere for its service. The service would of course include a thorough internal clean, to remove

137

also any traces of Battle's last battle. I didn't know or care about the details but I had no doubt that they had been worked out to the last degree.

As he let me out of the passenger cabin door, he patted me on the shoulder:

'As I said, Dave, I don't think you're a fool.' I could be relied on to do the sensible thing.

I looked straight at him. I had a thousand things I wanted to say that would tell him he hadn't succeeded, he hadn't scared me, I could and would stand up to him. The trouble was, none of them would be true, and I badly needed a proper pee.

It was, I suppose, the most obvious answer of all; I unzipped myself, found with difficulty my shock-shrivelled prick and urinated on the steps and wheels of his plane.

To my eternal shame, he roared with manic laughter.

Then he reminded me of his warning:

'Remember, Dave, remember what I told you. You know me, Dave – I will know and I will do as I say.'

I did know him. And I believed him. I was finally scared – scared for my life and the lives of the people I loved – as I'd never been before, not even at those moments when I had directly confronted death. He turned away as my knees buckled and I grabbed hold of the steps to stop myself sinking to the ground.

# CHAPTER NINE

'Woolf against Orbach, for hearing. All persons having naught better to do draw nigh and enjoy the performance. Honourable Mr Justice Orbach presiding.' The clerk swished his gown around his shoulder like Zorro and kicked me in the shins.

My counsel at the bar rose.

'M'lord, in this matter I appear for the plaintiff, Mr Woolf, and m'learned friends, Mr Tweedledum Q.C. and his junior Mr Tweedledee appear, well, as it happens, for your lordship. This is an action for a declaration, m'lord, that, not to put too fine a point on it, your lordship is stark, staring bonkers.'

'Mr Austin-Smythe-Filibuster,' who had taken the case at the last moment when the fifteenth barrister I had instructed found himself unavoidably professionally detained elsewhere, 'do you take exception to my hearing the case, in view of the fact that I might be considered in some sense partisan?' Orbach interrupted the opening.

'Good Lord, no, m'lord. I am sure your lordship's considerable reputation for impartiality is more than protection enough for my client.'

'Yes. That's my own opinion. Nonetheless, I thought I ought to mention it.'

'Your lordship is too kind. Too, too kind. I am much obliged. Would it be convenient to your lordship if I were to continue with my opening?'

'Is it really necessary, Mr Bumsucker? I have read the papers. I mean no disrespect to your client, of course, but it is hardly, well, a complicated matter.'

'Your lordship is quite right. I shan't trouble your lordship *any further. Perhaps in those circumstances I can rest my case?'*

'It's entirely a matter for you, Mr Lickspittle; please don't let me interfere in your conduct of the case.'

'What about me?' I hollered. 'Don't I get a say in any of it? It's my case, after all.'

'Oh, sit down, Dave,' Orbach said. 'You know you're a lousy lawyer, and a worse advocate. You haven't presented a case in court for more than a decade. Besides, you have most competent counsel appearing on your behalf.'

'Look, Russel,' I said heatedly.

'Mr Woolf,' he was horrified. 'In my court, you will address me in the proper manner. Everything must be done in the proper manner.'

'Right on, bro,' someone in the public gallery called out, sounding suspiciously like Carson.

'All rise,' mumbled the clerk in his sleep.

'Usher,' Orbach instructed. 'Open the window. Drop the clerk out of it.'

'M'lord.' The usher did as he was told.

'Look, Russel, this just isn't fair,' I protested.

'Fair?' screeched Orbach. 'Fair? Who said that? I decide what's fair. I know what's fair. Arrest that man.'

'Fuck it, Russel, this time you've gone too far. Even your sweet-talking counsel can't get you out of this one.'

'Tell us about it, Dave, tell us all about it. Come on, come on up here, sit on my lap and tell us about it. It'll be alright. There, there. Don't cry. Usher, bring Mr Woolf a Southern Comfort.'

'Russel, you killed your best friend. And his wife. Who you fancied.'

'Knickers. Prove it.'

'Prove what? That you fancied her? There's . . . ' I was about to tell him there was a letter that proved it, but I remembered my duty to my client – privileged information.

'Not that,' he snapped crossly.

One of his counsel rose; it was difficult to know which one.

'M'lord, I must object to your lordship's tone . . .'

'Sit down, fool. You're supposed to be on my side.'

'Am I? Sorry, m'lord, m'learned junior's mistake.'

'I invited you to prove that I killed Mick and Eartha, Dave. Well? Well? What was my motive? It's ridiculous. They were my best friends. I was the godfather of their daughter. I had to take her in because of their deaths. So much for motive. Anyway, the crash report was inconclusive; the coroner returned a verdict of accident; the insurance paid out. Besides, how could I have done it?'

'Walker did it for you.'

The well of the courtroom erupted in laughter. Even I was laughing. Choking on my mirth, I went on.

'You let his son off from going to prison . . .'

'For a pathetic little wank with a couple of willing youngsters. Oh, really, you've got to do better than that, Mr Woolf.'

'I agree,' Schofield announced. 'This case is totally out of order.'

Behind me, Tim tugged at my gown.

'Sit down, Dave, you're making an ass of yourself.'

I mooned him and ignored him.

Alton began to cry.

Frankie popped up from behind the judge's bench demanding:

'Give him to me.'

In the witness box, Jada sang a few bars from 'Desolation Angels' which quickly descended into 'Rock Of Ages'.

I said:

'Then there's Waterbottom. What did you have to do with that?'

'Hang on, Dave,' Orbach protested. 'I ask the questions here. This is a trial, not an investigation. Members of the jury, disregard that last remark.'

The twelve cardboard cut-out men good and true flopped forward as far as the floor and sprung back up into place with nary a sound.

'Waterbottom's not even a runner, and you know it. Move along, move along, get to your best point – if you have one.'

'Battle,' I said firmly. 'Brian Battle.'

'Who?' answered Orbach.

*I tried to tell them but I couldn't get the words out. How could I describe it? I had been there. I was, however unwillingly, however unwittingly, an accomplice. My mouth opened and shut and opened and shut to no effect. Someone else was tugging at my gown.*

*'I told you, Woolf, in no circumstances; the Pulleyne scandal never happened; this isn't happening; five times nothing is nothing; it's all in your head; it's all a dream.'*

It wasn't Schofield tugging at my gown, but a uniformed police officer shaking me by the shoulder. I woke up with a start and banged my chest against the steering wheel. I was still parked on the side-road by the airport. It was just after dawn.

'Are you alright, sir?'

His car was parked in front of mine, preventing a quick getaway. He said:

'I wonder whether you would mind stepping out of the car, sir.'

Awkwardly, I got out. He didn't try to help me.

'Have you been drinking, sir?'

'What?'

'I asked, sir, whether you had been drinking.' He was extracting a breathalyser from its case.

I cackled crazily.

'No, officer, I haven't been drinking.'

It was true: the one time in my life a police officer asked to breathalyse me was the one time in my life when I wasn't half-cut.

* * *

There were two reasons I didn't drive back to London straight away. One was, I was still shaking so bad I wasn't sure I could handle the car. The other that I didn't want to face my family. For a lot of years, I'd been pretending to be a tough guy, handling occasional but very real physical fear with gallows-humour. Just like everyone else. It wasn't easy admitting the truth was that I was far more coward than anything else. What Tim had said at the club was right. Orbach scared me. We used to

142

say in the sixties, he scared me shitless.

I had a theory. Becoming a proper, full-time judge had been both Orbach's saving coup and his major error. Until then, though isolated in his personal life, he had contacts and influence, even power, principally through his work; information and circumstances and people he could use to his own ends; like he'd used others during Disraeli Chambers, maybe like he'd used to find something out for me during Mather's – I now firmly believed in order to put me into his debt – and like he'd then used me and others during Pulleyne. Like, too, he'd used his position as an Assistant Recorder to manipulate Nick Walker.

Once he was a full High Court judge, his access to people and his room for manoeuvre were restricted. His power and influence had been formalised. He couldn't call up anyone in the legal profession or any of the other established institutions without attracting attention to himself; there were fewer places he could safely go without a legitimate explanation; he had placed himself under the microscope of an abstract integrity which can only be sustained by minimal activity.

This was the trade off: he gave up his freedom of action for an effective immunity from prosecution, an immunity of which he'd tested the fibre during Pulleyne. Which threw up another question – why fight it? Even if, and I was still a long way off, I was going to be able to put together a package convincing enough and sufficient to justify publication, with the only consequence that he had to resign, wasn't that exactly the deal he'd made with himself?

The answer wasn't as obscure as it might have seemed to someone who didn't know Orbach. It was one thing for him to accept intellectually that there would forever remain a risk of discovery and to guard against it; it was another actually to confront it and admit it was happening – happening to him. Perhaps there was another level to it, too; perhaps, though he'd theorised that he could accept push if it came to shove, in reality he was incapable of doing anything other than he had done all his life – fighting it, fighting back, fighting 'them', whoever for the time being might be his enemy. Like a *schmuk*, I'd stood up to be counted.

* * *

'So what're you going to do?' Carson asked with her mouth full of muesli.

I had driven to the club and let myself in. I had rung Sandy and told her I was alright, I'd be home later, I'd explain when I got back. She had been so worried she had even rung Orbach to make sure nothing had happened on the flight.

'What did he say?'

'He said it was fine. He left you in Southend.'

'To tell the truth, I feel asleep in the car.'

For some reason she believed me. She said in a small voice:

'Dave, are you alright? What's going on, Dave?'

'I said I'll tell you when I get back. Honestly. Go to sleep, San.' She must've been tired: she didn't tell me off. 'I love you. Kiss Alton for me.'

I replaced the receiver sadly.

After the local law let me leave, I drove back to London slowly, carefully and thoughtful. I tried to keep the image of Battle's final fling out of my mind. I tried to put my fear and my guilt to one side. I set out to think it through.

The nightmare helped. It reminded me of the essentials. Orbach was the law. Orbach, with Schofield and Dowell in support. They were not there to protect the man; just his office. I knew and liked and respected Tim, and for all his manner sensed that beneath Schofield's callous exterior lurked an essentially decent man, one who would at the lowest prefer people not to be unnecessarily nasty to one another. If I could put a strong enough package together, I had a good chance of abridging the professional career of Mr Justice Orbach much as Pulleyne's had come to a premature end.

The difficulty was that I could not go so far as to put Orbach away. The Mellor charge depended entirely on

Walker. Jada's instincts were not admissible evidence. Eartha's letter was ambiguous. Even in a court, Walker would not make a compelling case; a good brief would easily be able to get Orbach off. I knew, however, that there would be no trial, of either of them: Schofield had as good as said it; it was an essential premise. They would rather not charge Walker than have Orbach's name dragged into his defence.

So far as Waterbottom was concerned, there was even less evidence to connect Orbach. I was not certain in my own mind that Walker had been in touch with him beforehand. It was a messy killing, and probably unnecessary; I doubted Orbach would have sanctioned, let alone conceived of it. Again, however, if I – or anyone else – pointed the finger at Walker, he would threaten to involve Orbach and charges would have to be dropped as soon as they realised that it was not a wholly hollow hazard, that a sufficient connection to withstand superficial scrutiny could be sustained.

There was only one case where there was independent evidence. Battle. Me. My word against Orbach's. My word against Orbach's and Walker's. My word against an open journey taken by Orbach – foolhardy indeed if the purpose was a public viewing of a private execution – and a journey Walker would, so Orbach claimed, by the time I could cause any enquiry, be in a position to prove had never taken place. Once again, the conclusion was inescapable: no trial, no incarceration.

The most I could achieve, therefore, was the Schofield-style 'quiet word' that compelled Orbach to resign. This was not a solution that suited. The man had terrified me beyond terror; he had threatened the only things in life I have ever held precious enough to want to go on living for; he had a camel-like capacity to harbour grudges, a Sicilian approach to revenge, an elephantine memory, skill and money; he would know my part in his downfall, and Jada's when her book was published. Even if forced to quit, even if – as he had said he might do later on in life – he went abroad, I and my family would remain forever vulnerable. It was not something I was prepared to subject

145

them to; it was not something I was prepared to subject myself to.

There were, it seemed to me, only two ultimate solutions. The first was to do what Orbach wanted: drop the case, forget about him and it, go back to being a lawyer and a father – as he wanted to remain. The second was to push the logic of the situation to its extreme: if Orbach was protected by his position, if Walker was too, why should it not extend also to me?

\* \* \*

I was, however, not yet ready to confide my decision in anyone. I was about to embark on an extremely dangerous undertaking: I knew there were people – above all, Carson and Sandy – who would, once I had told them about the plane trip, go as far along the route with me as I wanted; while the choice to do so would remain their responsibility, it would also be mine – as I felt responsible for Battle. I did not wish to involve them unless and until it became necessary. I would not know whether it was necessary until I had worked out the details. Until I did so, it seemed to me that caution called for an apparent abandonment of interest.

'I don't feel I have any choices, Carson. I'm going to do what he says. I'm going to go back to London, and I'm going back to the office, and I'm going to tell Mister-mister Nigel-nigel Morris-morris it's a load of crap and I can't waste my time on it anymore, and then maybe I'll forget to bill him or maybe it'll be even more convincing if I do.'

'What're you going to tell Sandy?' Why did I have the idea she didn't believe me?

'I'm going to tell her the same damn thing. I'm going to tell her I'm convinced there's nothing in it and that's that.'

'What're you going to tell Jada?'

'I'm going to tell her to grow up. Just grow up and don't be so stupid: you can't do everything you want in this life; that's why there're laws; being gorgeous and

146

brilliant and half-orphaned and a pop star doesn't make her any different.'

'And what're you going to tell Dowell?'

'How the hell did Tim get into this? I might've told him at the beginning but he told me to take a running jump.' I groaned — it was entirely the wrong expression to use and equally entirely accidental. 'So I don't have to tell him anything.'

She shook her head.

'Uhuh. As soon as Battle surfaces, he'll be onto you.' This was true.

'Who says he surfaces? The fishes'll eat him. How can they i.d. him? He had no identifying clothing — not even a watch.'

'I dunno,' she admitted. 'They do, though, don't they? Besides, someone's bound to report him missing sooner or later.'

'I don't know,' I said with false bravado. 'He was pretty much of a slime; I doubt he was married; his parents probably denied responsibility for him five minutes after he was born. With the current turnover in Fleet Street, no one's likely to notice at his paper.'

'Crap.'

'So, already, I don't have all the answers. I never said I did.'

'That's even bigger crap, Dave. You're not telling me the truth.' Her eyes met mine and glowered. 'How dare you call me back from Oz and then hold out on me?'

'*Chutzpah?*' I suggested lamely.

* * *

After I had talked with Sandy, telling her too what had happened on the plane, I crashed out. She left Alton off at the childminder so I could get some sleep and went into the office. I was only just in bed when the phone rang. It was Jada Jarrynge. She had rung the office and demanded my home number. When you're a pop star, you can do things like that; they wouldn't have given it out to the Lord Chief Justice in person. She omitted the courtesies altogether —

perhaps Orbach had more of a hand in her upbringing than I had appreciated.

'This is Jada. What happened last night? What are you doing with him?'

'What do you mean?'

I forgot he had told her he was going night-flying with me. She reminded me and added:

'Why?'

'Ah, right. Well, that's about it. You know we're moving into a house near his. He was talking about flying and, uh, that was it: he told me he sometimes went night-flying and asked me if I'd like to go. I said sure, why not. It was something new, you know? That's all, just a new experience.' And then some.

She breathed heavily into the phone. If I had taped it, I probably could've sold it for a smash hit.

'What did you find out? What is this? I agreed to look after Frankie; I thought – this was something you were doing for me. I had to cancel a recording session. Just so that you could do something new?'

She sounded incredulous. I couldn't blame her.

'Listen, Jada, I was going to talk to Nigel Morris today but, uh, you know him, I didn't have enough years to spare.' She didn't laugh. Maybe she didn't know him that well. Maybe I wasn't funny anymore. I didn't laugh either. 'I've done a lot of work on this thing . . . I don't think it's going anywhere . . . You know, when you've got a certain amount of experience, you get a nose for it: I don't think it's there, Jada – you know?' If I said 'you know' once more, I'd scream.

More rhythmic breathing.

'Jada? You still there?'

'What did he give you? What did he pay you? Why are you backing down? You believed me; you told me about him; you know it's true. He buy you off, or what?'

'Hey, c'mon. Those're heavy things to say. Nobody buys me off. I don't have to take that kind of shit from you; you know, what are you – just a kid? I don't have to take it – you know?' I didn't scream. Even I couldn't rely on my word.

148

'Oh, yes, sure I know. I know what this is about. I know what all you people are about. Remember: if you aren't with me, you're against me.'

She hung up at about the same time I slammed down the receiver in my own unjustified indignation.

* * *

I figured I'd better get my version into Morris first. I called but he was in a meeting. I left a message. When he called back, he rang the office instead of the home number I'd left for him. He only tied up the main line for half an hour. By the time he got through to me, he'd already talked to Jada.

'Working at h-h-home?'

'We're moving soon; thought I'd do my share of packing.'

'I r-r-r-remember when we moved. I never thought, looking at my b-b-b-books on the shelves, how many p-p-p-packing cases I'd need. June w-w-w-went . . .'

I groaned. Unlike on earlier occasions, when I'd wanted him to get straight to the point, my aim this time was for him to let me do so. I started talking over him.

'If you've spoken to Jada you'll know I've come to the conclusion there's nothing in the case. You're not going to be able to publish. It's a libel – and I think it probably qualifies as criminal libel.' I knew not much more about criminal libel than the civil variety: but I knew it existed, and had been used once or twice in recent years, and if telling the world that a judge whacked off your parents didn't qualify, I had a hard time thinking what would. Queen eats baby for breakfast? Archbishop's silk underwear secret? Prime Minister's hair out of place? President tells truth?

'I s-s-s-see. Don't you think, don't you think we ought to discuss this. There's a v-v-very nice cocktail bar near the office: I could buy you one of their extraordinary con-con-concoctions. They do one that . . .'

'I don't want to. I'll write you a letter; you consider what I have to say; if you still want to meet and discuss it, OK, it's your money, your time.' I'd reached a compromise over billing: I wouldn't charge for any of the time I'd spent working on the case; just for all the time I'd spent listening to Morris.

'B-b-b-but . . .' he was still protesting as I replaced the receiver: 'The co-co-co-cocktails are ex-ex-ex-exquisite . . .'

\* \* \*

This is how I passed the next couple of days. Sandy was happy for me to take Alton to, and pick him up from, the childminder; she told me where to get cartons for packing; she even let me do the shopping though I got most of it wrong.

In my place, she went into the office for most of the hours it was open. I think she would have enjoyed the role reversal if she wasn't worried about me. It was more her firm than mine, and it gave her an opportunity to see how much damage I'd done during my tenure. We didn't talk much, though: she refused to ask what I was going to do, unwilling to be accused of nagging, waiting instead for me to tell her, and I decided there were a lot of programmes on the television that I was really quite addicted to.

Nor did I go to the club; nor did Carson ring me. She was sulking; I was skulking. I know she went into Nichol & Co, who were her theoretical employers, and Sandy said she was working on a couple of cases, to help out, to have something to do. She also said they'd had lunch one day, and a chat the other, but the way she said it was like a cross-examination where there's nothing left to lose, bluffing for an answer. I knew Carson was disappointed, maybe angry at me, but she would remain silent – for a while at least – to give me an opportunity to make up my mind.

In the end, though, Carson's patience gave out and she called round, during the day – the third of my retreat – bearing a bottle for me and a bunch of flowers for the house.

'Got it bad, boss, huh?' She glanced at my already full glass and, ostentatiously, at her watch.

'Have you come to lecture me, or to have a drink?'

'Both.'

I got her a beer from the fridge as she stretched out comfortably on the sofa. Half the room was now taken up with boxes: we'd run out of elsewhere to store them. In another few days, there'd be a couple of rooms at the new house which would be sufficiently ready for us to start carting over the breakables we didn't want the removal men to handle, and a few pictures which it would be convenient to hang before the day of the move itself. We had seen too many friends move into half-decorated, half-improved houses, and live out of boxes for years, adjusting to their incomplete homes until, it seemed, they were happier than if the work finally came to an end. We didn't want the same.

'You looking forward to moving?'

'You mean what I think you mean?'

'Sure.'

'No, then. No, I'm terrified of it, terrified of seeing him, terrified, even, of seeing *her*,' Frankie. 'Terrified how I'll react.'

'Waddaya gonna do, then? Ask Sandy to leave you here for the new owners? Hide in a back room? Emigrate? Forget it,' she pre-empted any flip reference to going back to Australia with her.

I sighed.

'I suppose it's time.'

'Certainly is. Time for what?'

'Time to tell you what's on my mind.' I paused to gather my thoughts, to find the best way to tell her. Confident as I had been until then of her support, I suddenly realised that I didn't know her that well, that no one knew anyone else that well, to be a hundred per cent sure they would go along with the wildest and most dangerous scheme.

'I've been thinking about a lot of things. The choices're much less straightforward than you seem to think. In fact, I think there's only one that makes any sense.'

'Tell me.'

151

I was about to do so when – with impeccable mis-timing – we were interrupted by a ring at the door.

He started talking before he was into the living-room:

'I don't believe it. I really don't believe it,' he howled. 'They had floods in Bangladesh, a war in the Middle East, dictators in South America; here, there've been tube crashes, train crashes, plane crashes, football crowd crushes – and yet you haven't been involved. I don't know why not. You're a one-man walking disaster area.'

'I resent that,' Carson piped up.

'Right. One-person,' Dowell snarled back at her. He could give as good as he got.

She started to tell him that wasn't what she meant when she realised it wasn't what he meant either.

'What are you talking about, Tim?'

'I'm talking about one death soon after you mention Southend to me maybe I could eventually have persuaded myself to swallow as coincidental; not two.'

'Who's the second?' I asked with sweet-toned innocence.

'Your friend Brian Battle, the one you said you were looking for in Southend, from the same paper you claimed you were working for. Seems he went swimming; correction, diving.' He was sufficiently at home to fetch his own glass before he sat down. 'Sky-diving,' he added unnecessarily melodramatically. 'From an airplane that maybe came out of Southend Airport. Without a parachute.'

'This Orbach's plane that Dave originally asked you about? The one that crashed?' Carson asked disingenuously, to remind him it wasn't a connection on its own.

'You,' he wagged a finger at her, 'you keep quiet. You're far cleverer than him, and if I'm going to trip him up I don't want you running interference, right?'

I wasn't sure if it was a mixed metaphor or not, so I asked:

'Start again, Tim. I've had a lot to drink. I'm taking a break from work.'

'Yeah, I know. Like a fool, I thought you'd be at work, went to your office first.' Where Sandy had told him I could be found at home. 'And to add to all these coincidences, you happen to decide to take a break. Really,' he exclaimed. He shook his head: 'Stop pretending, Dave. Stop pretending you don't know. Stop pretending it ain't serious, Dave.' His tone turned quite gentle, 'It's getting heavy again. How long do you think you can go out playing cowboy without somebody blowing your head off, Dave?'

I conceded nothing. I repeated:

'So far, all I know is that Brian Battle, you say, is dead, and I think you're saying he fell – but maybe you're insinuating he was pushed, as I say I don't know – out of an airplane that might've come from Southend Airport, which you think connects to me because I asked you about a plane crash which involved Orbach and that's where the plane he owned flew out of and Carson was down there recently but alibi'd for when Wetbum got it. Is that it? Even for you, it's pretty thin, isn't it?'

'That and he was helping you on the Orbach case.'

'Is that something you know or just a wishful guess?'

'Both more or less. His editor didn't know what he'd been working on, but he'd already filed his expense claim which gave me Southend. I was referred to a man called Nigel Morris, a book publisher who I'm going to put under arrest for speech impeding the police with their enquiries.' He was talking about my Morris. 'He claims he doesn't know what Battle was doing for you, but agrees he lent him you to assist. He won't tell me why until he's spoken to his boss – he says his boss is out of the country and, allegedly, entirely uncontactable. I don't believe him; everything I've read about his boss says you can contact him in the bath. But there's nothing I can do at this stage; he's consulting the group's own lawyers.'

'This ain't necessarily criminal, then?' Otherwise he'd be talking obstruction as he had with Carson over Waterbottom.

'Not necessarily, not yet. He was naked when he was found. Given the height from which he fell, we're talking a small aircraft. Probably five, six thousand feet from the damage.' I omitted to tell him how close he was.

153

Broken bones, crushed vertebrae, he gave us a few other distasteful details which told me they couldn't be sure what sort of state he was in before he took a dive. 'But he died of a heart attack of course.' I nearly had, so why shouldn't he?

'And it definitely came from Southend?'

'No, it could've been Humberside, Norwich or Ipswich – or maybe even Cambridge or Stansted. Could have come from the continent, too. But Southend has five, six flying clubs, which is a lot, and it's nearest.'

'If he was naked, how d'you i.d. him? He was carrying his passport maybe?'

'There's a dental computer at Eastbourne. The Dental Estimates Board keep it; they've just got a new system up and running; when you've got a body you don't know who it is, one of the first things they do is X-ray the jaw and teeth and feed it in.'

Without thinking about it, I was gnashing my own teeth and stroking my jaw. I didn't like the idea they were on public record; it was an invasion of my privacy. Anyone could find out how I had neglected my gums.

'If it doesn't kick anyone out, it's either a foreigner or someone with perfect teeth. Even private dentistry's on the records. Usually, it'll produce anything from one to half a dozen people it might be. From then on, it's relatively straightforward. In this case, because his record showed up his occupation as a journalist in London, they faxed a photo through to the Met. where it was matched with his press pass picture, from where it led to Waterbottom and you.' And Dowell.

'How long had he been in the sea?'

'Probably a couple days. The temperature's been volatile, which makes it harder to pin down. He was trawled the night before last,' he added, literally fished out. 'Now it's your turn to do the talking.' He tapped his glass impatiently but it wasn't another drink he wanted. 'What was he up to?'

'He was on what we like to call a frolic of his own, ducky.' A job on the side for which his employer would not have to take responsibility. Dowell, a former law student, might remember the phrase. 'He did a bit of research for me and then decided to do some freelancing; so how can I know what he was doing?'

I waited for him to argue. When he didn't I added:

'I don't know where he'd been or why. That's it. You can book me for interfering with an officer and all that jazz, if you like. But you haven't got the basis for it; you won't be able to hold me even overnight; it doesn't help you get any answers.'

He sighed loudly, satisfiedly. I thought he'd been taking it all too calmly so far. He had simply wanted to confirm I was going to lie to him. He had something else up his sleeve.

'Well, if you won't tell me anything, I'll have to tell you a bit more, won't I? I think I, er, forgot to mention, I've already got some information. Yesterday, they checked all those airports for private craft flights over the last few days and particularly for night-flights.'

He watched my face drop – to the ground, where I keep my brains.

'Another bit of odd coincidence,' he continued. 'Remember the name we mentioned before? Sir Russel someone? Had a flight out a few nights ago. I saw him at the lunch-break – pardon, luncheon adjournment – today. Naturally, I was most deferential, especially as he hasn't got such fond memories of me, apologised for disturbing him, genuflected, kissed the hem of his robes, touched my forelock. I explained we were making enquiries of everyone who took their planes out of certain airports – the ones I told you – whether they'd seen anything suspicious, whether they happened to lose any passengers, that sort of thing.'

'And?' I croaked.

Carson got up and filled my glass for me and, rather than miss anything by going into the kitchen for a beer refill, poured herself a shot. Dowell held his glass out but she shook her head:

'Not yet.'

'Mr Sir Russel Justice says he neither saw anything suspicious nor did he lose any passengers. He says he only had one passenger, who he assures me will confirm what he says, and who was definitely still with him when he landed. Get it?'

I was clenching so hard, the glass shattered in my hand. I've heard of it happening, but I'd never seen it and it's never happened to me before. I jumped up cursing. Fortunately, it had not cut me. As Carson went inside for a cloth, I started to lick the sticky Southern Comfort off my fingers – waste not, want not – when Tim grabbed my hand to stop me:

'Slivers,' he warned.

'Ta,' I said faintly.

After we'd cleaned up, Carson announced she was going to make coffee.

'This is no way for two responsible people to spend the afternoon.' She refused to say who wasn't.

We followed her into the kitchen.

My knees were weaker than when I'd left Orbach at the plane. This was why he hadn't killed me. They had to kill Battle – it was inevitable, possibly even from before Walker contacted Orbach, because he was already too badly damaged; it would all be superceded by harm done in a fall. Because they wanted to drop Battle, they needed a flight – and preferably a night-flight; a flight meant a record; a record needed an alibi.

I could always tell the truth.

My word against his. My life against his.

Tim babied:

'Talkie time, Davey.'

'Nothing to say. I was up with Orbach. Only me. We both came back. That's it.'

'And what did you see while you were up there?'

'Uh, stars, and, uh, clouds, and, well, more stars and clouds and of course we looked down at towns and the sea and stuff.' I gulped my coffee too quickly and burned my mouth. 'Shit.'

'Tut.'

'Tim, you're taking it all very calmly, aren't you? I mean, for you. Isn't this when you take out your rubber hose?'

He normally got quite pissed off when people got whacked. Quite but not very. But he was invariably furious if he thought I had anything to do with it.

'I know you, Dave. If something's going down again, I'm resigned to it; let's just get on with it.' It was the first time he'd ever admitted that, one way or another, we worked well together.

I snorted.

'You're snowing me, sunshine. I've got nothing to tell you and sweet-talk won't get it either.'

'Right, then. I'm going to ask you formally,' he took out his notebook. 'Sir, did anything strange happen, or did you see anything strange, while you were in the air with Sir Russel?'

'No.'

He shook his head sadly as he put his notebook away.

'Dave. I like you; I like Sandy; I don't want to see you hurt. I'm your friend, trust me.'

'Someone else told me the same thing just recently,' was as far as I would go. 'But I don't think you'd expect me to trust him either.'

# CHAPTER TEN

We sat up most of the night, me and Sandy and Carson. In the middle, one of Sandy's headaches came on and she went to lie down for an hour or so, but still sleep would not release her and she got up again, around three o'clock, to re-join us in the living-room, in the middle of our boxes.

Sandy was the hardest to convince. She scrutinised every element of my reasoning and the details of my plan the way sometimes I would come across her examining Alton, inch by inch of the perfect body she could not believe she had built, for the slightest hint of flaw or potential problem.

What I was trying to do was handle it the same way Orbach would. It was simple: Orbach had hurt me, Orbach was enemy, Orbach must die.

I pointed to the boxes.

'And the new house? Just forget it? You love it, San; I love it. It's the perfect place for Alton. It's our house.' Nothing we hadn't said many times since she'd decided we were going to buy it. 'We can't move into it if he's there.'

She shook her head.

'Not good enough, Dave. You can't do this so that you can have the things you want, we want. That's as bad as him. It's only an option if it's the only way to defend yourself, to defend us.'

'You should have seen,' I said also not for the first time, 'you should have seen Battle. Can you imagine how he felt, what he was thinking? Dowell said he died of a heart attack, of sheer shock; it may not have been for long, but he knew what was happening to him.'

'No, of course I can't imagine it. The closest I can get is to try and think how I'd feel if, say, Alton was ill, we took

158

him to the hospital, and they said – well, he's dying, he's going to die in a few hours or days. I couldn't cope with it – it's the unmentionable, the unthinkable. That's why, I suppose, that's why despite everything – everything I've believed about violence, everything I've believed about law, everything I believe about civilised behaviour – so-called – that's why I can even sit here discussing it.'

After a lengthy silence, she asked, as if Carson was not present:

'What about Carson? Is it fair to involve her? Remember. . .'

Carson cut her off:

'I know what you're going to say.' For Carson to participate was inevitably to evoke the memory of all she had gone through about her uncle – the publicity, her trial, being shunned by some people and congratulated for all the wrong reasons by others. 'It's the same thing. It's not immediate, hot-blooded, spontaneous. But you're – we're – not dealing with a hot-blooded man. The opposite, really. It's the only way. It's an absolute certainty they won't prosecute him. Either we lie down under it, or we put him down. There's no middle ground. It's not our responsibility; it's theirs – because they won't use the power they've got.'

I said much the same:

'It's them, not us. This is a situation that doesn't fit concepts of "civilised society". In a civilised society, an awful crime is always punished – unless of course it's perpetuated by the authorities themselves, in which case – give or take – it's not a crime at all. What we're saying is that because the authorities won't take any real action against him, they've adopted his conduct, absorbed it if you like.'

'With us or agin' us?'

As Jada had said.

'I suppose. In a sense, no. In actuality, he is one of the authorities. What I'm saying is, we're right outside all the known rules now. This is what the judiciary are: above the law, part of the penal system, part of the process for enforcing law and therefore no part of those who are intended to be enforced by it.'

159

'*Quis custodiet*?'

'They made their devil's pact when they made him a judge. And unless there's any chance – which there isn't – that they'll admit their error, sacrifice some of their authority, the mystique of law that says a High Court judge can never be crooked, then that's their choice. I ain't paying for it; you ain't paying for it; Alton ain't paying for it. The whole thing is outside the law; what he was doing in that plane was outside the law; the law has abdicated responsibility for this particular game; therefore, we've got to play it the same way it would be if there was no law.'

Which is when she conceded I was right; there could be no other outcome. It was a question of survival.

\* \* \*

It had to be done fast. Dowell was already too close. He was far closer than hard evidence permitted him to prove, either to the press-pack in hot pursuit and protection of their own or to his superiors, because he knew what people were involved and could probably guess how they were tied together. Once the destination of an investigation has been identified, it is twenty times easier to determine the route, to find the evidence that links the beginning to the end. In addition, we were now less than a week away from moving in as Orbach's near neighbour.

I didn't tell either Morris or Jada Jarrynge the full truth of what I was going to do. I didn't know how either would react. I told both of them that I was back on the job. I needed their help. But I told them only as far as they needed to know. If my cover-up theory was wrong, if anything went wrong with my plan, it was still not impossible that I – and maybe Carson, maybe even Sandy though I would not let her play any active part – would face charges, if only of conspiracy: I didn't want either Jada or Morris to be subject to the same risk.

Jada's main task was to convince Orbach; Carson's to enlist Stephen Walker; Morris's, despite what he claimed were his better instincts, to help me out again in the world of journalism: I had to remind him that he had hired me to provide sufficient proof to enable them to publish Jada's book; what I wanted from him would achieve that result.

I considered Orbach's four basic rules: people are predictable; they only do what they want; once they start on a course of conduct, they can't get off it; and, people are capable of being both good and bad. An Orbach plan meant confrontation, that was his forte; he liked to strip away the insulation and bring the bare wires close together, so close that the slightest tremor would cause them to touch and to spark; so close that, notwithstanding the danger, the thrill of the impact became irresistible, like a child reaching out to touch fire. All I had to do was to engineer Orbach and Walker into the right place, at the right time, and under the right conditions – nature, according to Orbach, would take over from there.

\* \* \*

Jada rang in before lunch. She gave me an avowedly verbatim account of her conversation with Orbach. He had not suspected her for a second. Why should he? This was the half-sister of his ward, who admired and respected him so much she had already told him he was going to feature in her book. It was an encounter between the citizen above and the child beneath suspicion.

She went to see him at the High Court, in his chambers, before his working day began. She told him she had been telephoned by a man, who wouldn't give his name. The man was demanding money, under threat of disclosing something extremely damaging about Orbach.

'Disclose to whom?' Orbach had asked, immediately but understandably visibly anxious.

'He didn't say; I didn't ask. I'm sorry, Russel, I was stupid; I panicked. I know there's nothing he could do to hurt you, but I was frightened. He said he was watching, watching the flat, then, while we were speaking,' she had proven her acting ability in the TV mini-series, 'he said I should ask you: you wouldn't want me to go to the police.'

'Yes, you did the right thing. You see, Jada, I've told you this before, the slightest hint of scandal – people like to

161

believe the worst, a judge, me – people have always liked to believe the worst of me.' His ego was all. 'Did you see him when you left your flat?'

'No. There isn't a phone box; it must have been from one of the other flats or houses on the wharf.'

'Not necessarily; it might have been a carphone. Is he going to contact you again?' He didn't doubt her for a moment.

'He said – he said he was going to come to the flat tonight. How did he get my address, Russel? What about my phone number? I'm scared.' She had appeared on the verge of tears. 'What's it about, Russel? Did you do something?'

'Yes,' he said tersely. 'I did. It was a long time ago. I'm not proud of it, you understand; it's something Mick and your mother knew about,' he invoked the uncontradicting dead. 'There were some people who had done me a lot of harm. They almost wrecked my life. Someone else was, well, threatening them. I could have warned them. I didn't. That's what he's talking about: it must be.'

Jada interrupted her account to say to me:

'It was what you told me about; the chambers. But twisted so it sounded like nothing serious.' She continued: 'I asked if he knew who it was.'

'Not for sure. It's possible, there are one or two people. You have to understand, Jada, I didn't do anything wrong. I just, well, I didn't go out of my way to help people who had hurt me.'

'I understand, Russel. I know you wouldn't do anything that was wrong. What do you want me to do? Should I go to the police?'

'No. It's impossible. What time did he say he was coming?'

'He didn't say. He just said tonight: anytime after seven. He said to have the money there.'

'How much?'

'Twenty thousand pounds. What do you want me to do, Russel? I want to help you. I want to do the right thing. Surely, if you talked to the police, if you explained . . .'

'I said, it's impossible.' He glanced at his watch:

'I have to be in court.'

'I've got a recording session tonight. I'll cancel it. I'll see him. I'll give him the money,' she had sobbed. 'I don't want anything to happen to you, Russel.'

'No. Don't be silly. I'll see him of course. I'll be there at seven. Don't worry. Keep to your session. Have you got a spare key?'

She shook her head.

'I can get one; I can drop it in here at lunch.' She did have one with her, but it would have been too obvious to admit it.

Before she left, he hugged her tightly to his robed chest.

'It'll be alright, you'll see. I'll take care of it. I always do, don't I?'

\* \* \*

Carson had the harder task. And the most dangerous. We had to take the greatest risk to ensure her safety. I felt like an assassin who had only one shot in his gun, and only one chance to use it.

Walker was only a locally powerful man. He was not a rich man, but a big small businessman, a local power in an insignificant community, impressive to the likes of Ambleton but not otherwise. He did not have troops to call upon, nor Orbach's skill at manipulating others to do his will.

No one is more dangerous than his Achilles' heel. Walker had one weak spot that we knew about: his son Stephen, with whom we had already established something of a relationship, though from the conversation on the plane – when it touched on Carson herself – it was not one to be relied on. If we could manipulate Stephen, I had no doubt at all we could manipulate his father.

She waited until mid-afternoon before going to the workshop to see Stephen. Fortunately, he was alone again. He didn't look displeased to see her: like other clumsy and physically cowardly people, he admired unduly those with agility and fighting ability; she had taken much of the lead in reassuring him; though uneducated, he was a sensitive man, and she had shown him consideration. We had forced him to acknowledge that his father had fixed his case for him, and informed him who had paid what price. The bonds of secrecy between us were not insubstantial.

Carson, too, later provided me with a full account though I guessed there was a lot more re-creation in it than reconstruction.

'Why have you come here?' He sounded less surprised than he ought to have been.

'You said last time that you wanted to help your father?'

'Yes, I remember.'

'I think he's in trouble, Stephen; I think maybe he's in bad trouble.'

'You said you'd keep him out of it,' he accused half-heartedly but without challenging the assertion.

'We have, this far; we can only do so much. We're not responsible for everything he does.'

'What're you saying? What's he done?' He asked listlessly, a protest without conviction.

She had been surprised initially at how easily he accepted the details as she laid them out for him. Later, as they drove together to see his father, he said he had read about Battle – it was a bigger story locally than nationally; without wanting to admit it to himself, he had sensed his father's involvement; he confirmed that he had – reluctantly, he insisted, only under questioning by him, not until after my second visit – told his father about us. He realised his father was distressed, he knew something was badly wrong – he just hadn't known what to do about it, or even how to ask. Without telling his wife how it had all started, he hadn't been able to seek her guidance. Carson was quickly his confessor. He was ripe for penance.

'I want to see your father, Stephen.'

'What for?'

'I told you – Dave told you – we're not interested in hurting him; it's Orbach we're after. But your father, well,' she shrugged, 'he's the key, the only key.'

He thought about this for a while, then shook his head:

'If it's like you say, then he's safe, isn't he? I mean,' he had the grace to blush, 'now.'

'Waterbottom didn't have anything to do with the original fix, did he?'

'I don't know.'

'Well Battle certainly wasn't anything to do with it.'

'So what?'

'So if it can come out once it can come out again. Don't you see, Stephen? It's not going to remain hidden forever. It's going to happen again and maybe again and again. There're some things, well, you can't keep hold of forever . . .' She hesitated, then plunged on: 'Some things have to be undone, Stephen.'

'What do you mean? They can't be brought back,' he said dully, halfway to her answer.

'Big wrongs, Stephen . . .' Require big rights.

'Right,' he muttered.

She said, almost tenderly:

'It's time for him to do the right thing, Stephen; you too.' She reminded him it was on his account it had begun.

'I know,' he said quietly. 'I know what you mean. What do you want me to do?'

'I want you to try to persuade him to help; I want you to fix it for me to see him.'

'He won't see you,' he shook his head.

'Not on my own, no.'

\* \* \*

'What's this about?' Nick Walker asked aggressively as soon as his son and companion were shown in. 'Who's this?' He studied Carson curiously, then snapped his fingers. 'I know you. You were . . .'

'Correct, I was; but I have an alibi up to here and I've already been eliminated from their enquiries by the police. Have you?' She went straight onto the offensive.

He paled but blustered:

'I don't know what you're talking about. Why should they want to talk to me? I'm on the police committee. I'm a councillor. What are you doing here?'

'Calm down, Mr Walker; I'm not here to do you any harm; I promise you.' Compared to what he deserved, it was the truth.

'Why were the police looking for you?'

'I'd been seen with Waterbottom.'

Nick revolved the swivel chair behind his desk and scowled at his son:

'Why've you brought her here? What's this about?'

With difficulty and perhaps without precedent, Stephen stood up to his father:

'You should listen to her, Dad. Please. I know . . . I know what this is about.' He had flushed, then said in a rush, like he'd been rehearsing it in the car: 'I know about the Mellors, Dad. I know what happened at court. I don't . . . I didn't . . . I'm sorry, Dad,' he tailed off in a gruff whisper. 'I never meant to cause you trouble; I never meant you to do something like that on my account.'

Walker was torn in two. He knew he ought to deny any knowledge of what his son was talking about, because Carson was present; if he denied it, he was also denying his son in his moment of shame. He said cautiously:

'You've never been a trouble, son; the things that have happened – well, they happened, right. I wanted . . . I've wanted to help you. You've nothing to apologise for. But, mind now, I'm not saying I understand what you mean about the Mellors, right.'

'Or Brian Battle?' Carson asked.

'Who's Brian Battle?'

'Don't you read your paper, Mr Walker? You recognised me quick enough.'

'The journalist in the sea, right. What's it got to do with me? I didn't know him. I never met him.'

She snorted. It didn't require any acting ability.

Walker avoided his son's eyes. The son who could positively link him to Battle and who was on this woman's side. He was visibly shrivelling before Carson's eyes.

He placed his certainly sweaty palms face down on the desk as if he was about to use them to lever himself into an upright position. Carson said:

'I've got a proposition for you, Mr Walker; it's an interesting proposition and I think you'll regret it if you don't hear me out; maybe for the rest of your life. I know your son agrees with me.'

'Go on.' He struggled for an appropriate sarcastic epithet with which to cling on to his pride. 'Entertain me.'

'It's all about Orbach. All and only. He's all I'm interested in. If you help me get him, you can put all of this behind you.' She was unmoved by the overwhelming enormity of what she was saying; so apparently was he. She paused to watch his reaction; behind the scepticism lay a glimmer of hope. 'I'm working for someone whose name you'll know, the singer, Jada Jarrynge. You know her name?'

He shrugged indifferently.

'I don't listen to music much. I don't have the time.'

'Did you know Orbach has a little girl living with him? A little black girl. Her parents were the Mellors, who died in a plane crash; a plane you had the maintenance contract on.'

'I remember. Yes, there was a child. I knew she went to live with Orbach. Right.'

'The woman – Eartha – had another daughter – much older – that's Jada Jarrynge.'

He was more interested in hearing where this was leading than where it came from.

'Jada knows the crash wasn't an accident . . .'

'That's rubbish; there was an investigation; no one had tampered with that plane; people who fly, they know the risks . . .' The sequence of Carson's argument was too quick to accept without an automatic denial.

'The investigation was inconclusive. What is conclusive is that you rigged a soft sentence for Stephen, from Orbach, a few months beforehand.'

He still wouldn't look at his son while he challenged her: 'So what? It's a coincidence. You can't prove there's any connection.'

Carson shook her head.

'No. That's what I'm here about; to try to persuade you to help us prove it. There's no other way.'

167

'Yes, right, why should I do that? Even if it were true – which it isn't,' he remembered to add. 'I'd be putting my head in a noose.' As England has no death penalty this was not quite accurate, unless he meant he'd rather top himself than do time.

As in the law of physics, she was using the sheer weight of what he had done against himself.

'They won't prosecute. He's a High Court judge – you know that. It's what he's always told you,' she guessed. 'It's true; and if they can't prosecute him, they can't prosecute you.'

He shook his head slowly, bewildered.

'Then why should I? Why take the risk? What can you do with it?'

She said:

'I want you to talk to Jada, Mr Walker; I want you to make a statement to her; it's enough for her to get the child away from him; it's enough to get him off the bench, Mr Walker. That's what she wants; it's all she wants.'

'What would be in it for me?'

Carson had gone as far as she was able on her own. Stephen chipped in on cue:

'Dad. Listen. You can't get away with it. I've seen you, the last week; you're unhappy, Dad. It'll come out in the end and then, well, it's not just you, is it?' It was Stephen, too, who would be exposed, which would make all of it utterly pointless.

'Mr Walker, listen to your son, listen to me. Orbach's crazy. You must know that now. Do you think he's going to leave you out here, leave you alone, with what you know about him? How long for?'

'There was never any trouble before . . .' He meant after the Mellors died.

'He wasn't there, Mr Walker, was he?'

It was a significant difference from Battle.

'What about Woolf?'

'He's already made a statement to the police that he saw nothing: even if he changed his statement, they couldn't use it to prosecute because of the risk a jury wouldn't believe it. Mr Walker, what we're asking is

168

for you to help us – all of us, Jada Jarrynge, Dave, hell England,' she appealed to his patriotism: he was, after all, a Conservative councillor. 'Help us get rid of him. I'll be honest with you: there's no way we could ever link Orbach to the Mellors' death without you; not enough.'

His eyes narrowed.

'There's no way you could ever link it to me, either – without me, right.'

'Correct. Especially so long ago. But it's not the same for Battle. And who knows what'll come up about Water-bottom.'

Stephen shook his big head slowly, awed by the schedule of the dead for whom his father was responsible.

'Dad. Dad. I don't know what to say. I feel, like, well, I'm to blame, 'cos it started for me, 'cos I called you when Battle came. But I never, I never thought . . . I'd never have believed . . .'

'But you do?' Nick Walker snapped as he swung towards his son. 'Why? Why believe her? Why believe her instead of me – instead of your father?'

There were tears tumbling slowly and singly from Stephen's eyes:

'Tell me then it's not true, none of it; tell me, Dad; I'll believe you.' He sniffed: 'You know me, Dad, I'm not that clever, I don't do everything right, I don't see everything right, everyone always said I was stupid but you never did, Dad.'

They sat in silence for what Carson insisted was at least five minutes, but was probably about thirty seconds. Eventually, she broke it.

'Listen to me, Mr Walker. You're scared of Orbach. Everyone's scared of Orbach. He's used you, Mr Walker, taken you over; you're not your own man anymore.' There was a latent challenge in this: she wondered if he would spot it; it was the reason Stephen's support was so essential. 'Help us now and you're free of him. He'll have no power left; he'll be a broken man; there's no risk: no prosecution, Orbach finished, you're off the hook, Mr Walker – the hook he put you on.'

For a time she thought she'd lost but the imperative of his son's presence brought him to the otherwise unachievable pitch.

'It's true,' he mumbled. 'I never wanted to. I put myself in his debt; I never knew what it might mean. You've got to understand. Stephen,' he spoke as if he had forgotten he was there, 'it would have finished him, finished his marriage – she would have left him – the way his mother left me.' He buried his head in his hands and his shoulders jerked, but there was no sound of tears. His son got up and walked awkwardly around the desk, resting a meaty hand on his father's shoulders.

Eventually, he looked up, but he didn't brush his son's hand away.

'I lost my head. I didn't mean to kill Waterbottom, Orbach didn't know about that beforehand. I didn't hurt Battle that badly, not to begin with. I've never, well, never killed anyone before, not with my hands,' he corrected before Carson could mention the Mellors.

He hesitated again but now that he'd begun it was pointless not to finish: 'I've never even fought anyone really. I went to see if Battle was telling me the truth. To see if he'd told anyone else. Funny thing was, such a little man, he stood up to me better than Battle. I hit him too hard. I don't know if it killed him, the first time. But after that there weren't any choices left and, well,' he added apologetically, 'it seemed – just then, not now – it seemed as if it couldn't make any more difference.' Not to him; only to Battle. 'It was Orbach worked the rest of it out. No,' he looked Carson straight in the eye: 'I was responsible too. Right. I know that. I'm sorry for what I've done. I can't make it right any other way. I'll do it. What do you want me to do?'

\* \* \*

The encounter between Orbach and Walker was over much quicker than I had expected. But, then, there was a number of aspects of it that I hadn't expected. For example, I hadn't expected Walker to be armed. Orbach, on the other hand,

170

obviously had. The very first sound we heard, almost as the door opened, was some sort of thump, a howl of pain, a grunt and then the noise of furniture falling. For a couple of minutes, there was silence, save for a brief series of clicks I couldn't identify – maybe Orbach was doing rosary.

'What's happening?' Jada whispered.

I shrugged. I didn't know.

After a while, Orbach spoke.

'Come on, Walker, get up, I didn't hit you that hard.'

When he got no response, we heard him moving about the flat, then running water – the cold jug cure. My heart went out to Walker – Sandy sometimes did it to me when I o.d.'d on Southern Comfort; there's nothing worse.

'You bloody fool, Walker. What did you think? I'd wait patiently until you pointed it at me? Did you forget I knew you belonged to a club? I didn't, I never forget – anything.'

I cursed myself for my stupidity and carelessness. Walker was supposed to have believed he was going to see Jada, was supposed to have decided to help, but I ought not to have expected him to be entirely without suspicion. Orbach himself had told me that Walker was a member of a gun club. I hadn't warned Carson.

And what else did I expect Orbach to do? I had intended him either to suspect or even to feel sure that Walker was who he was going to meet at Jada's flat. I wondered what he had hit him with and where. It was difficult to imagine Orbach in the act of physical violence: I associated him exclusively with its planning; I had forgotten my own theory – he had no one left to do it for him.

It was possible the scene I had set was about to come to an unscheduled ending. I couldn't think about the implications while I was listening, but it might go beyond what even the silken Schofield would be able to keep a lid on, and in turn that would render my part of it more open to scrutiny than I had intended.

I was listening from the flat roof. The recording session Jada had planned for that night was in her own home. Friends from the music business had wired it as professionally as any spies might have done. We had wondered about setting it up for vision too: a remote- or sound- or movement-triggered video camera. But there was no way to eliminate a whirr within the apartment without the sort of sophisticated equipment it would have taken much longer to acquire. There would be no other sounds to cover it up. I didn't think Orbach and Walker would be playing music to dance by.

Stephen Walker had wanted to come with his father, Carson told me later. His father refused, ordered him back to his wife and children. Stephen had reluctantly obeyed. He had asked his father to ring him later and then, when his father was already in Sandy's car, as he walked Carson around to the driver's door, he asked her too to let him know. She squeezed his hand:

'It's the right thing, Stephen.'

They had driven in almost total silence. Once, Nick had asked what part of London they were passing through. Just once, he repeated what he had said at his own office:

'I'm sorry for what I've done; I am, right.' As if he was trying to remind himself.

She told me later: 'I ought to have been scared when he said he didn't want Stephen to come with him.' The man had personally and brutally murdered two men within the last few days. 'But I didn't even think of it until we were almost there.' Nor did she think of it when he went to fetch his coat – and gun. 'He was too pathetic; he was like a child who had been found out doing something wrong, being taken to his parents for punishment. It made me think – killers aren't so different; they're ordinary people, too; people like you and me.'

We looked at each other; we had disobeyed the same commandment. We belonged to the same club – those who had passed judgment on another human being. Orbach had done it; we were doing it to him.

As they reached Jada's door, Carson told him to go ahead alone, she had to go back to the car. He looked at her strangely, like he knew, but all he did was nod and point at the door to the flat to check it was the right one. She said:

'Go on in; it's open.'

* * *

'Put it away, Orbach,' Walker said at long last.

'Why did you do it, Walker? Did you really think she'd meet you here without telling me?'

'I don't know what you're talking about.' Then: 'You're the one who got me here. Is this what for?' In his shock, he believed Carson was on the other side, Orbach's side. 'Go on, go ahead, do it,' Walker dared. 'I'm not afraid, right.' I could smell his sweat glands from the roof.

'I said tell me why you thought you could get away with it.' Orbach's authority did not seem to have been undermined by the challenge. 'What were you going to sell her? How much were you going to tell her? How dare you? How dare you approach my family?' His voice rose in controlled anger.

Jada whispered:

'Shouldn't we do something?'

I shook my head. I wasn't armed.

'You can't do nothing,' she hissed.

'Watch me, Jada. Just keep telling yourself, it's your mother's killers talking.'

'Why did you bring me here?' Walker asked.

'What game are you trying to play, Walker? You rang Jada. You came here. You were going to tell her about her mother, weren't you?'

Silence. I imagined Walker frowning with effort. The idea of Carson as Orbach's moll no longer rang true. Slowly, unsure of himself, Walker said:

'Yes, I was. Not for money, right. It's gone too far, Orbach. First the Mellors, then Waterbottom, then Battle. I was frightened. She frightened me. My son wanted me to talk.'

'Your son? How does he know? You told me you'd never . . .'

'I didn't,' Walker said. 'Your woman did,' he probed.

'Jada? What are you talking about, Walker? Make sense, man.'

'Not Jada. I never met Jada. I came here to meet her, right. So I was told,' he added.

'What do you mean – "my woman"?'

173

'The Australian. The one who was there before.' Which had led Orbach to me.

'Woolf's girl,' Orbach snapped.

It was a good thing Carson wasn't with us on the roof or there would have been another outburst of violence. She had gone back to the car to await the outcome and to cover the door to the building faster than we could if it proved necessary.

'Tell me exactly what happened, Walker? This is a set-up. Good Lord,' the point finally dawned. 'Jada? Jada's a part of it?' He sucked in his breath so loudly it registered on the tape-recorder. In a puzzled tone, he said: 'But I trusted her. I loved her almost as much as I love Frankie. How could she?'

'You killed her mother,' Walker said as if it was something he might have forgotten. 'We killed her mother.'

'Yes, yes, I know,' he brushed it aside as trivial. 'But she didn't. How could she know? Woolf. Woolf told her. Why would she believe him? When? Since the flight?'

'You said Woolf's a private detective as well as a solicitor, right.' Walker was surprisingly in command. 'Who was he working for, Orbach?'

After a moment, Orbach answered:

'Jada. Jada was who he was working for. It has to be. What has she told Frankie?'

There was another, much longer silence. Then Orbach again:

'She set this up. She set me up. She set you up. What for? I wonder. Yes, I see it.' His voice was clinical now, analytical. 'They thought we'd fight, perhaps they thought we'd kill each other, that's it, that must be it. What do you think?' He didn't wait for an answer. 'Perhaps they're right,' he mused. 'Perhaps that's right. I shouldn't trust you. I can't trust you. You've told your son . . .'

It was the wrong person for Orbach to mention. It made Stephen, too, vulnerable. As long as Orbach was alive, his son was as much at risk as Nick Walker. Orbach must have realised the mistake, because next we heard Walker.

'What are you going to do?' he asked, the pitch of his voice the only indication to us on the roof that the question might not be entirely disinterested. 'Here, Orbach? Here in her apartment?' Then: 'Go on,' in a calm, resigned tone of voice. 'Go on then. It doesn't matter. It doesn't matter anymore. I'd rather. Go on, Orbach, do it,' he shouted.

I had physically to restrain Jada during the prolonged silence that followed. Once I was sure she was back in control of herself, I crawled to the side of the roof and waved down at Carson to warn her it was coming to a head. She pointed at herself and then at the building's front door to ask if she was supposed to go in. I shook my head violently enough for her to understand that she was to stay in the car and out of sight.

When I got back to the tape, nothing was still what was happening. Jada was biting her lower lip. I lit a cigarette. She didn't tell me not to. Then I heard a chair scraping as it was pushed back. Orbach said crisply, as if announcing his decision in court on a point of law: 'No. It would be too easy, far too easy.'

There was a loud clank, like something thrown onto a hard floor or table top, then the sound of the door pulled shut behind him.

Jada rose. I pushed her back onto the roof-top and told her to pack the gear up and, to make sure it was done before I entered the apartment, switched off the tape-recorder myself. Unless she made a deliberate decision to turn it back on, she would not now be able to hear, which was what I wanted. Then I dropped back through the hatch into the corridor. Orbach had gone. The door was shut. I used my key to let myself in. I tried but failed to do it silently.

Walker was still sitting, presumably in the same place he'd been told to sit when he came in. He turned to look at me. He'd last seen me in the pub in Southend. He nodded, as if he was expecting me. He picked up the gun and pointed it at me.

'Ah,' I said brightly, but mostly because it was the only sound I could squeeze round the lump in my throat. 'I don't think that's a good idea,' I said eventually.

He said tiredly:

'You're full of good ideas you are, right.'

'I didn't start it, Mr Walker. You can't pretend it's not your responsibility.'

'No? People've got away with worse, right.'

'I don't know; perhaps. I'm sorry we tricked you.'

'You used my son,' he said flatly. 'You tricked my son too.'

'Only a little bit, Mr Walker. I promise you only a little bit.' Why did he snarl at my use of the word promise? 'You had to see for yourself, to see you'd never be safe from Orbach.'

'Why did I have to see? Do you think I'm that stupid? I believed your girl: she was working for you after all, wasn't she?' He rushed on: 'I knew it for myself. I've always known it would be me took the blame, not him.'

'That's not quite what I meant.'

'I know what you meant, right. Don't treat me like an idiot.' He didn't like it any more than I did. 'I've done bad things; I know that; I told your girl, I'm sorry for them; but I'm not a fool, right. I just wanted, always, I just wanted my son . . . I wanted my son to have a better home than I ever gave him. Can't you understand that? Have you got a kid?'

'Oh, yeah. And I want to live to see him grow up. I need your help, Mr Walker, to help me do so.'

He looked at me peculiarly. He was right to tell me not to treat him as an idiot. He was way ahead of me. He said:

'He won't go up.'

'I think I can make him.'

He shook his head slowly, still not lowering the gun.

'Until now, I would have said the only man I knew who could make him do it was himself. Maybe, I don't know. You've got this far.'

He was talking about the same thing Orbach had taught me: all you can ever do is make people do things that – at some level – they want to do. I said:

'The trick is to make him think he wants to do it.'

'How?'

176

I moved slowly, the gun following me, to the cane chair in which Jada had sat the night I visited her and extracted a small microphone. He smiled thinly:

'I thought of that. He didn't.'

'Why didn't you tell him?'

'He didn't want to listen anymore.'

'No. But he will.'

'I won't,' he said suddenly. 'Not to him, not to you.'

'Wait,' I said.

He turned the gun around and placed the barrel at his mouth.

I said:

'If you do it, you leave your son to Orbach, Mr Walker.'

'It seems my son can take care of himself,' he said, though not without a measure of doubt. He gripped the barrel of the gun between his teeth.

I tried another tack.

'Fine. But you know what I want. If you won't help me – be there to help me – I'll ask Stephen to, Mr Walker. You know he will.'

His eyes widened, then blinked once to tell me he had understood; it hadn't made a difference.

I lunged across the room as he pulled the trigger. I fell into his lap as we both belatedly realised that nothing had happened. Stunned, he slumped back, the hand carrying the gun pointing loosely down at the floor. I crawled off him before he thought I'd confused father and son and took offence. He let me take the gun from his hand. I opened it. The chamber was empty and, when I extracted it, so was the clip. I realised then what the clicking noise had been after Orbach hit Walker: he had been unloading the gun; he had never intended it to be used – not by Walker, nor even by himself, not even at the very end when it seemed as if he was threatening to kill Walker. What the hell was he playing at?

# CHAPTER ELEVEN

The next day was the last day. It was the beginning of our final weekend in Sandy's house. Completion was due right after the long, end of May, Bank Holiday weekend. Jada could not stay at her flat until it was over but was unwilling to stay away from town. Carson took her to the flat above the club overnight. In the morning, they all came over, along with Tom, to help Sandy in the final packing and other preparatory removals.

I had work to do, one more piece of the puzzle to put into place: it was the piece for which I had needed Nigel Morris. The meeting could not take place any sooner; nor could it be postponed. Reluctantly, Morris deserted the magnificent Mimi and met me by arrangement in a pub near his office. He was accompanied by a gap-toothed, black-bearded, bulky, ugly, unkempt man wearing a worn leather jacket, a battered hat and smoking an untipped Gauloise. Morris introduced us:

'Dave W-woolf, S-sean McCarthy.' He turned to McCarthy: 'D-dave has told me what he w-w-wants you to do; it's got the p-p-papal blessing.' Their mutual boss, the newspaper magnate who owned the book publishing company. 'I don't know exactly why D-dave w-wants things done this way,' he held up a hand to forestall any interruption by me, 'I don't w-want to know.' He was a shrewd man. 'I've sp-spoken to the l-lawyers: th-they can't see anything il-l-legal in it except l-l-libel and I have D-dave's w-word,' he looked at me balefully, as if there could be nothing quite so unreliable, 'It won't be shown to anyone who could s-s-sue.' This was true: it is not a libel if the person written about is the only person to whom you publish it.

He got up to leave. The floor creaked as he exited. McCarthy said, 'Did the earth move for you too?'

'Another drink?'

'Sure,' said Sean.

To gain a little time to get the measure of the man, I asked about his relations with Brian Battle. I had assumed they were friends.

'Lord, no. The man had no friends. He was a pig. That was why he was loaned out to Morris. That was why the editor agreed to his taking a break. Anything to get him out of the newsroom.'

'It was just an impression I got, from your piece on him.' An account of his death that doubled as an obituary: they didn't want to waste too much space on him.

'I took everything I thought and turned it on its head. Worked well, didn't it?'

I said:

'You couldn't care if they don't catch his killer, then?'

'Yes, I'd care. He took my bloody chance away.' His eyes narrowed: 'What's this all about?'

'What have you been told?'

'You want a story written – a dummy Sunday – tomorrow's date – it'll probably never get published properly.'

'Right.'

It wasn't completely correct, only in part. With Orbach dead, Jada's thinly-veiled accusation would be publishable. Though it would arouse press interest and possibly some modest investigation, none of the participants would be available to feed it or to keep it alive. Later elements of the tale would have to remain unpublished – I was doing this in order to survive, not to put my own head into a noose.

I selected my words with extreme care and prejudice.

'I have someone so important there is no prospect at all of his being prosecuted, nor of any paper – including yours – risking publication of what I have.' No paper would go ahead without their own research: authentication of tapes, sworn affidavits, they would be bound to give Orbach the opportunity to comment, and the sheer enormity of that exercise is what finally would persuade them to abandon it or turn it over to the authorities, which in the circumstances would be the same as spiking the story or, as they probably do nowadays, wiping the floppy disk.

He looked at me sceptically:

'I didn't think she went in for cold-blooded murder, not personally.' I took it he meant the Prime Minister not the Queen. 'So as it can't be published, you want to make it look as if it can be, has been. Right?'

I nodded once. He was stumbling preciously close to the whole point: the purpose Nigel Morris had the foresight to foreswear all knowledge of. The evidence of the confrontation between Orbach and Walker would not be enough on its own: Orbach would laugh at a mere recording; would tell me I would never get it published. McCarthy asked me:

'Why?'

'I want to spook him. I think I can spook him into panicking. I think that might, uh, let's just say it might be a helpful thing to happen.'

'Help who? Help what?'

'Help make sure he doesn't get away with it,' I turned and looked him straight in the face. 'Or anything like it again.'

He understood I was saying it was in his own interests not to press me any further. He said:

'I know about you. I know a hell of lot about you.' He told me. He did. He knew most of what there was to know, informally, off the record, the same Fleet Street scuttlebut Nigel Morris had picked up but in much greater and more thorough detail. He said: 'And none of it ever gets printed, and no one ever gets into court. That's your style. Right?'

'Seems that way,' I admitted. 'Not of my choosing, you understand.'

'What you're saying,' he concluded, a crafty smile creeping across the black holes in his mouth, 'it's going to happen again. Only this time, you want me to help you control the outcome. Is that about right?'

'Something like that.'

'You've got nerve. You want me to set up the best story of my life, and never see it in print. You want me to trust you to know what the right outcome is. I just want to be sure I've got it right.' He shook his head in mock disbelief.

'I want you to help make sure Battle's murderer doesn't walk free. And, well,' I shrugged, 'for what it's worth, your employers seem to trust me.'

He thought for a moment, then asked:

'What do you need me to do? When?'

I told him. He frowned, then nodded:

'Not much time. But it can be done. It'd be a change to write the truth for once. I just hope you're right; I hope it is the truth.'

'It is,' I said as I flashed him the tape. 'You got somewhere we can listen to this in private?'

* * *

Which is how, very late on Saturday night, instead of relaxing for the next-to-last time in our old home with my old woman and our young child, I was a few houses down from where we'd be living come Tuesday, banging at the door, waiting for Orbach to answer it, so I could play at newspaper delivery boy.

Nick Walker had gone straight back to Southend by taxi. I had no doubts about his commitment to the cause. Unless Orbach, too, had gone directly to the airport, Walker would be ahead of him. If he flew off without my final shove, I was so much the cleaner and that was so much the better. No part of what I felt involved the necessity for me to do it for myself.

I had spoken to Walker twice during the day and Orbach still hadn't shown up. Earlier in the evening, while they were still unpacking – by the sound of it, with the help of a couple of bottles of wine – at the new house, I rang for Sandy to pop into the street and she came back to confirm that there were lights on in his house.

He came to the door. He nodded at me, as if he had been waiting for me. He was wearing slippers, but was otherwise dressed. He had on the Norwegian cardigan with its steel buckles in which he had greeted me when

181

I first went to his Highgate apartment during Disraeli Chambers, or one that looked like it. He was freshly-shaven, his customarily unruly hair tidily in place, his eyes shone brightly, excitedly.

I asked if I could come in and he held the door back for me. He put a finger to his lip as he led the way to the livingroom. I knew from an earlier visit that Frankie still sometimes suffered nightmares from her parents' death, and accordingly slept with the door open. We didn't speak until we were out of her earshot.

Then I handed him the first, previous night's copy of the next day's paper, holding it open so that he could read the headline:

'MR JUSTICE MURDERER: POPSTAR JADA'S J'ACCUSE!'

* * *

He stood as he read the story on the front page, spiced with selections from the transcript of the tape we'd made, including Orbach's opening remarks, and the exchange between Walker and Orbach in which they'd said:

'It's gone too far, Orbach. First the Mellors, then Waterbottom, then Battle.'

'Your son? How does he know?'

And:

'You killed her mother. We killed her mother.'

'Yes, yes, I know.'

He tossed the paper aside as if contained nothing that interested him.

* * *

'I suppose it goes back a long way. I don't know. How far back does one have to go to find out who is the real self? A minute after birth, an hour, a month, a year? I was one of six children. Five of them, pouring over the cliff of my psyche like lemmings,' he repeated a pat phrase he had obviously used often before. The outrage was emphatic: 'my' psyche. 'That surprises you, doesn't it? You thought

182

I was an only child, a spoiled only child. Or did you think I was born a bastard who wouldn't know if he had any brothers and sisters?'

He laughed briefly.

'Well, I wasn't an only child and I wasn't spoiled. Anything but. Oh, of course we had all our material needs taken care of, we wanted for nothing that way. My father wasn't wealthy. He was a doctor. The money came from my mother's side. But it was a big family to cope with, even for the times, though they both came from yet larger. My father was one of ten, my mother one of seven. My father suffered from his inability to provide for us all, to the high standards my mother expected. It made him broody, withdrawn, but subject to occasional outbursts of anger and affection in equally immoderate proportions. My mother, the princess: she saw no reason why so many children should interfere with her social life; that's what nannies were for. My father had a different idea of what nannies were for; we got through them fast; that was his revenge.'

He paused to recollect the point of his account.

'Yes, that was it. You see, from the very beginning, from as far back as I can remember, I always felt I was different, I was special, I wasn't like others – ordinary people. Does every child feel that way? I don't know,' and he didn't want an answer in case, belatedly, it undermined this all-important criterion by which he was to have lived the whole of his life.

He went on: 'I was disappointed; from the earliest years of my life: disappointed that I'd been born to these banal people, disappointed in the boring ordinariness of my siblings, disappointed I had to compete with them for my parents' attention and affection, disappointed I had to do all the things expected of me that I hadn't determined for myself, disappointed down to the last detail – the hand-me-downs and small meannesses and ostensible generosities that were never what I wanted but always what someone else thought I wanted or thought I ought to want. Disappointed, too, that others didn't seem to understand my particular, special position.'

183

He stopped for a full minute, then:

'I haven't spoken to any of my brothers and sisters in, oh, five years – not since my mother's death, when we all went to the funeral. My father died a long time ago,' he added parenthetically. 'We were such strangers, we weren't sure whether to offer each other condolences. There's a lot of accident in life. I thought, who is that man – the accountant with the balding head, the paunch bigger than mine, the ill-fitting suit and above all with the wife I had not met since his wedding and the adult son I had perhaps met twice in my life. This is my older brother I am talking about; I told myself I was supposed to love him, care about him, care if ill befell him – but I wouldn't have noticed if he was no longer alive and I doubt I would have gone to his funeral if it was inconvenient for me to do so.'

He was bragging about his uncompromising honesty.

'And the others – in their different ways, their different identities, their different lives – meaningless. No love, no feeling, nothing. What offended me most was my middle brother – I was second from last – he's a very successful man, in the city, and he was making a big show out of us, out of the brothers and sisters, a show for the wider family and friends, as if there was still something there between us all, as if there ever had been. Well, I suppose it's his trade: selling stocks and shares in companies without assets.' Hypocrisy had always been his biggest bugbear.

I could and perhaps should have stopped him but I wanted to know; before it was over, I wanted to know. He continued:

'They told me, later on, but when I was still a youngster, they told me I was always the one who was the worst trouble. As a baby, I screamed the loudest, I made the biggest mess, I was naughty – always naughty, they called me. But not a nice naughty, as you might use the word about an impish child, a child with spirit, a child who challenges the rules because he wants to understand them or even because he wants to beat them. They meant evil naughty.'

He spoke with pride of the profit he had extracted from this putative peculiarity.

'I'm not sure why. At least, not why it began. I don't believe in inherent qualities, or defects; I don't believe anyone is born bad or whatever word you want to use. But something in the aspects of my family cast a shadow over me from so early on I can't remember a time without it. I can't remember a single moment of happiness in my childhood; I can only remember always, always the bitterness of the struggle.'

'Struggle for what?'

'I'm not sure. To survive is the expression that comes easiest to mind, but survival was never really in doubt. Perhaps that's it. Perhaps I didn't want to survive. I think . . . I think I was always so damned disappointed, each day disappointed, and hoping against hope that something would happen to give me some sense of joy, or hope, but it never did. I think, above all, I was disappointed in myself. I think that's true. I think that dates from a very early age. I was disappointed in me.'

'What does that mean?'

'Just that I didn't admire myself, I didn't think I was making a good job of being me, of demonstrating how different I was from all the others. They weren't noticing, so I was failing. In turn, I grew contemptuous of myself, for my failure. Do you see?'

Again he did not wait for an answer.

'I went through phases. When I first went to school, for the first couple of years I was always top of the class. It was a great shock when one week someone else came out equal first. Then I stopped, just like that. During one term, I went from the top to nearly the bottom. They don't do it anymore, even in that sort of school,' he meant private, fee-paying schools; 'But then they marked us each week. What was I trying to do?'

I watched him speculate, visibly straining with the effort. He said:

'It's difficult to know, without discounting hindsight. I wanted to be liked. I'm sure of that. Perhaps I stopped working in order to make myself more popular. Why was I unpopular? Because I was always top of the form? Because I didn't conceal my satisfaction at it? Because I competed

185

too openly for it? But if it wasn't there to be competed for, to be satisfied about winning, then what on earth was it there for?'

This was one I thought I could answer:

'To show you knew how to be a good winner?'

'How to play the game?' He smiled: 'Perhaps.' He wasn't interested in my interventions. 'Then there was the Jewish thing. I suppose I could put it like this,' he started to explain, as if he had forgotten that I was too. 'As an outsider, you think you always have to try harder just to keep up – it's their culture, their world, they belong and it seems as if it must all come so easily to them. But actually I didn't need to try harder. I was at least as good as them all along, probably better. So then I went to the other extreme in order to try and fit in; the desire for assimilation, the immigrants' traditional weakness. I was probably working harder to come bottom than to come out top. What do you think, Dave?'

This time he seemed to want me to speak.

'I don't know, Russel. I've never known; I mean, I've never known what makes you tick the way you do. I've only ever known that something was very badly wrong with it.'

'It's as good a definition of insanity as any I ever heard; fortunately,' he replied dryly, 'not one known to the law.'

Another prolonged pause. He got up from his leather armchair to fetch and place within easy reach the bottle of scotch from which he'd earlier poured himself an uncharacteristically substantial slug. I already had my bottle at my feet.

'I don't want to relive my schooldays. I think I've probably described the path enough for you to understand it. Veering between showing them what I could do when and if I wanted and showing them too how I could turn it all on its head, mocking them by failing as much as I was mocking them when I won. It was all so easy. They never understood: not my parents, not my teachers, not my brothers and sisters either. I could do whatever I wanted and they never found out how I was fooling them. They looked for reasons, psychological explanations, just some way to understand the way I swung to and fro. It was the same when I left school.'

I knew he had not followed the conventional route from school to college to bar course into practice. He had been at sea for a while, in the merchant marine – the Norwegian merchant marine, which was the origin of his relationship with that country and knowledge of its tongue. Then he had come back, done exams at a crammer and gone on to study law at university. I was to understand now that he had been poking two fingers at their system by leaving school when he wasn't supposed to, simply in order to come back and show them it was not for want of ability to master it.

A pattern was emerging. Thus, he had become a left-wing lawyer, which traditionally was a course followed by those lacking a marked academic bent – whether from want of interest or ability; accordingly, Orbach had also to show off by becoming a successful scholar in his subject. He was one of the founders of Disraeli Chambers: therefore he had to break up with them and prove he could make it at the straight, non-political bar. He had bettered law, so he had to better life without it. He had become a judge, an administrator of law; he had become its abuser.

I don't know whether it qualifies as schizophrenia. I ain't that educated. It reflects a profound root ambivalence, designed, I suppose, to isolate and protect his individuality from any possibility of routine definition or classification, and perhaps I could identify it because there lurked traces of it within me too – to belong and yet retain my independence; to enjoy the fruits of professional qualification but not to be constrained by its disciplines; to defy the notion that because you are good at one thing, you cannot be as good at its opposite.

Sensing the course of my reflections, he said:

'I must admit, I've never really understood why you made life so difficult for yourself, Dave.' He was trying to understand me; I was trying to understand him.

'Me too,' I murmured, unwilling to have the spotlight shifted or to engage any further on any more personal a note with him.

187

'You seemed to have so much going for you,' he disregarded my reluctance. 'Sandy was a good, solid, reliable partner; you had between you enough spirit and cash to get your own firm off the ground without having to spend too long putting up with someone else's way of doing things; then you blew it all. Why?' He'd envied me? Back in those early years, when I'd always envied him?

I said quietly:

'I just found, well, too much pain, too much human pain. It affected me; I couldn't ignore it; so I had to isolate myself from it. I thought you understood that; I always thought that was why you concentrated on civil law rather than doing crime.'

He shook his head.

'No. Crime was no challenge intellectually. That's all.'

After a brief pause, the bracket closed, he added:

'There's something else I wanted to say. It's been a burden, always a burden – being me I mean.' I wasn't surprised, but I didn't interrupt. 'I felt guilty – now there's another traditional Jewish trait for you. Because I was making such fools of them, I felt guilty; but I couldn't stop doing it; I've never been able to stop. I never could; I couldn't imagine what life would be like if I did; this was the only me I had built, that I knew; I couldn't let go of it, but I would have given anything to have it taken away from me.'

* * *

We sat up through the night. Snatches of conversation stay with me, though not in actual or logical sequence. Orbach saying:

'I had thought about it – we had even joked about it, how I half-hoped they would have an accident. Then he' – Walker – 'said to me: "I'll do anything . . ." to keep his son out of prison. And I thought, "anything". I wondered if he meant it. I wondered if he knew what it meant. I wondered if this mealy-mouthed mechanic had any idea of the things it could mean, of the things I had managed

188

to make "anything" mean. I don't think, at the beginning, I planned to do it. It was more a matter of putting him into my debt, knowing the possibility was there. Then I suppose it took on a life of its own.'

* * *

'Why did you stay with Margot for so long? I mean, once it was clear that you were not going to continue as lovers, as a couple.'

'Why separate? We were each other's best friend. I have a higher regard for Margot than for anyone.'

'Didn't you think, well . . . Didn't you perhaps want someone else?' In his early days at the bar, he had been powerfully attractive to – and commonly, almost indiscriminately, attracted by – women.

'I don't think I did, really. Perhaps it's why it didn't work out fully with Margot, either. I didn't really like the constant intimacy – especially physical: too much familiarity; too little respect.'

'Respect?'

'Yes. Respect,' he insisted. 'Respect for me, the real me, the private me. I think the period between Margot and my separation as lovers and her departure was the best: I had a sufficiency but not an excess of companionship; the fact that I still lived with her, that I shared a home with her, was an effective bar to a full, new relationship – we had lovers, we both did, but of necessity they were held at a distance, and of course, therefore, did not last. I was protected, insulated, but not isolated.'

Throughout he was detached, relaxed, occasionally sipping his whisky but showing no signs of being affected by it, nor of tiredness. I, too, was drinking much less than usual, seeking to keep a clear head. Though I was tired, I was not anxious to bring it to an end. I knew what I intended, but – confronted by his calmness – I was no longer so confident that I could cause it to come to my conclusion. I needed, but did not yet know how to compel, his co-operation.

189

'Were you in love with her?' Eartha.

'In a way; as an ideal; as a fantasy. But only in that sense.'

* * *

'Didn't you ever mind what you were doing to the law?'

He sneered.

'Their law? No, that was part of the point of it. Pulling down Pulleyne; putting myself up there in his place.' He chuckled with satisfaction. 'I've done things to them far worse than any one could imagine, and yet it still will not make any impact. You know, if this was Russia, they could at least wipe me out of the history books – the law reports is what I mean. But here, they can't do that. There's an irony for you: my judgments will be cited in argument in courts for decades to come; and only an inner core, a clique, will know. Who's the winner, Dave? Them or me?'

The word 'judgment' struck a nerve.

'It's an odd word, isn't it. it. Woolf's judgment: does it mean the judgment given by Woolf, or that imposed on him?'

I'd rather he substituted his own name.

* * *

'I still want to know, Russel. Why? How could you?' The Mellors.

'I could not believe they were going to do it. I just could not believe it. First they gave with one hand – bringing me into Frankie's life and Frankie into mine . . . You know, it wasn't just a formal, distant, godfatherhood. I always saw a lot of her, they always involved me. They knew, well of course they knew I could not have children, so they were doing it partly for me but also for her. That makes them sound more selfish than I intend. I just mean, they could feel confident in her interests that I would have more time and energy and love and support to spare than someone

190

who had his own children, or might yet.'

'Just not how much?'

'Yes, that's the best way to put it. They unlocked something I no longer believed existed in myself. They held out a hope for me, and they were planning to take it away. Explain that, Dave? How could they do that? It was cruel. Wasn't it? Wasn't it?'

'Ach, Russel, I can't say that. What about Frankie?'

'What sort of life would she have had? In Bolivia. For God's sake, whoever heard of Bolivia? What do they know in Bolivia? How much would I have seen of them in Bolivia?'

'Them?'

'Yes, yes, them,' for the first time, he sounded anguished, disturbed, confused. 'Yes, alright, I admit it, that is what you want, isn't it? Yes, I probably was in love with her. If you want to put it into little categories you can understand, Dave, I shall not contradict you.'

'No,' I shook my head sharply. 'It's you who doesn't want to admit it's that banal. You can't face the thought it was the mother, you wanted Eartha, it was that basic. God, why didn't you go to bed with her?' He'd slept with another man's wife once before. 'Hell,' I expostulated, 'why didn't you kill him? At least I could understand that.'

He laughed in short bursts:

'I should be recording you. Are you recording me now?' he asked, so many hours into the conversation it was as unimportant as he made the question sound.

'No. What for?'

'They might catch up with you yet. They can be such crafty buggers.' Crudity came uncomfortably from his lips. 'They might find a way, Dave.'

'For what? Tell me what my crimes are, Russel.'

He thought about them. Those which were identifiable were minor, certainly insufficient to justify the risk of scandal. Save one, yet to come.

Not for the first time, he could read my mind.

'You could even get off that too, couldn't you? Conspiracy's always such a difficult conviction.'

He knew all along what was planned for him.

I shrugged.

'If they charge, I'll plead.' Guilty.

'Why?' He asked idly.

'I don't know,' I admitted. 'It would seem the right thing to do. I've done things that are legally wrong – before now, too – but none of them have been morally wrong. At least, that's what I believe.'

Until the last moment, this was the only exchange about how the night was to end.

\* \* \*

'It wouldn't have worked.' He admitted he had thought of killing only Mick. 'She wouldn't have had me. So I would have lost a friend, without gaining a wife or a child.'

'Why wouldn't she? Hell, you're not an ugly man; I remember a time, you had no trouble finding women. Why wouldn't she?'

'I think . . . I think she would have had too much delicacy.'

'What do you mean?'

'Can you see it? Mr Justice Orbach, highly educated, white middle-class male, with his working-class black wife?'

'You weren't a judge then,' I reminded him.

'No, but she would have known that was what I wanted.'

There would have been no question of postponing, let alone abandoning, his ambition in favour of his wife.

'Do you think about them? About Mick and Eartha?'

'Of course,' he appeared offended I might think otherwise. 'Often, perhaps daily. Frankie and I talk about them. And Jada. Ah, Jada.' She was not someone he wanted to think about but he had to come to it. 'The book, it was the book, wasn't it? She said she was putting me in her book; this was what she had put in the book?'

'Yes.'

He held up the newspaper:

'They were going to publish it, but wanted proof first. Yes, I see. That was how it was.'

'Right.'

'But how . . .? Why . . . ?'

192

He was having difficulty formulating his question, so I did it for him:

'Why did she suspect you? Well, she suspected her parents' best friend who didn't want them to leave, helping them learn to fly, buying a plane with them, apparently doing everything to facilitate it, and I suppose at some level she sensed what you felt about Eartha and then she also knew Eartha was frightened of you . . .'

'What do you mean?' he cut across my recitation. 'She was not frightened of me. She loved me too. I know that.'

'No, she was frightened of you. Look at the inside account.'

He picked up the paper he had thrown down earlier, after reading only the front-page – possibly he hadn't even noticed there was a follow-on inside.

The oddest thing of all that I remember is that he read it almost out loud, his lips moving like an ill-educated person reads. He could skim a law report and absorb ten pages in a minute. They invented speed reading so others could compete with Orbach. When he was in practice, he used to need to extract the essence from a hundred-page bundle of documents in no time at all, often well after a case had commenced, perhaps while it was continuing in court. He was expected to do the same on the bench. Now he read word for word, like each one was a struggle.

I knew when he came to the vital letter. Tears fell from his eyes, first in a slow dribble then in a flood, onto the newsprint, making it wet, so that when he put the paper down and wiped his face he left it streaked with black lines as if he had been wearing mascara. When next he spoke, it was to say:

'I'll get ready.'

I rose to follow him.

He shook his head.

'There won't be any difficulty.'

* * *

While he was gone, I rang home. It was approaching morning, but I doubted any of them had enjoyed any real sleep, Alton excepted. Carson picked up the phone on the second ring:

'Boss?'

'Yeah. Where's Sandy?'

'She had another headache; I made her lie down.'

'Jada?'

'Oh, she's here. You wanna speak?'

'No. Go up and tell Sandy you're both going out, or if she's asleep leave a note. Then take my car and come here, both of you. Wait in the car till I come out.' I had Sandy's car, for the longer drive.

When he had not reappeared after fifteen minutes, I went up to find him. He was kneeling by the bed of the deep-sleeping Frankie, sobbing quietly into the sheets. I said quietly:

'Russel.'

He got up slowly, leaned over to kiss her cheek then covered her carefully with the sheet again. On the way down the stairs, he asked:

'Jada?'

'Of course.'

'She's young. You'll help?'

'We'll help.'

We waited in the hall for the sound of my car drawing up. At this time of the morning, it would only be Carson.

'Sandy's a good woman, Dave. Hang onto her. Don't make a mess of it again, eh? If I'd ever found someone like her, well . . . well, I never could have, could I?'

'Why not, Russel? Why not if you'd only let yourself?'

'Let myself what? None of them ever wanted me, not really, not for more than a moment. They enjoyed the heat I gave off, the sensation of power, the man on the rise, but the last thing they'd ever have wanted was to stay with me. Margot was the only one strong enough to cope, and sometimes even she feared she was drowning under it.'

'You didn't have to . . . You didn't have to be so strong, so hard, not if it made it impossible for you to live with yourself, or with anyone else.'

'You should have been a shrink, Dave,' he laughed. 'No, you shouldn't. The first pretty patient to sob on

194

your shoulder would end up with her legs apart on your couch.'

Though his earlier crudity had seemed so out of character for the Orbach I had come to know in this last round of our acquaintanceship that started with Disraeli Chambers, this second venture reminded me of an Orbach I'd long since forgotten, and that he had too; a man capable of humour, ordinary activity, a bit of banality, a glass of beer in the pub with the lads. It isn't an achievement to write books about; it's how much of the world lives; it just wasn't enough for him.

\* \* \*

As we emerged from the house, Carson flashed her car lights to let me know she was there. I said to Orbach:

'The best thing would be for you to get into my car, let me give your house keys to Carson.'

I thought for a moment he was going to do what I told him. Instead, he crossed the road to where she had parked, walking around the car to the driver's side. I followed. Jada looked terrified. Carson used the central locking. I signalled her to lower the window electrically, just an inch or two.

Orbach thrust the keys in at Carson then spoke across her.

'I'm sorry, Jada, I'm most terribly sorry.'

Jada wouldn't look at him. She stared straight ahead out of the windscreen. Then she said:

'It's too late, Russel. Tell it to my mother and Mick.'

'Take care of Frankie,' he started to say, but Carson had already put the window back up. It wasn't his right to say it.

# CHAPTER TWELVE

As we left Cloudesley Road, I could see in my rear-view mirror Carson and Jada letting themselves into Orbach's house. I presumed everything had been left to Frankie; we hadn't talked about it, but there was a realistic possibility that my new neighbour would be a famous female pop-singer and actress. Sandy would be pleased, it would boost house prices.

With one exception, we drove in silence until we neared the airport. The exception was soon after we were on the road, when he asked:

'How much does Jada know, about . . .'

'I told her you would be leaving the house; not coming back.'

'That's all?'

'That's all I told her,' I admitted it was possible she would have guessed the rest. 'Why?'

He didn't tell me. Thinking back on it, it seems he was pleased by my answer, pleased she didn't know, pleased she hadn't sanctioned my solution.

As we turned off the A127, he asked: 'Do you understand yet, Dave?'

'I don't know,' I admitted. 'It's hard. I understand bits of it. Does it matter?'

'Try to understand, so some day someone can explain to Frankie. I did love her, I do love her, more than anyone. I know that does not sound well from me, and I know what you think about Eartha, but I loved Frankie more purely than I've ever loved.'

We turned into the airport. It was open for business. I drove down the road to where the flying clubs were sited.

He added:

'You've done well, Dave. This, not the alibi, was what I wanted to keep you alive for. You're a little on the predictable side, but that suited my purpose, and you don't let go. Now there's a final judgment for you: after all your efforts to be anything but, you're a reliable man. Lucky Alton, lucky Sandy.'

He got out and slammed the door, walking away, I thought, without another word. Then he returned to the car. I lowered my window. He said:

'I hope Jada or Carson will remember to pick up the paper before Frankie gets up. They shouldn't destroy it. It's a collector's item. Unique. It was very clever, but I'm not sure if it was necessary.'

'Wasn't it, Russel?'

'We'll never really know. I knew it was a fake, though, from the beginning.'

'How?'

Did he really know or was it one last claim to omniscience? It was punitive to demand an answer but until he gave it I would not know of whom.

'They would have been banging at the door, the telephone would not have stopped ringing, someone from government would have been there before you were, Dave. I know how they work; I know how they think; just as I know how you do.'

I had neither caused nor compelled his co-operation: it had been his choice; at the end, he had to tell me that he had done it, not I; that was his game.

\* \* \*

I watched from the car as he boarded his plane.

From the hangar, Walker emerged, dressed in an overcoat. It looked odd. It was no part of the script.

I could not hear their exchange at the cabin door. Orbach tried to shut the door, Walker was holding it open. They were gesticulating at one another. Walker pulled out a gun and thrust it straight at Orbach's face, with no attempt at concealment. Orbach backed into the cabin and Walker climbed in after him. I understood Walker's amendment to the agreed plan.

In a few minutes, the 'plane began to taxi onto the runway. I drove quickly to the small, fenced area between the terminal and the control tower from which spectators were able to watch. There was a handful of casual observers, commenting on the different craft, a couple of them with cameras.

I watched and I watched as the plane flew out towards the sea, smaller and smaller until I could hardly identify it in the distance.

At the last moment, the dot in the sky turned red and smoke billowed out of the craft as it floated slowly back towards us, clearer and clearer, confused only by the cries from those around me, until it fell out of sight beyond the hill.

I remember clearest of all the long, painful silence that followed its departure from our vision, then the solitary boom as it finally shattered on impact and we could neither see nor hear anything yet knew it all. I drove back to London.

\* \* \*

Only Sandy and Alton were at the house. I had expected Jada and Carson to bring Frankie back rather than to remain in Orbach's house, but Sandy shook her head.

'Jada wanted to be there with her. I think she wanted to be alone with her but Carson insisted on staying.'

I nodded detachedly. I was not interested in the domestic details.

Sandy looked at me quizzically, critically.

'No, I suppose you aren't.'

'What's that supposed to mean?'

We were in the kitchen, now bereft of all but the basic amenities. I was tired; I wanted to sleep; I didn't even want a drink.

'Just what I said.'

'Hey, come on, Sandy, I'm hardly in the mood for a feminist analysis of my failures as a father and partner . . .'

She shook her head, also tiredly.

'That isn't what I meant.'

'So?' I asked irritably.

'Just that – you aren't interested in the details, the details of what comes after.'

'What're you saying?'

'Jada and Frankie have to go on living. It's hard to imagine a more difficult circumstance. But you wash your hands of it.'

I was stunned: after what I had just been through, the last thing I expected was one of Sandy's verbal assaults.

'You knew what was happening,' I protested, as if she was criticising what I had done with Orbach.

'I knew. That doesn't make it right.'

'Shit, Sandy, it's more than a bit late for this.'

'No, I don't think you understand what I'm getting at, Dave.'

I waited for her to explain.

She said:

'I'm not saying you – we – were wrong to go ahead with it; I agreed, it was the only thing to do . . .'

'Oh, hell,' I cut across her. 'It was what he wanted. He didn't have to go up. He guessed the paper was a dummy. It was his choice.'

She shrugged; the facts rarely concerned her.

'I'm not talking about his choices, Dave; I'm talking about ours.'

Maybe the reason I was still in love with her was because I still didn't understand five per cent of how her mind worked. The day I got to ten, I swore to myself silently, I'd leave.

'I agreed. I'm not denying that. I agreed so as to protect you, us. But it has to be an end, Dave, an end to the whole way of life you've been leading – and a beginning. That's what I'm trying to get at, I suppose,' she admitted she was almost as confused as I. 'The thing's done; it's time to face up to the consequences, and all that it's left behind, and to make sure the same things don't happen again. Do you understand?'

I understood, but I was still angry. There were times

199

to talk, and times for support. I know what Sandy would say. She'd say she had to get at me when I'm weak and vulnerable because the rest of the time I just don't listen. So all I said as I got up was:

'You do choose your time, Sandy,' and swung out of the kitchen to head up to bed without waiting for her answer.

\* \* \*

I crept into bed without washing and fell into unconsciousness without another thought.

When I awoke, it was late afternoon. The house was deserted. I found a jug of coffee and a note in the kitchen. It told me that Sandy and Alton had gone over to Cloudesley Road, to go with Carson, Jada and Frankie to the fair on Hampstead Heath, the lower fair, opposite the Freemasons' Arms on Downshire Hill. The note didn't suggest I join them, but the detail left it open to me to do so.

I took my time washing and dressing. I felt both annoyed and relieved. Annoyed, because though I understood the logic of taking the children to the fair, something else, something less raucous, seemed to be called for on this day; relieved because I didn't want to talk. I almost didn't go after them, but in the end what I wanted least of all was to be left alone.

It was a bright, sunny day. I found them without difficulty. They made a distinctive group. Alton was in the backpack, but Jada was wearing it along with huge sunglasses and a floppy hat that were almost completely effective to disguise her. Frankie was the star of the show, leading both Sandy and Carson by the hand. I was surprised but not displeased to find Natalie with them. My family. I felt proud.

I watched from a distance for a while. Then Frankie was dragging Sandy towards a whirly-gig, one of those infernal constructions made of cardboard and stuck together with glue that go round and round and up and down all at the same time and that she hates as much as I do. They were all laughing at Sandy. I ran across to say I'd go instead, but they were already ensconced, a metal bar across their waists, and they only just saw me as I arrived, Frankie giggling, Sandy with her teeth clenched in fear, before the machine began to move.

My teeth too stayed clenched for Sandy's strain as long as they went round. My beautiful woman. The others' attention had switched to the dodgems; they were still debating whether to have a go when Sandy's agony finally drew to a painfully belated close. I helped her off as Frankie, with barely an acknowledgement of my presence, galloped away to catch up with her sister. I put an arm around Sandy.

'Hi.'

'Hi,' she replied, neither her face nor her tone telling me whether or not she was yet ready to forgive and forego the morning's argument.

'Are you OK?' I asked, giving her the opportunity to answer whichever way she wanted to take it.

'I feel a bit giddy.' She clung onto my arm for support rather than to tell me what I wanted to know.

The others decided against the dodgems and strolled back to us via a candyfloss stand. Sandy called out:

'Not for Alton.' Then she looked at me wryly. 'Jesus, my head hurts. What a time for a headache. Jesus,' she screamed suddenly, grabbing the back of her neck.

'San? San? What is it?'

She sunk to her knees and keeled over face down on the ground. I dropped to the ground beside her, gently rolling her over.

'San? San?'

\* \* \*

I don't know what happened next. There was a crowd and voices and then a St. John's Ambulance man and a police-woman and they were carrying her between them to the carpark and thrusting her into the back seat of a police car and I was running after them and another car – a complete stranger's car, I don't to this day know whose – drove me the minimal distance – just a few hundred yards – to the

Royal Free, where Alton had been born. At that moment, I didn't even know where Alton was. I didn't even care.

They raced her into casualty and I went along with her into the examination room. I said yes when they asked if she was my wife. So she was in all but law. I answered a couple questions then someone said she wasn't breathing and they pushed me out while they were shoving a tube down her windpipe; someone else was examining her eyes. Outside I found the people I had thought of a few minutes before also as my family. I snatched Alton and hugged him to me and hissed at them:

'Go away, go away, go away, we don't want you here.'

Jada covered Frankie's ears with her hands but that was the only movement amongst them until Natalie stepped forward to relieve me of Alton before he drowned in my tears.

'What's happening, Dave?' Jada asked.

Carson walked away to make her own enquiries.

'I don't know. Just . . . She has these headaches . . . You know that . . . no, I keep forgetting, you didn't really know her till just now . . . She's always had these headaches and then when she came off the whirly-gig, well, she said she felt giddy then she said she had a blinding headache then . . .'

Frankie started to sob:

'She didn't want to; it's my fault.'

I got to her before Jada and hugged her tighter than she'd ever been hugged:

'It's not your fault, sweetie, it's not your fault, I promise it's not your fault, don't ever, ever say it.' It was all pointless if she, too, was damaged by it.

Somehow time was slipping by and they wouldn't tell me what was happening. Carson came back and said they'd taken her to the neuro-surgical unit: we were lucky, it was the centre for neuro-surgical problems for the whole of the North West Thames Area. Then she disappeared again and I could see her at the phone bank but I didn't know who she was phoning.

It went on for what seemed like forever. They didn't let me see her. A doctor came and talked a foreign language to me.

'She has a ruptured beri aneurysm.'

I looked blankly at him. He thought I wanted an explanation but all I wanted was to be told my wife, my life, Sandy, was alive and would get better.

'It's a congenital malformation of the blood vessels around something called the Circle of Willis. Well,' he laughed nervously, 'I don't suppose that means anything to you. Has she suffered from these headaches for long?'

I'd told them when we came in about her headaches and that it wasn't the first, though self-evidently the worst.

'Forever,' I said listlessly. 'What does it mean?'

'The vessels control the blood supply to the brain. The malformation has probably been present since birth. I suppose, the only way to describe it is like a blow-out in the blood vessels. It's caused a brain haemorrhage in the internal part of the brain. Like a stroke in effect. We've been doing a C.T. scan.' At the raise of an eyebrow he elaborated: 'Computerised Tomography. Basically, this will show if there's a sub-arachnoid haemorrhage secondary to the ruptured aneurysm and, well, whether it's operable. It'll take a couple of hours to complete.'

He was beginning to wonder about examining my own pupils when Carson drew him aside:

'This's going to take a while?'

'I'd say so.'

They whispered together for a while then Carson came back:

'I'm going to send Jada and Frankie home with Natalie and Alton, Dave. Have you got the car keys?'

I handed them over without protest. They hovered around me, touching, kissing, murmuring: I hated them, they were all so fucking healthy.

Only Carson stayed.

'You got enough cigarettes, Dave?'

I shrugged. She reached into my jacket pocket and squeezed the pack.

'I'll go get some more, huh?'

'Right.'

While she was gone, Tim arrived. He was who Carson had been calling. I understood why: he was authority, but a bit of it that was – in the last resort – on our side. He sat down beside me without a word and we sat there for a moment until I looked at his face and he saw it coming and put his arm around my head and pulled it into his shoulder like he was my father. I didn't care what it did either for our future relationship or his jacket. Someone had to be strong.

'It's my fault, Tim. You know?'

'I know. I got it on the wire hours ago. As an accident of course. One thing's got nothing to do with another, Dave. There's no connection.'

'Wrong, Tim. I'll tell you how it is,' I said dully. 'I've been playing God, playing with death; this is his message back telling me who's really in control. Get it?'

He shook his head sadly.

'She's not dead, Dave. Don't give up hope.'

But his tone told me he'd already spoken to the doctors and hope was merely a way of bridging the time between love and death.

\* \* \*

I can't remember much after that. I remember Carson coming back and she and Tim consulting quietly, first with one another and then with a different doctor from before. Then Carson went back to the house and Tim sat with me until they came to tell me:

'She's had a cardiac arrest, Mr Woolf. There's no chance. If we operate, well, she won't be the same, she, er, well, she won't be . . .'

'He's not her husband,' Tim cut in. 'Someone has to contact her parents. I'll ring the local police,' he placed a restraining hand on my wrist before he got up and was led into an office to make the last call.

'I need to see her, doctor,' I pleaded.

'It's not a good idea, Mr Woolf; it's better to remember. . .'

'You're a fucking shrink, already?' I grabbed his lapels. 'I know more about death than you'll ever know; I know about it, I've been there all my life.' I was shouting so loud the whole hospital was watching and Tim came back from the office to stop me: 'I'm going to see her.'

So they left me alone with her, just like in the movies with machines with lines and bleeps and tubes running out of every part of her and her eyes were shut and something was pumping up and down listlessly beside her and I kissed her on the lips hard like maybe she'd respond and then in anger in fury in next-to-hatred I was shrieking, thrashing out, breaking the connections, screaming:

'Don't, don't, don't dare fucking leave me, I'll never forgive you. Sandy, Sandy, please, please, I love you . . .'

Until they dragged me out and held me down and plunged a needle into my arm and thankfully I too could die.

\* \* \*

*It was a blast from the past that caught me just as I was going back to sleep again:*

'Dave?'

'Ug.'

'Dave, this is Sandy . . .'

*Sandy? Sandra? Sandra Nichol? My former partner? The woman who had personally, single-handedly, totally and utterly destroyed my career without hardly a helping hand from me? That Sandy?*

'How are you, Sandy?'

'OK I guess. I'd like to see you. Are you free for lunch? I'll buy . . .'

*She was there before me. She looked good. She was in a dark suit which meant she'd been to court. Her hair was permed which she didn't use to do. But she still didn't need any makeup. And hadn't put on a pound.*

*She was making me nervous. We'd been together five minutes, plus five on the phone made ten. She hadn't torn my head off once yet.*

'How's Bernie?' I asked after the waiter'd gone. Bernie had been her bloke for six years when I met her; a decade of loving service by the time we broke up.

'We split up,' she said defiantly.

'And the other one?'

'That . . . that didn't work out either . . . I've missed you. Missed working with you, I mean.'

'What is this, Sandy?'

'Maybe I like you,' she said softly. 'What about giving it another try?'

'Jesus. You make it sound like we were married!'

After we'd ate, we went for a walk. We walked along to Kensington Palace Gardens, and through to Hyde Park.

We sat and watched the ducks. They were cute. There were a lot of people in rowing boats. They weren't so cute.

We looked each other in the eyes. Something was stirring. It took me a while to recognise what it was. She didn't resist. I'm not even that sure who it was finally took the plunge. Me or her. It was just happening.

'This is crazy,' I murmured after. 'I've known you ten years . . . We've had some of the worst times of my life together!'

She laughed:

'Such nice things you tell a girl.'


'Was it true? When you said that you weren't sleeping with him anymore?'

'Yes. That was true.'

All I wanted was the truth.

I got up to refill my glass.

She bit her lower lip nervously:

'Make me another drink, Dave.'

G-and-T, like the good English lady she wasn't.

When I took it to her, she grabbed my wrist:

'He . . . he never suggested . . . what happened, in the park . . . that's the truth, Dave . . . I swear it . . .'

'That's supposed to be some big deal?'

'That's supposed to tell you . . . Oh, shit, I don't know . . . I wish . . . I wish I had got in touch with you

206

before . . . It's a funny old world, isn't it, Dave? You can know someone so well, and not at all. Or, different sides of them. But,' she smiled wryly, 'it isn't news to me that I . . . liked you . . .' That wasn't news to me either. The news was . . . that I liked her too.

I was standing at the sideboard, doing what came most naturally within reach of a bottle. She got up and stood beside me, again placing her hand on my shoulder:

'Just let me say this, then.'

Her voice was choking. I glanced round. She had tears in her eyes. I turned away. I didn't need it.

'We haven't slept together for years . . . He's gone on coming to see me . . . turning up late . . . like he did the night he talked to me about you . . . a bit drunk . . . wanting . . . trying to . . . you know. I just want you to understand it's me that's said no . . .'

'So what, Sandy? So fucking what?'

'You're hurt, aren't you, Dave?'

'Who? Me? Forget it. I don't get close, and I don't get hurt.'

We were both more than a little pissed. Otherwise, she might have let it go then. Instead, she whispered: 'Are you sure?'

'What do you want from me, Sandy?'

She grinned:

'You know . . .'

I did know. What she wanted. Just then.

I glanced at my watch. It was nearly ten o'clock. She followed the movement of my eyes.

'What's that for?'

'I wanted to know what time to put down that I stopped work . . .'

'Bastard . . .'

'Do you still know what you want?'

She nodded. She was shivering.

I would have left. Only. I was too.


Kat had booked a table at the Cafe Pelican on St Martin's Lane. I wasn't complaining. Kat was paying.

'I know about you and Sandy,' she said.

*It wasn't exactly a state secret, but we'd been out of touch for a long time and, so far as I knew, she and Sandy had never been close. I wasn't pleased she knew; I've never been able to think of an answer to female solidarity as an excuse not to hop into my bed.*

'How?'

'I heard. I can't remember who from. It doesn't matter. It didn't surprise me. I always expected it.'

'You did?' I was truly shocked.

'Sure. Anyone could've guessed you'd end up together. You were made for each other, like a couple of old trees planted next to one another in a clearing in the forest.'

*There were two calls on the answering machine when I got home. The second was from Sandy:*

'Dave, it's me. I was wondering how you were feeling. I really am sorry about Katrina, Dave, I liked her too. Oh, shit, I hate these machines. I need to talk to you, Dave, it's time we talked. We can't keep carrying on like this, Dave. We're off more than we're on. Oh, I shouldn't have started. Look, just ring me, please.'

*I didn't ring Sandy; it was too late, and I was too tired. Oh, shit, as she would say: I didn't ring Sandy because I couldn't face talking to her. I have a real problem with Sandy. A bit like the old Groucho Marx line, how can I stay with anyone who'd stay with me? I love Sandy, just about as much as Katrina had always assumed, long before I knew it; but it's easier to list the things that are wrong with our relationship than to remember what's right.*

*I was just about to leave for Companies House when the outside line rang:*

'Dave Woolf.'

'Sandra Nichol,' she said dryly.

'Sandy. Hi. I was going to ring you. We ought to meet,' I said.

'What a good idea. I wish I'd thought of it.' Ouch.

'I'm ringing from the Law Society. What about lunch?' Double ouch. I couldn't lie my way out of it: my lies last in her presence like ice in a blast-furnace.

'I, uh, was figuring maybe you wouldn't want us to be seeing each other if I was working on it,' I said lamely, once we'd settled into a corner with our respective refreshments: white wine spritzer for her.

'And for the month before? Maybe you were waiting for the case to begin?' Sandy has a tongue you could circumcise with.

'Fine, you wanna row,' I downed my drink: 'Let's have a row already.' I got up to fetch another. I can't fight with Sandy when I'm sober: it's an unequal contest; I'm not saying I win when I'm drunk, but at least it don't hurt so much.

She looked at me curiously when I returned, like she was trying to figure out what she'd ever seen in me. I wondered if she'd tell me. I reached out and took her hand:

'I do love you, you know.'

'Yes, I do know. It's not about that, is it? I'm getting too old for all of this, Dave; I don't want to spend my fortieth birthday wondering whose bed I'll be sleeping in, or sleeping in my own alone.' It was hard to think of her as beginning the approach to forty: she looked ten years younger.

'What do you want to do, Sandy?' I didn't want her to say it, but I could neither say what it was she wanted to hear nor else could I bring it to an end myself.

'I don't want to give you an ultimatum, Dave, but I can't keep on like this. If you can't – oh, shit, I don't know – I want to say "grow up" but it seems such a trite thing to say. Just that, though: grow up; we're both getting older; we've both got to start settling down or we'll wear ourselves out. Think about it, Dave, think about what I'm saying. And remember, if you don't want me, someone else just might, y'know.'

Now that the case was coming to an end, the rest of my life started to come back into focus and a bit of it was missing. It was a long time since I'd seen or spoken to Sandy. I punched the number I knew as well as my own, as indeed once it had been.

'Hi,' she sounded brisk.

'Bad time?'

*Pause.*

*'No.'*

*'Uh, well, you're obviously glad to hear from me.'*

*'Of course I'm glad to hear from you, Dave. I've been meaning to ring you. We ought to meet.'*

*'That was what I was thinking, kid.' She's four months older than I. 'I'm just about wrapped up here, at Mather's. 'Nother couple of days.'*

*'Yes.' Her enthusiasm and curiosity knew no bounds: they weren't even acquainted.*

*'Sandy, what's up?'*

*'What's up?' her voice raised. 'You let me walk out of a pub, on my own, in the middle of the day, without trying to stop me; you let me walk out of your life without even saying so long; you ignore me for weeks, then you ring up cheerful as a sand-boy, and you ask me – what's up already?'*

*I hadn't said 'already', had I?*

*'Look,' I said, calming and conciliatory, 'this hasn't been a lot of fun . . .'*

*'What's the matter? Weren't the high-class bimbos falling over themselves to hop into bed with you?'*

*Well, uh, yes, as a matter of fact.*

*'Oh, shit, we always argue on the phone. We'd better meet,' she conceded reluctantly: 'How about the twenty-third?'*

*If phones could see, I'd've boggled down the line:*

*'Sandy! That's nearly three weeks away!'*

*'Well,' she sulked, 'I'm pretty busy right now.'*

*You love someone in as many different ways and for as long as Sandy'n'I've loved each other, there's some things don't need spelling out:*

*'You're seeing someone, aren't you, Sandy?'*

*Silence. Then:*

*'I don't want to talk about it on the phone, Dave. Maybe I could make next Thursday, later on in the evening . . .'*

*'Tell me, Sandy.' Tell me Sandy: I love you; I know I'm a jerk; I know I've been fucking around with someone else, but I always thought, you know, you understood the way I was, am; I always thought you, you loved me anyhow, at any price. That was what I wanted, Sandy; that's what I*

*needed; someone to love me more than life itself; someone to love me as much as Robin loves Mick.*

She said flatly:

'I warned you, Dave.'

And so she had.

'You take care, Sandy. You take care, you hear? Doesn't matter how long; I'll still be here, well, there anyhow. Y'know, I'll still be around for you. You've only got to call; it'll always be true.'

I replaced the receiver gently before she could catch me start to cry.


The phone rang.

'Hi, it's me.' This is a universally accurate opening, but in this case it meant Sandy. 'Are you coming up this evening?'

'Am I allowed back in?' I asked dryly.

I could hear her smile down the line. In the case of anyone else, this would be a universally inaccurate proposition, but not when it's Sandy.

Every time I finish up with someone else, and go back to Sandy, I can't remember why I left. There's no one who's a patch on her, or with whom love-making comes as close to transcending isolation. If I say there's no one who's as good as her I don't mean that she's invariably kind, or sensitive, or moral, or unselfish. She has the sharpest tongue of anyone I know, can be intolerably demanding in the most irritating, petty ways, can cut someone down to size swifter than a Samurai's sword and when she wants something, heaven help anyone who stands in her way. What I mean is: no one else I know has got all their appealing and unappealing qualities in such perfect balance.

'Dave, I'll leave the office on time – get here early?'

'Can't, San. I've got an appointment at nine o'clock.'

'I want to talk to you, Dave,' she insisted. 'Can't you change it?'

'Would you believe – Russel Orbach wants to see me? At his new house?'

'Ah.' Sandy knew Orbach too. 'Try to keep it short, then. That shouldn't be difficult.'

'Sure. I won't be late.'

211

*I was just about to hang up, when she said:*
*'Dave?'*
*'Yup.'*
*'Oh, nothing.' And she hung up.*

I arrived at Sandy's considerably sobered. She, on the other hand, was a wee bit pissed: squiffy, she liked to call it. I didn't ring the bell: I had my own key to her house.

We kissed and hugged and wriggled against each other hornily. Someone I knew once referred to bad sex as like chewing someone else's stale gum. Sandy was rare fillet steak cooked at the Savoy Grill. I bore down on her and we tumbled onto the sofa. We both liked it that way: sudden, urgent, half-dressed, just the bits that counted.

After, while she went to wash, I poured us each another drink.

'Did you eat?'

I told her I'd eaten with Orbach:

'And, wait for this, his ward. He's got a child living with him.'

'Poor kid. How awful for her.' She meant living with Orbach, not her parents' death. 'What's she like?'

'Well, you know, she's a child. Isn't that enough? I mean, she's black, she's smart and she's incredibly beautiful, but she's a child all the same and you know how I feel about kids.'

'Oh, yes, I know,' she shut her eyes for a moment. 'But it's all a pose, isn't it, Dave? You don't really hate them, do you? I never thought you did?'

'Well, you know how it is. If I ain't got one, I don't see why anyone else should.'

'Did you never . . .' She hesitated, but plunged on: 'Didn't you ever, just once, think it might be nice if you did?'

'What? Me? Have a kid?' I laughed so hard I nearly fell off the sofa. 'What if it turned out like me?'

'I know,' she said gloomily. 'That's what's worrying me.'

'But, San, you're forty!'

'Gee, kid, you say the most romantic things. I know I'm forty. So are you. So what?'

'But I thought . . . well, you know. Shit.' I got up and went into the kitchen to fetch more ice. I turned the tray over and the cubes spilled out onto the floor. 'Shit,' I said again: 'Shit, shit, shit, shit,' I flung the tray after them.

I started to pick up the ice-cubes but I couldn't. Either they kept slithering about the floor, or else I couldn't see straight. I was kneeling on the floor, grabbing at ice-cubes, crying like someone had died. I didn't hear Sandy come in until she knelt down beside me and took my head in her hands, kissing my wet eyes until they were clear enough to see she was crying too. She said:

'I'm sorry, I'm sorry. I had no idea it'd upset you like this.'

I pushed her away.

'Don't be stupid, San, I'm not upset. I'm happy, you schmuk.'

'This's why you didn't want to see me last night? Why?'

She couldn't meet my gaze: she'd spent last night wondering whether to keep it. I got up and went and sat on the sofa with her, putting an arm around her shoulder. In the end, I just whispered:

'Thanks, San.'

We took the Passat because though I drive like a pig Sandy was now too big for comfort in her Peugeot GTI.

In a moment of rare – perhaps unprecedented – honesty, I said:

'I still can't relate to the idea of being a father.'

I saw her smile out of the corner of my eye. She said:

'You think I feel like a mother?'

'Well, I suppose I thought, you know, carrying it around all the time . . .'

'I don't know, Dave. What I feel is a big, heavy weight, which could be a blob or a child but is somewhere between. It's a heartbeat, not a human yet. I think, well, I don't know what a mother's supposed to feel like, do I? Maybe this's how I'll feel when it's born, too.'

213

The party was in full swing when finally we arrived. I was getting drunk too fast and having thoughts that didn't work. Sandy whispered in my ear:

'They're on the edge, Dave, on the very edge. She told me, upstairs: she didn't want to get married so soon; it was the only way they could be together. He's just doing what he thinks he ought to do. Tell me, Dave,' she hissed, 'we're not doing it just because we ought to, are we? You're not, I mean, are you?'

I shook my head and put my arm around her waist:

'No, Sandy, I'm not, we're not.' I leaned down and kissed her cheek and felt unaccountably sad: 'We're doing it because probably we didn't ought to.' She turned her head and right in the middle of the party we did what no one is supposed to do at such an occasion: we kissed full on the lips, just as if we loved one another.


I got a little calm time with Sandy before it happened: in between spasms of labour-pain we still weren't prepared for notwithstanding the classes. She said:

'What I have to do to get you to pay me any attention.'

After I'd brought her up to date on the events of the last two days, she said:

'Is Carson alright? Are you alright?' She wasn't asking about either our physical or legal condition but about things we'd been forced to do.

'It's been heavy,' I admitted, my eyes searching hers to see what else she might be asking.

The intermittent outbursts of agony left her calmer than normal between.

'I'm glad. Glad she was with you, Dave. Glad I found her for you.'

I nodded.

'There's things you do that I know I'm not a part of. I know I can't be; I don't want to be. But over the last few days, I've been thinking: maybe that's for the best; maybe that's part of why I've gone on loving you when you've given me a million reasons not to. I do love you, Dave, I do.'

I squeezed her hand in reply.

*'And . . . And I know you love me too. So I'm glad you had her to share it with. It makes me a bit a part of it too.'*

*And then Sandy was screaming a meaningless noise and I was screaming with her and before I knew it a third voice had joined us. A tiny head, a tiny body, a squirming, squiggling, squawky little thing emerging half-afraid half-defiant from between Sandy's legs and somewhere back in the mists of time from between mine too. It sounded to my ears like it was crying: 'gimme a Southern Comfort, wanna stay up for Hill Street, gotta Camel?' Then I can't remember a couple of minutes maybe, including that one, until a nurse was showing me the child saying:*

*'It's a boy,' in case I couldn't tell the difference.*

*I leaned over him and kissed his tiny wrinkled head once for me and once for Lewis like he'd asked me to do; and to pacify all the available gods I baptised him with my tears.*

\* \* \*

It was alright. It was alright after all. She was not dead; she was still there. It was all a dream; just a bad dream.

\* \* \*

The light woke me up.

Tim was standing in the doorway, watching, concerned, wondering if I was going to be alright, if I was going to be able to take it, able to withstand the shock, to withstand the pain.

I wasn't.

I opened my mouth to scream.

Not a sound came out.

Stupidly, all I could think was, we hadn't finished our fight. Sandy and me.

215

All Sphere Books are available at your bookshop or
newsagent, or can be ordered from the following address:
Sphere Books, Cash Sales Department, P.O. Box 11,
Falmouth, Cornwall TR10 9EN

Please send cheque or postal order (no currency), and
allow 60p for postage and packing for the first book plus
25p for the second book and 15p for each additional book
ordered up to a maximum charge of £1.90 in U.K.

B.F.P.O. customers allow 60p for the first book, 25p
for the second book plus 15p per copy for the next 7 books
thereafter 9p per book.

Overseas customers, including Eire, please allow £1.25 for
postage and packing for the first book, 75p for the second
book and 28p for each subsequent title ordered.